Marla looked down at the floorboards where she'd trodden just seconds ago. They'd fallen away, opening up into a void below. She shifted on the roof beam, inching her way to the skylight and welcoming the cool kiss of night air on her cheek. As she moved out of the path of the beam of moonlight for a moment, she saw a reflection through the hole in the attic floor. Black goggle eyes, looking up at her from a room far beneath. Perhaps a dead animal, fallen down there with the rotten floorboards, poor thing. But then the eyes moved, slowly, deliberately, and Marla knew what was looking at her.

She scrambled along the beam in clumsy crawling movements, scuffing the skin of her knees and wrists. The pain didn't even register. That hulking thing had seen her and was charging up the stairs for her right now. She had to get to the skylight. Her fingers brushed the dark, wet wing of a dead crow. She had no desire to join the poor creature, pinned out up here until her own dead organs blossomed with maggots. Marla heaved her upper body off the beam and out through the skylight, legs kicking up dust and animal filth below. Fresh night air choked into her, such a tonic after the corrupt honey of the attic. A moth flitted by, dust from its wings billowing like falling snowflakes in the moonlight. She was frozen in time for a spell, watching it. Then, with an almighty crack, the skylight frame gave way beneath her and she tumbled down the sloping roof, a scream caught in her windpipe as she fell.

To all ot Great missenden library !

THE
LAMPLIGHTERS

with Best wishes

BY FRAZER LEE

[signature]

Macabre
Ink

DEDICATION

To Laura, who lights the lamps so I may always find my way home.

.

ACKNOWLEDGEMENTS

Special thanks to Joseph Alberti for telling me about the real lamplighters. And to the real Marla Newborn, my thanks for allowing me to use and abuse your name. Thanks to Max Kinnings for introducing me to the British Library—and to the latter, where much of this volume was drafted, for its comfy chairs, quiet desks, and mountains of inspiration. Thanks to Jason Conway for conversations on the cobblestones, here's to many more. Cheers to Joseph D'Lacey (AKA The Adverb Killer) for friendship beyond the call of dutifully (oops). Heartfelt thanks to family and friends. Much gratitude and respect to Don D'Auria and all at Samhain Publishing. And my thanks to the two Davids at Crossroad Press for giving this book a new lease of life.

CHAPTER ONE

"It's the greatest job in the world."

Vera smiled as she said the words.

"All I have to do is turn on the damn lights, water the plants, a few chores…"

Static crackled in her ear—the phone line was lousy tonight.

"Are you still there?"

"Yes," came the reply, "but I can hardly hear you. There's a weird kind of…echo."

"It's Jessie's uplink," Vera chuckled. "We're not really allowed to call anyone from the island…"

"Sorry…how…calling me?"

Christ, the line was getting choppy. Vera pressed the cordless handset closer to her ear, then checked herself.

"As if that'll make any difference," she said. Probably talking to herself now.

The crackling grew louder. She could still hear her friend's voice, buried beneath layers of digital cacophony. A faint echo smothered by an avalanche of noise.

There was something else in the mix, too, an ominous growling hum like the electricity pylons near her home. Berlin, so far away now. Even as she thought it, the hum grew, drowning out what little was left of her friend's staccato tones.

And with a click, silence.

"*Scheiße,*" she cursed, stabbing the redial button. The phone was completely dead. Hacking an outside line was a fine art, she appreciated that, but Jessie clearly needed some new software. And she'd be giving that little bag of smoke back, too.

First things first. Vera put the handset in its cradle and headed for the kitchen. She walked over to the huge range in the center of the room and ignited all four of the gas taps. Then, crouching on her haunches, she turned the oven on full blast. The expensive smoked glass oven door afforded her a look at her own reflection. Only a month on Meditrine Island and already she looked five years younger. Amazing. Gone were the dark grey shadows around her eyes—even her signature brittle dry hair had a new luster. Berlin could take care of itself, thanks very much. The island really was like a fountain of youth, she thought as she rose and crossed to the patio door.

Unclipping the latch, Vera had to use two hands to slide the glass behemoth open. Whoever owned this house had a serious heavy glass fetish. Stepping out into the night, her senses were flooded. The island's fresh air was like no other, an intoxicating blend of jasmine and ocean spray. When she went back to the city, she'd have to remember to bottle and sell it.

Click.

Her quiet moment was suddenly blasted with fifteen hundred watts of raw security lighting as she stepped in front of the infrared sensors. She cursed the light for blinding her as she picked up the watering can, blinking away the white-hot glare. The light had brought the mosquitoes a-calling too. They whizzed around her as she dashed back into the kitchen.

Vera filled the watering can with cool, clear water at the bath-sized sink. This was the least tedious of her tasks—the plants were going to drink their fill tonight. Amidst such fabulous wealth, such meticulous order, it felt good that a mere backpacker could decide the fate of items so precious to their millionaire owners.

Millionaires? Billionaires, more likely.

She remembered Jessie's sardonic voice from the first time they'd hung out together, gossiping about who owned these mansions, this island. But Vera didn't really care who the owners were. That they were paying her handsomely to do a few chores was all she cared about. And the most strenuous chore was watering the plants. Easy money. "The job's a doozy," Jessie had giggled. "Doozy Jessie" had been working on the island longer than Vera and seemed to be going a little stir crazy…

As the water rose closer to the brim of the watering can,

the security lights clicked off suddenly. *Like everything else on the island, they ran to a tight schedule,* thought Vera. As she did so, milliseconds before the light bulbs faded, Vera saw something outside.

A figure.

She blinked twice, slow and firm. The ghost imprint of the blinding bulbs still there, forming crescent-shaped black holes in her mind's eye. Was there someone out there?

Vera blinked again, then swore furiously as liquid spilled onto her feet. Soaked, she closed the faucet and let the watering can rest in the sink unit. *Shouldn't have smoked that joint before coming up to the house,* she thought, sounding for all the world like her mother. Scatterbrain, she used to call Vera whenever she lost the power to function normally, everyday tasks becoming impossibly hilarious missions. She still wondered if her mother had known her daughter was stoned, or if she simply believed her child was missing a neuron or two million.

The old clumsiness was really kicking in now, as she left little pools of water on the tiled floor on her way to the patio. Putting the can down (yet more spills), she grabbed the door handle and pulled with all her might.

Swoosh.

The glass giant slid open easier this time. Vera bent down to pick up the can—then the smell hit her.

Something had invaded the envelope of jasmine and surf, corrupting the very night air with its presence. A hospital smell, harsh and synthetic, like the way her dentist smelled. She'd hated the dentist since she was a kid. Had he followed her here, to paradise, tracking her down after all these years to do all that work she had chickened out of? To tut and frown disapprovingly through his paper mask, noting her cannabis-stained enamel and ugly overbite?

She leaned out into the night air, her nostrils searching for the source of the stifling smell. It was mixed with something else now, like ripe leather.

Click.

He was standing right next to her, impossibly close. Vera's heart blasted into her mouth, choking her scream. The source of the smell regarded her idly, his black eyes like camera lenses. Cold. Unforgiving.

Before she could react, Vera heard a swooshing sound. The smell of rubber gloves perversely filled her nostrils, pushing all the way back into her throat as if someone really had jammed two fingers up her nose. The intruder's dark form was a monolith, burned into her eyes by the security lights.

Click.

Swoosh.

The bulbs faded once more. Vera's senses imploded as the sliding door crushed her skull against the alloy doorframe.

Crunch.

Swoosh, as the door slid back again.

Crunch.

Vera's body jerked uselessly then fell still; her brains spattered across the cool, thick glass.

CHAPTER TWO

"It's the greatest job in the world."

Marla Neuborn tried to look interested, although in truth all she wanted to do was read her book. That's why she'd come to the park, a bit of peace and quiet.

"Looking after these two. Aren't they just adorable?"

The girl who'd sat down right next to her on the bench clearly wasn't going to let up. She wanted a proper conversation, goddammit. Marla couldn't remember the last time she'd had one of those.

"Do you like kids?"

Marla closed her battered paperback with an audible sigh and looked up at the girl next to her. Pretty face, blonde hair— Marla suddenly felt a hundred times scruffier. Great, her mood had worsened. The girl sounded Swedish and just a little bit vacuous. If nothing else, at least Marla had the intellectual high ground.

"Yeah, I love them," she lied.

This appeared to delight the girl; a slightly insane-looking smile spread across her face as she looked down at the pram in front of her.

"You should be an au pair. I get to look after these two all day. They're as good as gold. And their parents are lovely…"

Marla had been an au pair, once. She shuddered as she remembered the tabloid headlines, "JUNKIE AU PAIR A MENACE TO TODDLERS—MOTHER'S ANGUISH OVER INCIDENT."

Highgate Park had been busy on the day of the "INCIDENT," swarming with au pairs like her, leaning on the handles of high-tech executive baby buggies, texting.

Marla had quickly maneuvered the kids to the playground area, as she always did. As she sat on a bench watching them attempting self-destruction on the swings, Marla had rolled a joint—as she always did. Kicking back and resting her head against the comforting hardness of the wooden bench, Marla had drifted off for a while enjoying the gentle birdsong and distant murmur of a jet plane.

Suddenly, a wailing scream broke into her reverie. Returning to her senses sluggishly, Marla peered through slightly red eyes to see what was up.

The children were screaming.

Marla ran. She ran and pushed through the little gate into the play area. An elderly woman was cooing over the children, trying to calm them down. The youngest was in a bad way, the broken bone protruding through her soft baby skin. Her face was a rictus of pain. A constant rising and dipping wail flooded from her agonized mouth like an air raid siren.

Sirens.

The ambulance had arrived soon afterwards, and the police car. Angry parents had pressed charges of course, and she'd been unemployed ever since. So here she was, out of work and money in London. The most expensive city in the world.

Christ, she had to get of here. The Swede had started speaking into the pram in sickening baby talk. Marla stormed off and started the long walk home, the only place she'd get any peace now.

Marla let herself into her bed-sit, cursing the stiff lock as it nearly ate her key. She could barely wait to lock herself in her dark little room and smoke herself to sleep.

But sleep would not come. Her stomach was howling for food, so Marla dragged herself off the bed and rooted through the grimy cupboards in search of sustenance. A can of tuna, a little past its sell-by date, and a couple of rice crackers would have to do. She had nothing else. Eating from the can (*most unladylike*) she surveyed her room with mild despair.

Apart from the bed, a few charity shop paperbacks and dirty clothes scattered on the floor, the only sign that anyone was living there was a clunky old laptop. She'd inherited the machine from Carlo, an old boyfriend of hers. Poor Carlo fancied himself as a bit of a web entrepreneur, but had left town in a hurry when immigration came calling. Marla decided to hold onto his computer for him, back-payment for listening to all his crappy jokes and even crappier chat-up lines. The damn thing barely worked at the best of times, but at least she could check her emails and look at job ads. The landlady let her use the phone line for free, as long as she stuck to the free dial-up service. Although "service" was stretching it a bit.

The modem crackled into life, sounding like the anguished wails of that injured child, and promptly crashed. A few more attempts and Marla was online.

"You've-got-mail," said the excited computer voice.

Why did it always sound so excited? All she ever got was spam mail about weight-loss pills and penis enlargements. Marla was clearly in need of neither; she tossed the half-eaten can of dry tuna fish into the trash and looked back at the screen. Her mail inbox was taking an age to load up.

"You've-got-mail."

Expletives tumbled out of Marla's mouth as dozens of spam mails racked up onscreen. "AS OF CONJOINMENT" one read idiotically, "WANT TO CUM LIKE A FIREHOSE?" asked another. *Jesus,* why did she even bother? She was just about to turn the machine off, when she saw it. There, tucked away among the junk mail was the subject line, "Re: Article Submission."

Marla clicked on it and gazed at the email header, almost unable to scroll down and read the rest. It had been a couple of weeks since she'd submitted the feature, a travelogue cannibalized from her diary entries while backpacking across Europe during more prosperous times.

She actually trembled when she clicked the mouse to read the rest of the email.

"Dear Ms. Newborne," it read—great, they had already spelled her name wrong, "Ran a similar piece in last month's issue. Please check before sending unsolicited work. We are not taking freelancers right now. Good luck with your career."

The mail wasn't even signed with a name, but from the mail address she could see it was from someone called Sandy.

Well, Sandy was a bitch whoever he/she was. At least they hadn't crucified her work this time. Still, it made Marla feel a little better to sign Sandy's email address up for a few porn sites and dieting newsletters before she went to bed.

Digging some dope from the stash sock under her bed, Marla rolled herself a little nightcap and imagined what tomorrow might bring.

Only disappointment, she thought as she stubbed out the joint. Moments later, and Marla's head was at one with her pillow. Her breathing slowed and became heavier.

Somewhere in cyberspace, a series of electronic pulses conspired together, drawing data from algorithms out in the ether. The data weaved together into text, words gliding towards a pre-determined destination.

Words that became a message, a whisper.

"You've-got-mail," said Marla's computer, and she stirred for a moment before turning over and drifting off into a troubled sleep.

CHAPTER THREE

Rain pounded on the window, waking Marla from her nightmare. She'd been crushed inside a pram, listening to her bones breaking. Peering through sleep-encrusted eyes she realized she'd left the computer on all night. Wonderful. She'd have to feed the electricity meter before she fed herself, as usual.

Yawning her way across to the kettle, Marla made herself a cup of coffee. She flopped down in front of the laptop and fingered the track pad, ready to shut it down. As the screen lit up in response to her touch, something caught her eye. One new email. She couldn't help but look, even though she knew it would end in disappointment.

"*FAO: Marla Neuborn—employment offer*" read the email header.

What the hell? Marla rubbed her eyes, looked again. *More junk, surely*, she thought as she opened the message. She began to wake up as she gulped coffee and scanned the text; *Dear Ms. Neuborn—acquired your details from agency—ideal candidate—a paradise of opportunity—immediate start…*

Spam. She hit "delete," turned off the computer and downed the rest of her coffee on the way to the shower room.

Marla tried to keep her soapy skin away from the slimy tiles and mildewed shower curtain. The landlady hadn't updated the facilities at the "Mansions" in years. And every day, Marla had to run the gauntlet of the hallway outside her room to reach the communal shower room. Sometimes, like today, she got lucky and didn't run into one of the building's lecherous inmates.

Marla dropped the shampoo bottle onto her foot. *Fuck.* As she bent down to retrieve it, the shower curtain clung to her in a vile embrace. Joining the assault, the showerhead began to sputter cold water onto her back. Cursing wildly, she retreated to the safety of the sink and rinsed her hair there. Looking at her reflection in the chipped mirror, Marla spied a pimple forming on her chin. Brushing her teeth angrily, she climbed back into her bathrobe and sloped out into the hallway.

Glinting eyes peered out at her from a crack in her neighbor's door. The dirty bastard was spying on her again. As she hurried by, she heard pornographic moaning from the TV set inside— the sound made Marla wince. This place was really beginning to get under her skin. She pushed her door. She'd locked herself out. *Oh no. Oh please for the love of God no, not again.* Now she'd have to face the landlady and get the spare set of keys, which would no doubt be accompanied by a lecture about not losing her keys. That lecture would be followed by the one about paying her rent on time. Marla suddenly felt suicidal. Maybe suicide wasn't such a bad idea. Just kidding, she reminded herself, but it wasn't such a bad idea, what she was thinking. The window to her room was still open after all. Strangely amused that her fear of her landlady was so great she'd be willing to risk life and limb to avoid speaking to her, Marla quickly ducked back into the bathroom.

Wrapping her bathrobe tightly around her, she opened the window as wide as it would go and looked out over the ledge. It was certainly wide enough for her to climb across, then she just had a short section of roof to navigate before she could climb in through her window. A pigeon flapped noisily from the eaves above her, egging her on with its dumb show. Marla clambered out, wincing at the chill air as it penetrated her bathrobe and whistled, freezing, around her nethers. Clinging to the arch of roof tiles above her, she set off along the ledge, walking sideways like a crab. The wind picked up and her bathrobe rose up, billowing out suddenly and making her shriek like an embarrassed schoolgirl. It wasn't long before she heard the wolf whistles from below. Great, someone had seen her—and invited his pals along to witness the spectacle, too. Let them look, sad bastards. She wished that pimple had been forming on her backside, let them wolf whistle at that for a while. Marla reached the sloping section of the roof as the aural humiliation of hoots and lascivious cries railed on below her. *Don't look down. Don't.* Gasps from below now as her foot slid off the side of the roof, loosening a tile, which smashed noisily on the ground far below. Then loud cheers rang out as she corrected herself and clambered on up the slope to her window. She climbed inside and turned to shut the window. As she did so, she glimpsed a face pressed up against the glass of the window nearest hers. Her neighbor. He was naked. She closed the curtains.

Grabbing clothes from the floor, Marla dressed in a hurry and stuffed her door keys into her pocket vowing never to lock herself out again. Her makeup bag was almost exhausted, so she decided not to bother. She'd save what was left for a hot date. She snorted. *Like that'd ever happen.*

Minutes later and she was downstairs. Envelopes lay in disarray on the doormat. More damn junk mail. Still, she picked them up and dutifully separated them into neat little piles for the Mansions' inmates. The landlady would like that. And a happy landlady was a forgiving landlady—she hoped, wincing as she replayed the sound of the roof tile shattering on the ground. Marla's rent check was going to bounce again this month.

Sighing heavily, Marla saw the logo on the envelope first. It was one of those clunky, important corporate stamps. Then she saw her name, and a single rubber-stamped word in red.

URGENT.

Wincing at the chicory taste of the coffee, Marla put the cup down and added another two sugars. This was the worst café in London, no question, but on quiet days they never hassled her to free up the table. And today she really needed to be away from her crappy bed-sit and out of the rain.

She picked up the letter and read it again, slowly this time.

Dear Ms. Neuborn,

I am writing with reference to a potential offer of employment. We acquired your details from the agency and believe you could be an ideal candidate. The position is one of housekeeping in a private Mediterranean community owned and operated by our parent group, The Consortium Inc. We are confident you'll agree that the job

placement offers a paradise of opportunity to the right person. Please
contact us to arrange an interview. Please note; should you prove to be
a good fit, the job requires an immediate start.
Kind regards,

J G Mathers, Human Resources
The Consortium, Inc.

Marla looked down at the cup. *The agency?* Surely, she'd
dropped off their records ages ago.

A sickly beige skin had already begun to form on her coffee.

Marla folded up the letter, paid the waitress, and headed for
the nearest phone booth.

CHAPTER FOUR

The voice on the phone had been friendly enough, but the Consortium Inc. Building was pure corporate terror. Nestled in among the higgledy-piggledy side streets of the City district, it had taken Marla three bus routes to find it. And so here she was, craning her neck up at it, a modernist megalith of black marble cladding and smoked glass. She took a breath, licked her lips, and stepped into the revolving doors.

Sealed off from the hustle and bustle of outside, the foyer was calm and still. Marla's footsteps echoed as she approached the reception desk. The receptionist peered at her through layers of makeup, took her name and directed her to the sixth floor. Marla shuddered as she stepped into the elevator—any minute now and they'd find her out, pull her file, hear from the agency about her Big Mistake. *It'd be a blessed relief,* she thought, *then I wouldn't have to go through with the damn interview.*

Ding. The elevator doors opened and Marla found herself in another reception area. This time, the desk was vacant, with a closed door just beyond it. Marla sat down in a brown leather sofa and waited. She was still, miraculously, five minutes early. The voice on the phone had seemed delighted that she could make it that very afternoon. *Wouldn't be so delighted if they'd read the tabloids,* she thought beginning to panic again. Palms sweating, Marla stood up and opted for pacing the room instead of sitting. It helped. Her heart rate slowed and her hands became merely clammy instead of wet hot.

"Ms. Neuborn?"

Marla turned, and the voice on the phone now had a face, handsome and tanned, with a prominent jaw and strong hairline. He'd either had work done, or simply looked after himself. Maybe a bit of both.

"Marla?"

His teeth were so white.

"Yes, that's me," she spluttered.

He thrust his hand out. Marla discreetly wiped her palm on her hip and shook his hand. What a grip—the guy definitely worked out.

"A pleasure to meet you. I'm Mr. Welland. But you can call me Bill. Come on in."

Welland's office was the cleanest room Marla had ever been in. Even her time in hospital had seen more dust than this. He asked her to take a seat and offered her a coffee. Trying not to recline into the soft comfort of the leather swivel chair, she refused the offer of a drink. *Probably spill it all over his desk in a matter of seconds.* Damn her nerves.

"So, I take it our letter came as something of a surprise?"

Marla cleared her throat, "You could say that, yes."

"But a welcome one?"

He beamed at her.

"Of course."

She leaned forward a little, intent now on giving it to him straight. "To be brutally honest, Mr. Welland…"

"Please, Bill."

"Bill. I had kind of given up on that agency…. I've sort of, moved on since signing up with them."

"No problem, Ms. Neuborn."

"Marla."

He grinned again. "Marla. Our company has very specific requirements; the right candidate for the right job. We put feelers out everywhere. We have employees from the world over, offices on every continent. I personally am a firm believer in appointments that are meant to be. Your resume and experience, coupled with your age could make you an ideal candidate for the job."

Marla braced herself for the questions. So long since she'd done an interview. *Deep breath, don't mess it up.*

"This isn't an interview, as such," Welland continued, as if clairvoyant. "No, I prefer to keep things as informal as possible. Our meeting is merely an opportunity to tell you more about the position and answer any questions you might have. Okay?"

"Absolutely."

Marla's voice betrayed her unmistakable relief. Welland didn't seem to notice, or care.

"This isn't your regular job, I can assure you of that. If I were to tell you that it would involve living in real luxury on a Mediterranean island would you have a problem with that, Marla?"

His eyes positively twinkled. *Smooth bastard.* Marla shook her head, smiling.

"Good. Now we're past that difficult question," he chuckled. "Onto the details.... the Consortium Inc. represents a quorum of very rich clients, who would like to stay that way. Each of the members has a variety of business interests, and the day-to-day running of these is handled largely by us. One such area entrusted to us is the safekeeping of an island community owned entirely by our clients. Are you with me so far?"

"I'm with you."

Welland rose and continued speaking as he glanced out at the gloomy city sky.

"The mansions on the island are inhabited very rarely, usually when our clients are taking their annual break or attending a special event on the mainland. This makes it very difficult for them to fulfill their resident status requirements; have you heard of those?"

"I'm.... No, I don't think I have."

"No problem, Marla, I'll explain. The system is exactly the same in Monaco and other...prestigious areas; wealthy homeowners are required to prove residential status in order to qualify for generous tax benefits. If they only use their homes for a week or two a year, they don't qualify. So, rather than lose out, they employ housekeepers to keep things in order for them. These employees use up a bit of gas, water, and electricity each day, tend to the grounds, and generally enjoy all that the lifestyle has to offer."

"Sounds too good to be true."

"Indeed it does," he turned smiling from the window. "Especially when you also take into consideration the fee you get paid on top. The Consortium holds a monthly salary in an account for you. Once your contract is complete, the money is yours."

"May I ask..."

"How much? Of course," he chuckled. "It's a little more than double what the agency was offering you, per hour, as a base rate."

Marla whistled. She could already see the possibilities; a University course, no more debts, no crappy bed-sit.... She snapped back into reality. *Too good to be true. Has to be.*

"I don't know how to ask this politely..."

"Go ahead."

"What's the catch?"

Welland chuckled once more. He reached into his desk drawer and pulled out a folder, sliding it across the smooth surface towards Marla.

"First catch; before we hire you, you must complete this written personality test."

I already have a personality, Marla was tempted to say. *I don't need to take a test. I hate tests.* She bit her lip.

"You don't have to do it right now. Mail it back to us and we'll let you know in a few days if you've got the job."

After a pause, he went on. "Second catch; if we hire you, you must agree to be available without interruption for a year. You will not be allowed to leave the island for any reason during this period. That includes illness, and 'acts of God.' If you break contract, your earnings account will be closed and no monies paid to you. However, I assure you that if your contract doesn't reach full term for any other reason, then you'll be paid in full. And the third catch is our secrecy clause; you shall at no point during your employment be advised of the exact location of the island and you will not be permitted to contact the outside world."

"So, no phone calls?"

"That's right. No calls, no Internet, no text messages. No physical mail."

Marla couldn't disguise her consternation at this restriction. It seemed such a bitter pill after all Welland had offered so far. The warm smile again. Those white teeth.

"I know it seems draconian, Marla. Believe me, the island is so beautiful you won't even want to contact the dreary old mainland once you're there. All our employees say so. Please, take the test with you and give it some thought."

Marla warmed a little. She picked up the folder and stood up.

"Have you been there? To the island?"

He led her gently to the door.

"You're kidding, right?" He grinned. "I started out just like you; as a Lamplighter. I loved it so much I joined the Consortium full time. I'm sure once you take the test, you'll work out just fine..."

"A Lamplighter?"

He flicked the light switch off, then on again.

"That's what we call the island workers."

Lamplighters.

Marla kind of liked that.

CHAPTER FIVE

All the way home, Marla had expected a camera crew to jump out on her. *Surprise! It was a set-up! There is no job, but you've been such a good sport….* She leafed through the personality test Welland had given her. Some of the questions were just plain weird, veering randomly from logic puzzles to the somewhat intrusive. Actually, a TV show set-up might be better than all this prying.

As she climbed the stairs back at her building, Marla had an acute sense that something was wrong. Turning the corner into the hallway, she could see why. The door to her room was wide open. She approached the doorway cautiously, gripping Welland's folder like a shield. Peering into her room, Marla's heart thumped hard with the expectation that an intruder would be peering back at her. But the room was empty.

Marla checked the door lock. The catch was a little screwy as usual and there was no sign that it had been forced. Must not have closed it properly on her way out for the interview. Jesus, when she wasn't locking herself out, she was having an open house party. She flopped down on the bed and smiled grimly to herself. The room was such a mess anyway it'd look like it had been burgled whether the door was left open or not. Then she froze. Her laptop was gone.

Moments later, Marla found herself banging on the door of the pervert down the hall. She almost had no recollection of walking to his door; the red mist had carried her here. What if it wasn't him? No. If anyone was going to mess with her things, it was that letch. She pummeled harder on the door, nearly falling inside as it opened. His confused face looked out, half in shadow.

"I want my laptop back, now," spat Marla, harshly.

"Your...what?"

"Don't feign ignorance with me, Mister. I know you took it, so just give it the hell back."

She shoved at the door, hard, knocking him back slightly. There was a faint odor coming from inside, like soured buttermilk. Marla didn't even want to guess where the smell had originated. She did a quick one-eighty of the room. It was immaculately tidy. No laptop. He must've stashed it somewhere, or sold it already.

"Where the hell is it?" She was shouting now.

"I don't know what you're talking about. Are you feeling all right?"

Marla's red mist solidified into a wall of pent-up rage.

"I've seen you looking at me. Watching my every move. Perving over me when I locked myself out. Biding your time until..."

"What's going on here?"

A sharp voice, from up the hall. *Brilliant.* Marla's landlady was standing there, fixing her with an angry stare. She opted for a defensive stance, raising her hands in surrender.

"My...my room's been burgled. My laptop's gone. I was just asking this guy if he knew anything about it..."

"Accusing me, more like," he said, indignantly.

The landlady cleared her throat. "Mr. James is one of my best, most reliable tenants," she said. Her voice wobbled with anger, sounding like a detuned radio announcer. "Unlike you, Miss Neuborn, he always pays his rent on time. I was just on my way up here with this."

She held out Marla's rent check. The bank had rubber stamped it. The words "REFER TO DRAWER" burned into Marla's eyes.

"You have two weeks' notice to vacate your room."

Marla's voice dropped to a breathless retort. "But my laptop has been stolen. I..."

"No buts, Miss Neuborn. I warned you last time, three strikes and you're out. This is the third and last time. And if you bother Mr. James again, I'll be forced to evict you immediately."

Marla glared at James. He looked as shocked as she did. Her eyes filled with tears. She turned and ran back to her room, slamming the door.

This time it closed properly.

CHAPTER SIX

A week had passed since she'd been given her notice and Marla still hadn't found a new place. For days now, she'd got up early and headed out to scour the newsagent notice boards and local classified ads—nothing affordable. She'd logged onto countless property websites, using the computers at the local library for lack of a machine of her own. If her friendly local neighborhood pervert hadn't done it, she could only imagine that bastard Carlo had broken in and taken her laptop. *His laptop.* Still she couldn't find anything affordable. Her overdraft was maxed out, and no credit card company would touch her—not with her rating. As usual, the agents were asking for a month's deposit plus six weeks in advance. *Daylight robbery,* frowned Marla as she headed back to the bed-sit, her home for one more week.

Crashing into the bombsite that was her room, Marla kicked aside yesterday's T-shirt, socks, and panties. She flopped onto the bed and squeezed her eyes shut in frustration. There had to be some way of appeasing her landlady. Anything would be preferable to the nightmare of moving. If she could just buy some time until she heard about the job.

The job. She'd almost forgotten to mail the personality test back to them after her scene in the hallway the other day. Surely, they'd had time to go through it by now? *Probably just a scam,* she thought bitterly, *they'll get back to me and offer me some crappy telemarketing gig.* Sighing, Marla curled up under the womblike darkness of her bedclothes, contemplating dull years of work cold-calling angry strangers through a plastic headset. Perhaps that was her destiny; maybe she should just resign herself to it.

It felt like only minutes had passed when Marla was awoken

by a sharp rapping at her door. Blinking tiny traces of sleep from her eyes, she mumbled, "Who is it?" The sharp knocking again, rap-rap-rap. Not her landlady again, not now *please*. Marla shook off the duvet and stomped sleepily over to the door.

It was Mr. James.

"Sorry to disturb you. Were you sleeping?"

"No, not really, I…" Marla tried to waken herself up. "I was just chilling, taking a quick nap."

"There's a phone call for you. On the payphone, downstairs."

"Oh, thanks."

Marla slipped out of the door. Mr. James stepped back to give her some room to get by. An awkward moment passed between them. Marla felt suddenly embarrassed about shouting at him, accusing him. She turned.

"Listen, by the way, I'm really sorry about the other day."

He smiled back at her, "It's okay. No hard feelings. And it sucks—about your laptop, I mean."

"Never really worked properly anyway," said Marla as she headed for the stairs. *I can identify with it*, she thought to herself.

"Ms. Neuborn? We received your personality test. I wanted to personally thank you for taking the time to complete it for us…"

The voice on the phone was just as friendly as before. Friendlier. *Here it comes*, she thought.

"And I wanted to be the first to congratulate you on making the selection."

What? Oh no, not another interview. I'll simply die.

"Ms. Neuborn? Are you still there?"

"Yes, I am still. Here."

"Pending contractual arrangements, we'd like to offer you the position of maintenance operative as part of the Consortium's island workforce."

"Oh."

Marla had a sudden, violent, urge to pee.

"Oh!"

"May I ask if you're still interested in the position?"

"Oh, yes. Yes. I am." The urge to pee stopped, replaced by vague thoughts of a strong alcoholic drink.

"Well, I guess that makes you a Lamplighter. Congratulations, Ms. Neuborn. And welcome to the team. We'll be in touch with all the details."

The walk back to her room was a blur. Marla sat down on the bed, not knowing whether to laugh or cry, her face a tragicomic mask of both reactions. She rolled a celebratory cigarette and breathed the smoke in and out deeply.

Only then did she notice something else was missing from her room, something that had definitely been there when she left to answer the phone. She'd seen them only moments ago. Her used panties, from yesterday. She dropped the cigarette into the ashtray and scrambled around on the floor for them. Gone. A sick feeling hit her stomach. Anger building inside her, Marla left the room, cursing the latch. She crossed the hallway and stood in front of Mr. James' door. Loud pornography bellowed from inside his room accompanied by his unmistakably urgent grunts and groans.

Marla returned to her room and started packing her rucksack. It was time to get away, far, far away, from this rat hole.

CHAPTER SEVEN

Welland was waiting for Marla outside Nice airport arrivals in a sleek black open-topped car. He grinned at her as she approached, those perfect white teeth gleaming in the morning sun.

"How was the flight?"

Marla smiled her thanks as he helped with her bag.

"It was Business Class."

He laughed in recognition as he put his sunglasses on. Marla hadn't flown for a while and had clearly never flown Business before. She looked so much more relaxed than she had on the day of her interview.

"Only the best for our employees, Marla. And you'd better start getting used to life's little luxuries. The island has more riches to offer than Business travel. Think of it as First Class," he winked slyly. "You're about to get an upgrade."

"My second today," giggled Marla.

The car's powerful engine throbbed as he hit the accelerator. Marla grabbed her own sunglasses as they drove out into the bright sunlight. The breeze blew through her hair like a cleansing breath. London and her depressing bed-sit already seemed to be a million miles away. Good riddance. She kicked back in the comfort of the leather passenger seat and looked at the passing cars.

"Comfy?" asked Welland.

"Oh, yes," Marla said as she stretched a little, catlike.

"Good. We have quite a drive I'm afraid, so just relax and enjoy it. There's a boat waiting that'll take you to the island. The exact location has to remain…"

"Confidential, I know."

Back in London, Marla had looked Meditrine Island up on every website she could find. It simply didn't exist—not on any map. Even Google Earth couldn't find it. Doubt had begun to set in, so Marla asked about it when the Consortium had called to confirm travel arrangements. "Meditrine Island" was merely a name, the friendly voice had assured her; the island could only actually be identified by its registration number, latitude, and longitude. "Please understand the Consortium's need for secrecy," the friendly voice had implored. "The assets of our clients would be under considerable risk if every Tom, Dick, and Harry knew where the island was located." If Marla had any doubts, the voice went on, they could cancel her flight at any time. Reassured, Marla had told them that wouldn't be necessary. *Let them keep their secrets,* she thought, *and I'll keep mine.*

Through her sunglasses, Marla watched the gray airport warehouses and car parks give way to green countryside. For a moment, the sun slipped behind a cloud and Marla shivered, remembering her vile neighbor Mr. James. Then the sun blazed back into the blue sky, warming away the gooseflesh on her arms and bathing her face in its warming glow. She vowed that would be last time she'd think of that horrible man, or her horrible past.

The past. She had considered calling her "mother" before jetting off, of course. She'd found herself standing at the payphone at her bed-sit, calling card in hand, scrap of paper in front of her with the number written on it in fading ink. Marla had even picked up the receiver, just for a second, before returning it to its cradle. *From the cradle to the grave,* Marla had thought bitterly, recalling a song she'd once heard at a club with Carlo. No, relations with her final pair of foster parents had ended very badly. Best to leave them that way rather than re-establish contact and then make them end even more spectacularly. What would she have said anyway? *Hello, Mrs. Gore, it's Marla, remember that fuck up of a foster daughter you couldn't wait to get rid of? Well, I got a job. A job on a faraway island...* They would just assume she was high again, or finally being sent to jail for her latest heinous crime. No, it was better to lock up the past and throw away the bloody key.

"We're here."

Welland's tones cut through her thoughts like the very voice of reason. He slowed the car to a halt and half-stood, pointing over the windshield into the distance. They'd arrived at a small harbor. The faint ding-ding of bells rang their greeting. Sun kissed the water, twinkling into the ocean's distance.

Marla looked out to where Welland was pointing and saw the speedboat, huge, sleek and black like his car. *He had to be kidding.*

"Your chariot awaits."

She looked wide-eyed at the impressive vessel. Its name had been painted on the front side, *Sentry Maiden*.

Welland took Marla's rucksack from the boot of the car and handed it to her.

"This is as far as I go," he said. "Island Security will look after you now."

"Thanks for the ride," said Marla, "You're not tempted to take some time off? Sunbathe?"

"Oh, believe me I am *sorely* tempted," he replied, "But, alas, duty calls. Catch a few rays for me, will you?"

Marla nodded. He turned back to the car, then paused.

"And have fun. But work *hard*."

His eyes shone for a moment before he replaced his shades. As the car roared away, Marla heaved the rucksack onto her shoulder and made her way over to the boat.

A heavy-set man dressed in a black, almost military, uniform waited for her at the foot of a steel ramp leading to the deck area. Rather uncomfortably, Marla clocked the holster on his belt. He was carrying a pistol. She'd been in London for so long, this was the only gun she'd seen outside of the airport.

"Miss Neuborn, I'm Anders, security operative over at Meditrine Island. I'm here to ensure your safe passage to the island. Your safety is my priority. My other priority, of course, is to safeguard the island. So, I'm afraid I'll have to take you through a quarantine procedure before you board."

"No problem. No problem at all," said Marla. This was getting kind of surreal.

Anders led Marla to a low building adjacent to the jetty

where the boat was moored. Stopping at a thick glass door, he took a plastic card from his belt and swiped it through a reader. The little LED light on the reader turned from red to green, there was a loud click and the door opened. Marla followed him inside and down a dimly lit corridor to another door. He used his swipe-card again and led her into a clinically white room. A long bench ran the full length of the wall at waist height. Anders closed the door behind them, then produced a pair of white rubber gloves from some secret pouch attached to his belt and snapped them on.

"If you'd like to place your bag on the bench, please."

It was more of an order than a request. Marla did as she was told and watched as Anders leaned over the bag as though he was going to launch into an impromptu exercise routine. Instead, he loosened the straps and drawstrings and began rooting through Marla's rucksack. She averted her eyes with awkward embarrassment as he hit a deep seam of underclothes. Unflinching, Anders continued his search of the main compartment until all her clothes and belongings were lined up on the bench in a parade of shame. Making his way through the side pockets and buckled top compartment, he stopped and pulled out her toiletry bag, then her personal music player. He stood and held both items aloft in his hand. Marla suddenly felt like she'd been caught with a full bag of drugs at some seedy border crossing. Tiny headphones dangled in front of her, conspiring with her toiletries against her.

"I'm afraid we'll have to confiscate these for the duration of your stay, Miss," snapped Anders, "The rules state that no liquids, gels, or other cosmetic items are allowed onto the island."

"But—how will I wash? What about my makeup?"

"Toiletries will be provided from the island's stores. You will have no need for makeup," said Anders, "In addition, no personal electronic device is to be taken onto the island by any employee, no matter how innocuous."

"I thought the rule only applied to phones, laptops, that kind of thing."

"That's fine. Your belongings will be returned to you on completion of your contract."

That's fine. Easy for you to say when you don't use eyeliner. One thing was certain—she'd be going on a spending spree as soon as she got paid. She watched Anders take her music player and little toilet bag, separating them out, and placing them into a plastic storage box a little further along the bench. She was going to miss her music almost as much as her make-up. *Thank God I didn't pack an electric razor, all Hell would break loose.*

Anders dropped suddenly into a squatting position, again looking like he might launch into an impromptu workout. He rooted beneath the bench and pulled out a cylindrical container, like a fire extinguisher but smaller. Returning his attention to the bag's contents, he pointed the nozzle of the cylinder at Marla's clothes and began to spray them with a fine white mist.

"Hey! What the hell?"

The mist smelled awful, like neat bleach. Marla had no desire for her clothes to smell of bleach. Anders continued spraying, like an automaton in a factory.

"What are you doing to my clothes? That stuff smells horrible!"

Only when he had sprayed every single garment, did Anders put down the cylinder and turn to address Marla.

"Apologies—strict regulations."

"Regulations about what?"

"Meditrine Island is home to more than just human beings. Dozens of rare species live there, too. Plants, insects, birds. You've traveled from an overpopulated city, rife with contaminants. We have to disinfect everything you bring with you to the island to safeguard the island's natural resources. I'm afraid I'll have to treat your shoes."

Marla climbed out of her shoes. As he got to work spraying them, she took in what Anders was saying. The environmental message sounded rather strange coming from such a militaristic man. *I'm being lectured on ecology by an armed policeman. Better listen up or he might shoot me.*

"Someone could have explained…"

"It's done now, miss. Just the clothes you're wearing to do now."

"The clothes I'm *wearing*?"

He gestured at another door.

"Showers are through there. Please use the disinfectant gel provided. Leave your clothes on the bench just outside the door and I'll process them while you shower."

Marla scowled at him.

"The smell fades eventually," said Anders brightly.

Marla turned and headed for the showers before she could say something she might regret.

A faint odor of bleach trailing behind her, Marla lugged her rucksack up the ramp and onto the deck of the sleek black vessel under the watchful eyes of Anders' deckhands.

"Welcome aboard the *Sentry Maiden*," saluted Anders.

Anders' men retracted the ramp and hauled in the docking ropes. The boat's engine started up in an excitement of white foam and, drifting forward and to one side, the craft began to pick up speed. Marla was on the final leg of her journey to Meditrine Island. She felt clean.

STRATUM CORNEUM

The huge man looked at Vera's lifeless body, coldly. Now the kill was over, his real work could begin. He always preferred them when they lay like this—silent and still, not raving and wriggling.

Selecting his finest scalpel from the workbench, he pressed a restraining hand down firmly on the girl's chest and cut into her, just below the neck. His hand as steady as a tiller's, he made yet more cuts in beautifully straight lines. Each one was a crimson ribbon, each one intersecting in his perfect design. Soon the girl's skin was divided up, like tectonic plates floating above the lava of her viscera.

Satisfied with his pattern making, he put the scalpel down and picked up the flesh-comb. He marveled for a moment at its sleek design, surgical steel head, ivory handle. Inserting it into the first intersection, he began to peel back the skin carefully. The red ribbons became folds of velvet meat, which he folded lovingly and placed in the basin next to the gurney.

The hardest part was always around the nails, and the face. His mouth locked into a grimace of concentration. The greatest care was required to lift these layers of derma without tearing them. Softly, softly, he worked the skin upwards from her face.

Then, disaster. He caught sight of his reflection in one of the girl's eyes. The dead black pool of her pupil revealed him at once. Why had he looked? Why was *she* looking? The connection broke the spell, and his concentration, at once. Before he could halt his movements, he felt the skin tear at the corner of her eye socket.

Clenching his teeth against the rage, he put aside the flesh-comb and put her eyes out. Both of them. With his thumbs.

There, she could mock his mistake no longer. He tore the scalp from her head with a violent wrenching motion. Plunging her blood-slicked hair into the metal waste bin, he struggled for a moment to regain his composure.

Exuding calm, deliberate breaths, he vowed to blind the next one before he skinned it. He couldn't afford the tiniest mistake. Absolute perfection was required of him, and of his prey. But the base matter before him was substandard, distracting him. For absolute perfection, he would have to wait.

He would have to be patient.

CHAPTER EIGHT

The crewmembers were a quiet bunch. At the start of the journey, Marla had tried to spark a bit of small talk with one of the security guards, a particularly handsome, dark-skinned guy about the same age as her, mid-twenties. He had politely all but blanked her, explaining that conversation with employees was forbidden while he was on duty. She'd smiled as she turned away from his stony face; she couldn't help it. His eyes had betrayed him, and for a split second he definitely checked her out, which was more action than she'd had in a long time.

Marla made her way to the head of the boat, enjoying the slightly scary incline and the rocking motion as it sped through the waves. Holding on tight to the handrail, Marla held her head high and breathed in the cool, refreshing sea air. Every now and then, ocean spray coated her skin and she luxuriated in its touch. The wind picked up a notch and the craft altered course slightly, prompting her to look aft. Beyond the rear of the boat, Marla could only see a wide expanse of blue, curving as if at the edge of the world. Turning back to the head of the boat, the same vista greeted her. She really was in the middle of nowhere, hurtling ever onwards in this black vessel to…where exactly?

Several minutes later, her eyes finally gave the answer. In the far distance Marla could just pick out a vague landmass. Anders hollered to his men, barking orders. Within seconds, the boat was a hive of activity, and Marla was ushered to the rear deck by Mr. Handsome.

"Almost home, miss," he said softly, out of earshot of his crewmates.

Home. Marla leaned back against the rear rails and craned her neck out to see. The island's details were becoming clearer as the boat ploughed on towards it. She could now make out sharp craggy rocks, with waves crashing onto them dramatically. Above this steep rocky perimeter were signs of lush vegetation, and terraces cut into the cliffs and hills. Nestled there were several white buildings, huge mansions the size of which Marla had only ever seen in the pages of celebrity magazines. The boat's engine slowed to a bass line throb, and the crewmen prepared the craft for docking at a wooden jetty. A security hut stood at the end of the jetty, guarding a set of winding steps that led up to the island.

Anders instructed Mr. Handsome to escort Marla through security clearance. He gallantly pulled her rucksack onto one manly shoulder and led her to the security hut. Another quick bag check—

This is worse than Heathrow...

—and Marla was soon walking the length of the jetty towards the twisting steps.

"Sorry I couldn't really talk to you earlier miss," said Mr. Handsome, "Anders runs a pretty tight ship."

"Literally. And please don't call me miss. I'm Marla."

He beamed. "Nice name. I'm Adam."

Marla smirked, wondering if his surname really was "Handsome." From the way the smile played across his jaw and cheeks, revealing deep dimples, she truly thought it should be.

Steady girl.

"Always good to see a new face around here," he continued, "Not often I get picked to go to the mainland. I enjoy it, you know, being on the boat."

She wrinkled her nose at the smell of her skin, still vaguely bleach-scented. Great, she smelled like the bathrooms at King's Cross railway station.

"When was the last time you were off the island then? And do they make you shower in this god-awful stuff too?" asked Marla.

He smiled. It was a nice smile.

"A few w... Hey, sorry. I'm not allowed to talk about stuff like that. More than my job's worth."

Marla laughed. A sharp, shrill cackle that echoed off the

rocks and left her feeling immediately embarrassed. Adam was silent. She looked up at him and realized he wasn't joking.

"You're serious, aren't you?" she said, a mixture of surprise and apology.

"Yeah. You think Anders is strict, just wait 'til you meet Fowler."

"Who's Fowler?"

"You'll find out in a minute. My orders are to take you to his office right now."

"Why?"

"Induction," said Adam.

"Induction? That sounds a bit ominous."

She fixed Adam with a concerned look.

"Don't worry," he said, "Just agree with everything he says, then you can get on with enjoying your cushy new job."

Marla laughed again, a little less shrilly this time.

Fowler remained seated behind the desk for a moment as Adam showed Marla into his office. The shadowy room was situated deep inside the red brick Security Headquarters, built on a flat promontory overlooking the jetty. Behind Fowler, a wide wall-to-wall window the size of a movie screen gave an impressive view of the ocean.

"Our new arrival. Miss Neuborn, Chief." Adam's voice was now stiff, formal.

"Thank you, Hudson," Fowler said, "and tell Anders I want to see him just as soon as I'm done here."

Hudson. Well it sounds a bit like Handsome, Marla thought.

Adam nodded, dismissed, quietly closing the door after him. Fowler gave Marla the once over before standing up and offering his hand.

"Welcome to Meditrine Island, Miss Neuborn. I'm Chief of Security Fowler."

She shook Fowler's hand. Christ, he had an iron grip. And long sharp fingernails for a guy.

"Please. Take a seat, Miss Neuborn."

She did so. Fowler remained standing. He wasn't an especially tall man and he evidently knew it. But now he was towering over her, the interrogator and his suspect. He pulled a series of documents from his desk drawer and placed them in front of her, not taking his eyes off her for one second.

"This is the new New Testament," he said dryly.

Marla picked up the first document, emblazoned with a "Consortium Inc." corporate logo. It depicted a world bisected by a flaming sword, around which was curled an angry looking snake. Subtle.

"Rules and regs. The only things that make my world go round. I need you to absorb these to the letter, Miss Neuborn. If you can do that for me, I'll be most grateful."

She couldn't quite place his accent. He sounded like a Scotsman who'd spent most of his life on a Texan ranch.

"I'll do my best," she replied.

Fowler's features dropped for a moment, then adjusted themselves into something resembling a friendly smile. Marla was suddenly finding it hard to keep eye contact.

"Music to my ears."

Finally, he sat down, stiff as a board in his swivel chair. Fowler truly looked like a man for whom relaxation meant a ten-mile jog through enemy territory, a heavy pack of incendiary devices on his back.

"Talking of which, music is not allowed on the island. Neither is liquor, or drugs. Especially drugs. Gatherings of more than two persons are also strictly prohibited. All these regulations, plus the rest, are in your dockets there."

"Gatherings..." began Marla. This was all beginning to sound a bit extreme.

"It may sound strict," Fowler interjected, "But security's responsibility to the Consortium Inc. is paramount. Your position here as a Lamplighter is built upon a set of values that we've worked hard to maintain ever since this community was created. Our contract with each other is one of trust. We trust you to abide by the rules—and you trust us to let you get on with your job."

He gestured at the documents on the desk. "Talking of such, your job specs are also in there. They detail your daily task rota, working hours, break allocation, and so forth. I already have a hard copy of your contract on file here, so that's all good."

At least I get to take breaks, Marla thought. She'd begun to think detention centers had fewer rules than this gig.

Fowler stood up again, offering his hand once more.

"Welcome on board, Miss Neuborn."

She looked nonplussed and really couldn't hide it.

"You'll get used to it in no time, have no fear," he continued.

"Thanks," she said as she shook his hand, already feeling a little wary of Fowler—afraid of him, even.

"Splendid. Now, exit this building, take a left and head up the path to the residential area. One of your fellow Lamplighters will be waiting for you there to show you the ropes. Ah, and don't forget your documents."

Marla picked them up quickly. The truth was she couldn't get out of Fowler's office fast enough. The air in there was just a little too close.

In stark contrast, the fresh island air outside was lovely. Marla made her way up the steep dusty path with Fowler's directions echoing in her ears. Bright mimosa flowers and wide carob trees lined the path, watched over by towering palms and massive euphorbia. The largest plants must have grown here for years, long before people had come to this island. And now she was here, too. All around her, crickets chirped and birds sang their welcome to her over the soft whisper of a welcomingly warm sea breeze. Taking a deep lungful of fresh, clean air, Marla closed her eyes and paused for a moment before pressing on up the slope.

Reaching the summit, she got her first look at how the Consortium Inc. members had spent their millions. Lush gardens framed by intricate walkways gave way to a huge swimming pool, and beyond that, a building. Not so much a house, but rather a palace, this fantastical construction of glass, steel, and white stucco caused Marla to gasp. She strolled into the gardens, turning this way and that to take in the elegantly informal planting, smiling at the way the afternoon sunlight danced through the trees and onto the winding stone path. As she neared the swimming pool, Marla heard faint splashing sounds.

The swimmer was doing a lazy backstroke, slowly making her way across the length of the pool. Reaching the end, she flipped over and pushed her way up and onto the little metal ladder that gave access to the poolside. Leaving wet footprints on the warm slabs, she walked over to a sun lounger and grabbed an oversized fluffy white towel. As she dried off her hair, she saw Marla approaching from the garden.

"Hey! You must be the new girl!"

Her voice matched her looks, American, sunny, and deeply curvaceous. A year or two older than Marla, perhaps. The yellow of her bikini suited her tanned complexion and infectious white smile. Marla felt as though a talking sunflower was greeting her.

"I'm Marla."

"Good to meet you. I'm Jessie. I guess you've already met Scowler?"

She gestured to a vacant sun lounger next to hers. Marla sat down opposite her as Jessie continued drying her hair.

"Scowler...?" Marla laughed, suddenly getting the joke. She was a little disoriented by Jessie's good humor, especially after Fowler's boot camp-style induction.

"I can see he's got you good and spooked with his induction crap. Don't worry, he's harmless really, just doesn't like us having too much fun. He's what you Brits would call a 'little Hitler,' y'know? Hey, I'll throw some clothes on and show you around, okay?"

"Cool. Thanks for doing this on your day off."

"Day off?" Jessie cackled, "Honey, this is a *work day*."

She shimmied away to get changed, singing to herself. Marla looked at the clear inviting depths of the swimming pool and marveled at what Jessie had just said. This was a *work day*.

CHAPTER NINE

Chief of Security Fowler shifted uncomfortably in his seat. His hemorrhoids had been giving him absolute murder for the last few days. Fowler winced as he tried to balance his buttocks on the support cushion above the vengeful assault being visited below. Admitting defeat with an exasperated groan, he decided instead to stand and look out the window. Watching a seagull riding the breeze above the perimeter fence, he caught sight of Adam, patrolling the pathway.

He hadn't been too sure what to make of the lad at first, a little too polite perhaps, a little *too* efficient. It made him suspicious. But Fowler had to admit Adam was much better than the last fellow they'd assigned from the mainland. Crossing the room, Fowler remembered how defiant the last one had been when his contract had been terminated. Things could have gotten messy, and he didn't take kindly to mess. He wasn't the worrying kind, but he made a mental note to keep a careful eye on Adam all the same. A blind man could have noticed the way the boy had looked at Marla Neuborn. *Pussy, the weakness of every single goddamn soldier in Christendom.* Doubly so on a hot island with strict no-swim regulations. Nope, one could never be too careful, and the security of the island was always at stake.

A knock at the door—three raps, rapid.

"Enter."

Anders stepped inside and closed the door behind him. He stood, staring at the back of Fowler's head, awaiting his orders.

"I understand there was another sighting?" The Chief

spoke without taking his eyes off the view out the window, his back still to Anders.

"Yes, sir. In the early hours. 04:00. On the dark side of the island again."

The dark side, that was what they called the steep rocky side of the island, all hidden coves and treacherous drops.

"And I suppose when you got there…"

"Gone, sir. Not a trace."

Fowler made a sharp smacking sound with his teeth. This wouldn't do. Would not do at all.

"Someone is breaking curfew on this island. You are to bring them in. It's your job. Are we clear?"

"Yes sir."

A hesitant intake of breath. Fowler could tell that Anders wanted to say more.

"Go on, Anders, speak your mind."

"It's just, by the time we get there to scope it out on foot it's like whoever it is out there sees or hears us coming."

Now Fowler turned to face Anders. Not amused.

"Stealth, Anders. That is the singular solution to your problem. Instruct your men to kill their flashlights, cut the damn chatter, and split up so they are patrolling singly. Then you might get somewhere."

His eyes burrowed into Anders' discomfort like dark little hooks.

"Is that helpful?"

"Sir."

"Double your efforts tonight. Get your men to spread out across the ridge bordering the dark side. I expect results. Dismissed."

The door clicked shut, leaving the chief alone with his sour thoughts once more. Sighing, he returned to his desk to conquer his piles and sharpen some pencils.

Marla struggled to keep up as Jessie flitted into the kitchen, looking fantastic in her loose summer dress.

"And this is the kitchen." Jessie gestured around her with arms flailing.

She performed each task gleefully as she reeled them off, "Here you'll be expected to switch on the lights, switch off the lights, turn on and ignite the gas, turn off the gas, open the faucet, close the faucet..."

Marla giggled as she watched Jessie's performance from the doorway.

"It's not all fun and games, though," said Jessie, beckoning Marla to join her over by the sink. She crouched down by the cupboard beneath it and opened the door. "The job's not over 'til the cleaning work is done," whispered Jessie remorsefully. "Make sure the place is spotless and old Scowler won't have anything to bug you with. I usually clean a couple different areas each day. Variety is the spice of life."

Marla peered inside and saw a collection of white, unbranded plastic bottles and dispensers standing to attention aside cleaning cloths and sponges.

"Strange—to see products without logos and wild claims on the packaging, I mean."

"Yeah, you'd think these guys would have enough cash to buy the premium brands, wouldn't you?"

"Maybe that's why they're rich. They accumulated the savings."

"Think you're onto something there."

They stood up again.

"Well, that's about it, really. Just use the gas, water, electric each day. Keep the place clean. Water the plants and keep the lawn trimmed back. Any questions?"

"Just one," said Marla, "Which room do I sleep in?"

Jessie roared with laughter.

"Oh, boy, they did a job on you didn't they?" She took pity, sensing Marla's genuine bewilderment. "It's okay, I thought I was gonna be lady of the manor when I first got here, too."

"I don't understand..."

"They kind of exaggerate the job spec before they hire you. We don't sleep in the main houses, but don't worry, there's a little summerhouse out back just for you. Kind of like servant's quarters, I guess..."

"Servant's quarters?"

"Yeah, kinda. But nicer..."

Servant's quarters. What century was this?

Suddenly, Jessie stopped still and peered out through the kitchen window.

"What's wrong?" asked Marla.

"Did you see him? Thought I saw someone standing out in the garden."

They both focused on the garden path, scanning the trees in the mid-distance.

"Can't see anyone. Weird..." Jessie's frown turned into her infectious smile again. "Hey, sorry if I spooked you, Marla. Come on, let me show you where you're gonna be crashing." Jessie crossed to the back door and opened it.

As she crossed the threshold, Marla glanced at the trees again nervously. Maybe she *had* seen someone standing there, just for a split second, watching silently. Stepping out into the warm summer air, she realized her arms were covered in goose bumps.

"Come on, toots."

Jessie was already halfway across the lawn. Marla followed her.

The summerhouse was nestled in an alcove of tall trees, separated from the side of the main building by thick hedgerows. Either side of the path leading to the front door was lined with pungent herbs. Marla's nostrils drank in the piquant aromas of mint and sage, rosemary and camphor. Jessie reached above the door, feeling along the frame until she located the key. She handed it over and stepped back so Marla could open the door herself.

"Welcome home, Marla."

Marla stepped inside as if she was entering a dream. The summerhouse was decked out like a fairytale cottage in a movie. *Summerhouse.* That made Marla giggle; surely every dwelling place on Meditrine Island was a summerhouse? This place was bliss.

Jessie grinned in recognition at Marla's happy silence. "Pretty neat, huh? I'll let you get settled in and drop by again later, okay?"

"Thanks. Thanks for everything."

Leaning in close, Jessie whispered in her ear, "We can smoke a joint together later. You smoke, right? I can always spot a fellow stoner…"

"But I thought…"

Jessie raised a finger to her lips, "Shhh…" She gave Marla a cheeky wink and left, closing the door behind her.

Marla set about exploring her new home right away. The comfortable living space was complete with a little wicker sofa, piled high with cushions. This led into a small galley kitchen, with bedroom and bathroom tucked away at the back under the protective shade of the tall trees. Unpacking her rucksack, Marla put her clothes into drawers and onto hangers then investigated the kitchen cupboards. She found them well stocked with tinned and dried food, preserves and snacks. Curiously, the food packaging was similar to the cleaning products she'd seen at the main house—plain white labels with the name of the contents, a use by date, and nothing more. A little refrigerator was sandwiched in between the doorway and stove, and contained dairy items and an icebox filled with frozen bread and bagels. Marla stood in the kitchen and gorged herself on cheese, crackers, olives, and sun-dried tomatoes. This was more food than she'd seen in days, and the tomatoes were the best she'd ever tasted, drenched in rich peppery olive oil. She sat down on the wicker sofa to digest her food for a while. Sadly, the sofa wasn't as comfortable as it had first looked even with all the cushions piled high. Still, she wouldn't swap this for all the soft furnishings in London.

Waking up with a crick in her neck, Marla realized she must've dozed off for quite some time. The sky outside had darkened to an almost green-blue color as the birds chirruped at the sun's descent. Stretching her arms and back until her neck clicked, she made her way through to the shower room. This, too, was well stocked, with fresh, fluffy towels and toiletries to replace the ones that security had confiscated. The little bottles were similar to the containers of cleaning products at the main house, plain white plastic with no branding, just some simple text to describe the contents. She opened the container marked "shower gel" and sniffed at it. There was no discernable fragrance to the stuff at all. Oh, well, better no fragrance at all than some horrid floral scent she didn't like, although the latter might help mask the remnants of bleach she could still smell on her skin. Marla turned on the shower and tested the stream with her hand. It warmed up in no time. *Naught to toasty in ten seconds.* She climbed in and water pummeled her body like a powerful masseuse; this shower was a million times better than the one she'd suffered every day back at the bed-sit. She let the water run down her face as she blinked away embarrassing memories of climbing out the bathroom window and shimmying along the ledge while perverts wolf whistled at her from the street below. *Best not think about that one.* Marla turned, arched her back and let the warm jet travel up and down her spine. She could really feel the tension being driven out of her now. *Another half hour in here ought to do it.* Then she heard the whisper.

"*Marla.*"

The voice was urgent and shocking to her. Again, goose bumps erupted all over her skin. She felt suddenly vulnerable, naked, and afraid.

"*Marla.*"

She turned the shower off and stepped gingerly out onto the tiled floor, grabbing the biggest, fluffiest towel and wrapping it round her body tightly.

"Who's there?"

Her heart leapt into her mouth as a loud knock resounded on the door. She looked around for something with which to defend herself, the sudden mad image of her brandishing a toilet brush like a weapon flashing into her head.

"*It's me—Jessie.*"

Marla opened the door, "Jessie! Christ, you shared the shit out of me!"

"I'm sorry, toots. I'll wait for you on the porch," she held up a freshly rolled joint. "Okay?"

Minutes later, dressed in clean jeans and T-shirt, Marla stepped out into the evening air and sat down next to Jessie on the porch. The joint was already lit, the fiery orange tip dancing like a firefly as Jessie passed it to her. Marla inhaled the smoke gently—it smelled pretty potent. She coughed, hard. This was the strongest skunk she'd ever tasted. Jessie laughed at her joyously. Marla started to giggle too, through her coughing rasps.

"Where the hell did you get this stuff?"

"I could tell you," smiled Jessie, taking the joint back from Marla.

"But then you'd have to kill me, right?"

"Exactamundo."

What sounded like an owl sang in the distance. Night had arrived.

"How long have you worked here, Jessie?"

"Oh, too long really. I came here just over six months ago. Was bumming around in San Fran with nothing to do, saw the job ad, and a coupla weeks later here I was." She paused for a moment, as if winding down. "Do you like it here, Marla?"

"Yes. Yes, I really do."

"Good. Hold onto that feeling for as long as possible, toots."

"What do you mean? Don't you like it here?"

"I do…I mean I did, I guess. But after a while, this place just seems to…." She paused. "I'm sorry, it's your first day. Not fair to put a dampener on things on your first day. My bad."

"No, it's okay. Go on."

"It's no big deal really. You do any job for a while and it becomes…just a job, y'know?"

Marla nodded quietly. *After a while, this place just seems to get to you.* Marla felt certain that's what Jessie had meant to say.

The trees creaked in the balmy air. From the shadows of their trunks, he watched the girls with hungry eyes. They were smoking and talking together, blissfully unaware of his presence. He sniffed at the smell of their smoke, absorbing their pollutants. He would know all of their scents soon enough. And they would know him.

CHAPTER TEN

Breathing frantically, Marla was running for her life. The path down to the jetty was treacherous, and she almost fell a couple of times as the gravel slid beneath her feet. Her pursuer was gaining on her. He knew the terrain. She could almost feel him on her back as she hurtled down the gangway and onto the wooden jetty. Her heavy footfalls echoed off the rocks as she sprinted, full pelt, towards the security hut. Then, *fuck*, she lurched to a halt as Adam stepped out of the hut in front of her, brandishing a pistol. *No*, she tried to cry as he lifted the weapon and pointed it at her head but no sound would come.

Bang.

The bullet pierced her forehead, burned into her brain and rested there, molten hot. Her knees became fluid and she toppled over the side of the jetty, hitting the water with a splash.

Splash. Marla awoke violently and turned off the alarm clock, blinking away her nightmare. Sunlight was creeping in through the window blinds. Her bedding was in violent disarray. That was the last time she'd eat cheese *and* smoke a joint before bedtime, she told herself. *Idiot.*

Showered and full of coffee and breakfast, Marla set out across the lawn to work. Her first day's work on the island. She took the key from her pocket and stepped inside the palatial house, again marveling at its size. A majestic staircase, which looked as though some visionary Swedish architect had designed it, swept upwards from the lobby inviting her to explore upstairs. Marla took a first tentative step on the stairs, as though not wanting to wake anyone who was up there, sleeping. Of course, no one was—but the feeling of being an intruder in someone else's house was pervasive, and it would take Marla some time to get used to it. Wandering around the upper floor, she looked inside each of the five bedrooms, each with its own luxurious en suite bathroom. The bed linen, towels, and rugs were of the highest quality, clean and white. What struck Marla most was the apparent lack of any personality in the rooms. There were no framed photographs, no pictures of any kind. No trinkets, ornaments, or little family heirlooms to give any clue about who lived there. One of the bedrooms belonged to a child—the tiny bed and nightlight told her this much. A closet door set into the wall tempted Marla with its mystery, but upon opening it she found it empty. No toys? No dressing up clothes? No televisions or multimedia players? She supposed the children of the rich owners simply brought stacks of toys, games, and gadgets with them. Oh, well, it was less of a problem for her to dust. She hated dusting ornaments with a passion and, shuddering at the thought, went back downstairs to the kitchen.

Sitting on a high stool at the vast breakfast bar, Marla leafed through Fowler's rules and regulations, incredulous at how many of the damn things there were. There was even a directive on the minimum amount of water to drink each day, for Christ's sake. Still, if it helped the owners to rack up their utilities points and keep her in gainful employment, Marla was only too happy to do as she was told. She filled a glass with water and took a sip. It was the finest champagne compared to the dreadful bed-sit water—"Thames water" her ex used to call it. No, the water here had no unpleasant chemical smell; in fact, it had no discernable odor of any kind. She drank again and decided its source must be a wellspring on the island somewhere. Hell, even bottled water never tasted this good. Having drunk her fill, Marla set about vacuuming the ground floor lobby, hallway and rooms.

It was a little weird not to see a huge television in the living room, as Marla was sure these people would have a gigantic wall-mounted flat screen monstrosity. She felt strangely pleased that there wasn't one. The islanders, despite their incredible wealth, apparently embraced the "peace and quiet" lifestyle in the fullest sense. Vacuuming done, Marla rooted in a utility closet and found a mop and bucket. Digging around in the cupboard under the sink she found some floor cleaning solution, clearly labeled yet un-branded like all the other household products. She filled the bucket with hot water and added a capful of the cleaning fluid. It fizzed a little as it mixed with the water, creating a little layer of bubbles like the head on a pint of beer. *Strange*, thought Marla as steam rose from the bucket in little kiss curls. The floor stuff was odorless and colorless, just like the drinking water—in fact, it looked like it may as well have *been* drinking water. But as she worked the hot sudsy mixture into the floor tiles with the mop, they began to gleam. *Must be organic. Only the very best for these guys*, she mused.

Working her way across the kitchen floor in sections, Marla mopped herself into the corner by the patio door. She stopped her labors for a moment to unlock it, using both hands to slide the thick glass open. The lush Mediterranean breeze drifted inside, and began to dry the floor right away. Marla drank in the fresh air and a smile curled at the corner of her lips. Once her morning chores were done, she'd go for a swim in the pool, where she'd met Jessie yesterday, then eat some lunch in the garden. As she gazed out, something caught her eye. Her greasy fingerprints on the glass door. And something else, rusty red, coated the door catch and the metal casing surrounding it. It looked like blood. Marla tiptoed over the still-drying floor and grabbed a cloth, which she moistened at the sink. Returning to the door, she rubbed at the dry red patch. It made a little pattern on the wet cloth. Instinctively, she sniffed at it, without getting her nose too close. It smelled metallic. *Rust*, she thought, *even paradise needs oiling occasionally.* She refolded the cloth and wiped the greasy fingerprints away, listening to the glass squeaking as she did so. Sliding the door shut behind her, Marla headed for the summerhouse where her bikini was waiting for her.

The ravenous eyes watched Marla's shadow lengthen over the patio as she walked away. Just out of her sight were more tiny red stains that lay concealed below the doorstep, where only ants could find them. The stains formed the signature of his handiwork—a flourish. He hungered to work again.

Lying back in the water, Marla peered up at the blazing sun-shine. *Should have brought my sunglasses*, she thought, then looked at her pale white arms glistening on the surface of the pool. *Christ, anyone looking at my skin will need a pair, too.* No mat-ter, she'd have a tan soon enough if the weather stayed like this on the island. Floating to the water's edge, she kicked off again from the pool side, its textured hardness feeling good on the soles of her feet. Marla swam a few lengths then, breathless, clambered out of the pool. She felt embarrassed about how out of shape she was, and made a pact with herself there and then to take a swim every day. Back in London, all the gymnasiums had been too expensive. Now she had an entire pool to herself, there was no excuse not to exercise. *Well*, she thought as she set-tled back on the sun lounger, *maybe I do have a couple of excuses, like sunbathing followed by a delicious lunch.* She closed her eyes against the sun, which burned red through her eyelids. Then her vision went black. The sun must have disappeared behind a cloud. She shivered, her skin still wet from the swim, and felt her nipples harden. Just as the sun came back out again, Marla heard a noise like a footfall in the grass. She opened her eyes and sat bolt upright. Had someone been standing there seconds ago, casting a shadow over her but saying nothing? *That's too creepy, stop scaring yourself, Marla.* But her arms and legs had turned to gooseflesh again and she felt so vulnerable lying there half naked and alone. *You're getting paranoid, dear,* she told her-self, *it's been a long time since you smoked grade-A skunk and maybe with good reason.* Wrapping a towel around her tight shoulders, she started walking towards the summerhouse. Maybe she'd get dressed and go for a walk, see if she could find Jessie.

She didn't feel hungry anymore.

Strolling down the path, away from the main house, Marla started feeling better. She was just being paranoid; after months of hustle and bustle in the big city, maybe all this peace and quiet was giving her culture shock. A butterfly flitted by ahead of her, disappearing into the deep, fragrant foliage at the side of the path. Lilting birdsong drifted down from the tree branches high above. She lifted her head, shades protecting her eyes from the sun this time, and let the warm glow spread across her entire face. Cicadas sang their joyous fanfare as she passed them. This place truly was like some kind of paradise.

Reaching the section of path that led to Fowler's Security building, Marla stopped for a while and gazed out to sea. She realized she had no idea where Jessie was staying and, post-smoking, hadn't had the presence of mind to ask for directions. Turning away from the ocean, she spied another path leading off inland at an angle to the one she'd followed. *Nothing ventured,* she thought and walked on. This path was narrower and more overgrown, with thickets and trees providing welcome shade from the heat of the sun. After a few minutes the path took a winding turn to the left, then back to the right into a thick wooded area. As she followed the twists and turns, Marla suddenly saw a figure crouching at the side of the path up ahead. She instinctively slowed her pace, trying to see if she recognized this stranger in the woods. As she neared the figure, his dark skin and hair became suddenly familiar to her. She remembered her anxiety dream from the morning and halted in her tracks.

Adam was on his haunches, studying something at the side of the path. He did not look up as Marla approached, but spoke as if he'd been expecting her.

"It's dead, I think…"

Marla bent over to take a closer look. A sleek gray cat lay in the dirt on its back, perfectly still. It could have been sleeping, dreaming of mice, but there was no telltale rise and fall of fur—no movement at all—it had stopped breathing.

"Poor thing. What do you think happened to it?"

Using a thick twig, Adam gently lifted the cat's head. Marla held a hand to mouth in horror. The cat's eyes were gone from their sockets and half the creature's cranium was open like a pumpkin with half the flesh scooped out. It looked as if something had taken a hungry bite out of its skull.

"Predator of some kind," said Adam. "Big, hungry and pissed off, whatever it was."

"Did the cat…belong to somebody?"

Adam stood up and turned to face Marla. She was glad; she'd much rather look at his features than the cat's.

"Don't think so," he replied, looking a little bemused by her stare. "The owners don't keep pets as far as I know. Still, I'd better report it to Fowler—maybe he knows something about it."

"Maybe it's his cat?"

Adam raised an eyebrow at her.

"No, I suppose he doesn't seem like an animal-lover, does he?" she joked.

"Doesn't seem like an *anything*-lover," laughed Adam. "So, where are you off to?"

"Oh, just out for a stroll. Actually, I wanted to drop by and see Jessie—thank her for showing me the ropes yesterday. Do you know her?"

"The American girl? Yeah, sure."

"Good. Perhaps you wouldn't mind showing me where she lives?"

"Course not. It's not that far. Follow me."

Marla followed him through the trees.

She glanced over her shoulder and saw that flies had begun to buzz and swarm around the cat's ruined face.

CHAPTER ELEVEN

They found Jessie sitting cross-legged on the lawn, with an upturned lawnmower in front of her. She was busy trying to dislodge something that had become tangled up in the blades.

"Hey!"

Marla got the distinct impression the greeting was only meant for her, as Jessie avoided looking at Adam. *She really hates authority figures,* thought Marla as she walked over to give Jessie a hand with the mower.

"Need a hand there?" asked Adam.

"No thanks," replied Jessie, still not looking at him. She launched into an awful rendition of "Sisters are Doing it for Themselves." If the cat Adam had found was still alive, it would have been screeching at the sound of Jessie's song.

Marla laughed. Jessie's goofiness was infectious. She glanced over her shoulder at Adam, "Cheers for showing me the way."

"Anytime."

As he disappeared into the trees, Jessie guffawed. "You don't wait long, do you?"

Marla's cheeks turned beetroot red. "I don't know what you mean…"

"Yeah, yeah, whatever. Smoochin' in the woods with Mister Security. And it's only your second day."

She watched as Marla's embarrassment became laughter.

"Come on," said Jessie. "Let's go inside."

"But…what about the mower?"

"Oh, screw the mower. Let me fix you a *mow*-jito instead."

Jessie had not only been good to her word, but had mixed the best mojito Marla had ever tasted. The summerhouse was messier than Marla's, with that lived-in feeling. Perhaps her own digs would look more like Jessie's after she'd spent a few months living there. Jessie drained her glass, made an appreciative smacking sound with her lips and refilled it.

"Drink up." She waved the jug full of mojito teasingly at Marla.

Marla smiled and knocked back the rest of her drink, then held the glass out to Jessie. She'd decided she liked Jessie very much.

"Thank you, bartender," she giggled.

Jessie giggled, too, and filled her glass. They both took noisy sips, enjoying the sharpness of the lime juice and the alcohol-laden ice. Like the weed from the night before, the booze packed quite a punch. Marla found herself wondering how Jessie got this stuff onto the island without being caught. She suddenly felt very green, like the new kid at school joining in with an illicit cigarette out of sight of the teachers. Then she chuckled, imagining Chief of Security Fowler dressed up in academic robes and a mortarboard.

"What's funny?" asked Jessie, smiling.

"I don't know… I guess I'm still just a little bit amazed by this place. By you and your incredible stash of illicit substances. I mean, how do you sneak this stuff in?"

"Like I said, I could tell you but I'd have to kill you."

"Promise I won't say a word to anyone."

"I'm sure you wouldn't. You're one of the good people, Marla, I can see that. But if I don't tell you, then you don't know, and if Fowler and his cronies ever pick you up and put the thumbscrews on you…well, you won't be able to tell them a damn thing."

Marla gulped. Jessie's expression was deadly serious, her eyes never leaving Marla's as she took a sip of her drink. Then Jessie cracked up, almost spluttering her drink everywhere.

"You had me going there," sighed Marla. "I'm so bloody naïve. But they're not really that bad, are they? Fowler and his boys?"

"Now that I won't joke about," replied Jessie. "The guy who walked you here…"

"Adam?"

"Adam. Now he seems okay, I must admit. But I'm sure the rest of them are mostly just bored and itching for a way to get back at that bastard Fowler. Boredom and rebellion, it's a pretty volatile combination, but one that has its advantages."

Jessie winked as she topped up her mojito glass again. Marla nodded. *So that's how she gets her supplies,* she thought, admiring Jessie all the more.

"He's cute, but be real careful." Jessie's tone had turned to one of wise-old-oracle. "If you get caught doing the nasty with Adam in the Garden of Eden, Fowler will have you deported before you can put your panties back on."

Marla blushed furiously and buried her face in her drink.

"Relax, I'm just kidding. Kinda," teased Jessie. "Have to take your pleasure where you can get it here. No games consoles round here, no movies or fast food joints. And no bars. Well, not of the licensed kind anyhow."

Marla put her drink down on the little glass coffee table clumsily. She was finding it hard to think clearly through the alcohol now.

"How many Lamplighters are there?"

"Just three of us, including you. Pietro totally loves himself and he can be a bit of a bastard sometimes. But he's a smoker, too, so that's cool."

"When will I meet him?"

"That's the hard part, see? The 'two-person rule' makes it hard for us to hang out. Took me a few days to figure it out, do the rounds. Hey, where there's a will there's a way, I'm workin' on it. But hey, none of exactly came here to make friends, did we?"

"What do you mean?"

"Well, think about it. Anyone who's gonna sign up for this gig only has one thing on their mind, right? The money. That and the so-called 'millionaire lifestyle,' which ain't all that it's cracked up to be, let me tell you."

"Seems okay to me."

"Like I said before, I don't wanna piss on your parade. But remember it's only your second day. After a couple of weeks, the monotony starts to set in, and when the weeks turn into months…. Let's just say the shine gets taken off it, okay?"

"And then what happens?"

"Oh, nothing much. Personally, I just find little ways of dealing. But even the joints and the alcohol get a bit tired sometimes. Hell, I'm sorry Marla, I don't want to bring you down. It's the booze talking," she raised her glass in a toast, "So here's to more booze!"

"I'll drink to that." Marla clinked her glass against Jessie's.

They had almost drained the jug completely. "Looks like it's gonna be a good night, my dear," said Jessie drunkenly before swaggering off to the kitchen to fill it up again.

Marla took another sip and remembered her dingy bed-sit, all the unpaid bills, and hassle from her landlady. It was easy to complain when you'd had too much of a good thing, she supposed, but she meant to enjoy every minute.

A sound like gravel being sucked through an echoing tube woke Marla. Her brain throbbed inside her skull as she struggled to open her eyes. For a moment she couldn't open her mouth, it felt so dry. Slowly and painfully sitting up, she realized she'd passed out on Jessie's bed. Focusing on the form lying next to her, Marla realized her head had been right next to Jessie's feet. The violent gravelly sound continued from the vicinity of Jessie's head. She was snoring as loud as a freight train.

Marla managed to stand up, staggering backwards and steadying herself against the doorframe. Holding her pounding forehead with one shaky hand, she made her way out of the bedroom, through the living area, and into the kitchen. She could just make out a few trees in the moonlight outside the window—it was the middle of the night. Grabbing a glass from the worktop, Marla opened the faucet and filled it with cool, clear water. She gulped the water down in one go, and filled the glass again. Then, a dull wave of nausea hit her stomach and bile rose in her throat. The glass wasn't properly clean. It still stank of mojito. Marla lurched over the sink and vomited, the entire contents of her stomach emptying into the sink, echoing off the unsympathetic steel interior. The water still ran mockingly.

If only she'd drunk her fill of that tonight instead of all those mojitos. *Jesus*, she suddenly realized, trying not to heave again, *we put away three jugs of the stuff.* The mere thought was enough to send her stomach muscles into involuntary spasm again and, horribly, she retched up what was left in her poor aching belly. Splashing some water on her face, Marla steadied herself against the worktop and peered at her reflection in the kitchen window. She looked like death, her pale skin and sunken eyes all the more pronounced in the silvery light of the moon. *I'll never drink again*, she tried to promise herself. *I know I've said it before, but I mean it this time. Never again.*

Then she saw the other face, looking back at her from the trees.

CHAPTER TWELVE

Jessie was wrapped up in the kind of warm candyfloss dreams that only snoring drunks can access. Languid waves lapped at her feet, gently tickling her toes. A tropical breeze massaged her naked body. Then the sound of Marla screaming penetrated her skull.

She kicked off the bedcovers instinctively and lurched towards the door. The scream had come from the kitchen—Jessie hoped the cockroaches hadn't come back. Turning the corner, she found Marla lying on the floor, surrounded by broken glass. Stepping carefully through the shards, Jessie crouched and tried to rouse Marla. Good, she was still breathing. She shook Marla's body a little harder.

Marla groaned and looked up at Jessie's worried face, a welcome sight after the face she'd seen at the window. There'd been something wrong with its eyes, she remembered that clearly. But what had happened next, how she'd come to be in a crumpled heap on the kitchen tiles amidst all this broken glass, was a complete blur.

"What happened? You okay?"

"I'm sorry. I was sick. Then I saw…I thought I saw…"

"Man, I'm the one who's sorry," said Jessie earnestly. "I mixed those drinks a little strong. Come on, let me help you up."

Groaning again as the room spun, Marla struggled to her feet with Jessie's help. She half-fell, half-sat on a stool and leaned on the counter to steady herself, watching as Jessie filled the kettle with water and switched it on.

"Hot, sweet coffee. This will save your life," Jessie said cheerily.

Marla watched almost incredulously as Jessie made the

drinks, a superhuman feat considering the amount of booze they'd put away only a few hours ago. As the steam from the kettle rose, fogging the windows, Marla tried to picture the face she'd seen—or thought she'd seen—on the other side of the glass. Hollow eyes, that's all she could remember. But even that small fragment was enough to give her the chills. She shuddered, and pulled a small shard of glass from her hair.

"I only came in here for some water. Must've dropped the glass. Sorry."

"No harm done. Here you go."

Jessie placed a welcome mug of coffee in front of her. Marla wrapped her hands around it, the warmth comforting her.

"You must think I'm such a lightweight..."

Jessie laughed as she swept up the pieces of broken glass in a plastic dustpan.

"I'm just glad you're okay. Nearest hospital is quite a boat ride from here. On second thought, you could've hurt yourself at least a *little bit*—we could've gotten ourselves some quality shore leave."

Marla's eyes drifted to the window again. She took a sip of the hot, sweet coffee.

"Could've sworn I saw a face at the window. A man, watching me. Scared me half to death, let me tell you."

"Who was it? What did he look like?"

"I don't know. All I remember is his eyes—he had weird eyes."

Jessie peered out through the window, leaning as close as she could to the glass.

"Well, there's no one there now. I've scared myself a couple of times with my own reflection. Happens from time to time, being so isolated up here. And you did drink quite a bit."

"I suppose so," sighed Marla, feeling a little foolish. "I'm too used to being surrounded by noisy neighbors, TV sets, stereos. And bawling children."

"It's only been a couple of days, you'll get used to the quiet," replied Jessie, upbeat. "And if not, we'll throw a party."

"No mojitos this time?"

"No mojitos. I promise. Come on, you should get some

shut-eye. You can have my bed, I'll take the couch."

Marla tried her best to protest but Jessie was having none of it. Leaning on Jessie for support, she sloped into the bedroom and under the covers.

As her head sank slowly into the soft pillow, Marla closed her eyes. The image of the face at the window and those desolate, empty eyes returned to her, keeping her from sleep. Finally, her body surrendered to fatigue and she drifted off, her breathing troubled in the still, silent night.

In the other room Jessie sat awake on the couch, watching the window and waiting for the sun to rise.

Security Operative Anders felt the chill from the night cross-wind in his knuckles as he walked, clutching the flashlight in his right hand. The thing was switched off as per the chief's instructions, but the weight of it in his hand was reassuring somehow. His radio was silenced, too, again Fowler's call, for fear of alerting his quarry to the presence of him and his men. Anders pictured them fanning out as they'd been instructed, slowly crossing the dark side's craggy terrain. His hearing seemed enhanced in the gloom and he turned at the sound of breath whistling through teeth, his fingers clenching tighter around the flashlight. He froze, eyes searching out movement, but none was there. Not breath, just the wind. He breathed now, a slow and heavy exhalation of compacted tension, and made his way down a crude stairwell of sharp rocks. The biting cross-wind diminished as he descended into the natural shelter of a steep-walled cove, the whistling of the wind giving way to stone cold silence. He listened to the echoes of his own gravelly footfalls, almost deafeningly loud in the still calm, and hurried on down to the cove in order to be rid of them.

Tidal erosion had turned the area at the back of the cove into a steep bank the waves couldn't quite reach. As he worked his way down the last of the rocks and onto the cove's sloping surface, Anders stopped dead in his tracks. Not a sound this time, but a real honest-to-goodness movement. It had flickered at the periphery of his vision where the sand of the cove met the sheer rock wall. He stooped, strafing the line of the rocks behind him, in order to get a better look at where the movement had occurred. His eyes darted across the rocky surfaces, which held shadows as deep as the folds of great velvet curtains. There. There it was again, a movement at the rear of the cove—too big to be an animal, he felt sure of that.

He felt his heartbeat quicken as he crept up the incline, stealing closer to the source of the movement. Here, the rock face folded in on itself forming a deep fissure as large as the prow of the *Sentry Maiden,* and just as black as her hull. Had his eyes tricked him, mistaking the great dark shape for that of an intruder? He took a few steps nearer the maw-like mouth in the wall, phasing out the distant crashing of waves and listening intently for a sound that might betray the interloper. But he was the interloper here. Anders felt it just as surely as the nervous breath that hissed from his lips, just as acutely as the chill that kissed the back of his neck. It was a mistake to come down here all alone, following ghosts and shadows. It was a mistake to be out of radio contact, facing a dark impenetrable black crevice with the tide at his back desperate to sweep him off his feet and beneath.

Anders, the interloper, clutched the flashlight like a weapon and turned. His terror-filled eyes gaped wide as a child's, imagining dark things and their violent greetings.

He saw only the sky, midnight blue, and the vague froth of white waves and laughed in relief. Nothing there except his paranoia. Time to declare the area secure and move to higher ground where he could no longer do such a good job of scaring himself silly.

He was about to begin his ascent when he felt great hands bear down on him, then lift him from his feet. The world tilted, spiraled. His fingers lost the flashlight, clawing desperately for his belt, his radio. Everything turned to white noise as Anders felt his face slam into the wall of rocks. He tried to cry out as this huge *something* broke his mouth over the jagged stones and put out his eyes.

And when pain finally found his voice, the sea swallowed his cries.

Dawn and the fresh perspective of a new day left Marla a little embarrassed about the night before. Jessie had spared her the humiliation of morning small talk by leaving the summerhouse before Marla had awoken. Not only that, but she'd left a fresh pot of coffee on the simmer and a breakfast of eggs and ham in the kitchen for her.

Marla ate a little, memories of throwing up still swirling in her gut. But the food and coffee put the color back into her cheeks and gave the acidity in her stomach something to chew on. She gazed out the window, sipping from a glass of cool water. Sunlight flickered through the trees where last night she'd seen those eyes looking at her. She chuckled to herself as she washed her cup and plate. *Damned mojitos.*

She made her way over to the main house, looking for Jessie so she could say her goodbyes and go do her chores. As she called Jessie's name, birds and insects seemed to chirrup back at her jokingly. The house was empty, as was the pool. Maybe Jessie had gone for a stroll—Marla made a mental note to do the very same after her work was done.

The power shower was a novelty that was never going to wear off for Marla. The steaming blast of hot water and suds almost had her hangover begging for mercy. Feeling considerably brighter, Marla threw on some clothes and walked across to the house. There, she scrubbed and cleaned the bathrooms, watered the plants and tidied up the patio outside the kitchen. Her exertions felt good, and it had been too long since she'd indulged in the simple labor of household duties. Any kind of cleaning at her bed-sit had felt like a betrayal to what was left of her self-worth, especially with the rent that witch the landlady had been charging. This was different though—an honest day's work.

Afternoon had set in by the time she felt she'd done enough to deserve a swim, and Marla donned her bikini and slid into the pool. The water was warm and welcoming on her skin, and she spent a blissful hour swimming, splashing, and floating in its depths. Relaxing on a sun lounger for a while, Marla realized there was only one thing missing from her perfect day—a book.

She cursed herself for not packing one. Reading by the pool in the glorious sunshine would be the icing on the cake she decided and, pulling her clothes on, headed inside the house to find something to read.

"This is fucking crazy," she said out loud to herself as she ducked under the bed to continue her search.

No books, magazines, in fact *nothing* to read in the entire house. Even the cleaning products had no labels—if they had, she'd make do with reading one of those at this point. Frustrated by her fruitless search, Marla scanned the children's bedrooms once again, fantasizing that a well-thumbed copy of *Doctor Seuss* or *The Little Prince* would peek out from an open drawer. No such luck—finding nothing, Marla conceded defeat and walked heavily back downstairs. Filling a plastic bottle with water from the kitchen faucet, she stepped outside into the afternoon sun.

Walking through the garden and onto the path leading away from the house, Marla suddenly felt a chill on the nape of her neck, like a shadow had kissed her. She turned and looked back at the house, scanning the tree line beyond. There was nothing there, no phantom stranger. She shrugged off the chill, which had now spread throughout her body, and walked on down the path. As she blinked, the sunlight made a red void behind her eyelids, and the memory of those dark empty eyes returned to her.

CHAPTER THIRTEEN

Marla was panting by the time she reached the top of the hill. Her walk had taken her to higher ground, and air fresher than any she had ever breathed before. The trees had thinned out long ago, leaving her atop a gorgeous expanse of scrubland at the edge of the island. Pausing for breath, she saw a white building about a quarter of a mile away, its windows looking out to sea. She took a drink of already tepid water from the plastic bottle and began plodding down the sandy track towards the building.

As she drew closer to it, she saw that the building was a mansion house, constructed in the same luxurious style as the one she'd been assigned to take care of. Nearing the gate, she squinted up at the glimmering glass and white stucco through narrowed eyes. This house was much larger than "hers"—whoever the hell owned this place, they were a damn sight wealthier than she'd ever be, that was for sure.

Marla paused at the gate, feeling all of a sudden like an intruder on someone else's property. *By definition that's exactly what I am*, she thought—*an intruder*. Avoiding the gate, she opted instead to follow the perimeter white picket fence round back and take a peek at the garden. Verdant grass and simple hardy planting made the space look more like a bowling green than a garden. The lawn had been extremely well-tended, and was currently being nourished by the gentle rhythmic drizzle from dozens of sprinklers. Marla kicked off her shoes instinctively. Her hot feet demanded this pleasure of her, and carried the rest of her body forward before her brain could resist. The wet grass beneath her feet was actual heaven, and she padded across the grass with a saintly look on her face, laughing as the sprinklers suddenly spurted a cool cloud of summer rain on her face. Lost in the droplets, she spun and laughed and danced between the jets.

"Who the hell are you?"

The voice was male, hard, and just a little Latin-sounding. Marla stood still and opened her eyes, suddenly feeling like a complete idiot. *Dancing in the sprinklers. In someone else's garden. Idiot.*

"I'm Marla," she replied. "The new girl."

"Ah, the new girl. I should have known. I'm Pietro."

Marla reached out and shook the hand that he'd offered. His grip was firm but his skin was very soft, almost feminine. Only premium cleaning products could soften a guy's skin like this—that, and never working an honest day in a lifetime. *This guy has to be a Lamplighter,* thought Marla, trying and failing to remember what Jessie had said about Pietro. She looked up from his hand to his face. Dark hazel eyes peered back at her from within the frame of his olive-skinned face.

"Let me fix you a drink," he said as he turned and headed for the house.

Here we go again, she thought as she followed him.

Still giddy from her dance, Marla's eyes wandered. Whoever this guy was, his ass was as pretty as his face.

The drink turned out to be a smoothie. An evil voice in the back of Marla's head seemed to be crying out for an alcoholic hair of the dog. It would certainly help take the edge off her embarrassment at being found dancing in the garden. Marla managed to ignore the evil voice, instead watching Pietro intently as he chopped bananas and juicy berries and transferred them to a blender. Marla watched as he added a little cream and a handful of ice and hit the button. The blades whizzed loudly and made little purple and yellow waves on the inside of the clear plastic jug. Pietro then poured the concoction over some more ice into a tall glass, added a straw from the cupboard and placed it triumphantly on the work surface.

Flavors exploded on Marla's parched tongue and she felt her shoulders relax instantly. She beamed at Pietro with the straw still between her teeth.

"You like?"

"I like," she replied. "Better than chocolate. You've mixed those before."

"I was a bartender back home for a while. Then I opened a little smoothie bar, but the local gangsters didn't like me doing business on their patch."

"Where's home?"

"Sicily. Palermo. You've been there?"

Marla winced as she remembered her ex, Carlo, and his attempts to lure her away on a dirty weekend to Rome. She'd tried to convince him to spend the money on taking her out to a good restaurant in London for once. He'd gone to Rome without her.

"No. I've never been to Italy."

"A shame. Palermo is beautiful, full of art and history. And you can swim in the sea there. I used to, almost every day."

"You sound homesick. How long have you been out here?"

"A little over nine months. Can't swim in the sea here. It pisses me off."

"But you have the pool, right?"

"Not the same, not even close. The sea is alive, a pool is just dead. Dead water."

"I've never, um, thought of it like that myself."

Pietro scowled, gulped down what was left of the smoothie straight from the jug, and began methodically scrubbing it clean at the sink.

Marla decided to break the cool silence that had crept into the kitchen. "Still, it's a bloody lovely island, you have to admit."

He laughed. "Bloody lovely? Whatever you say, *bella ragazza*."

"You're making fun of me now."

"I just don't see the point in being in a paradise if you can't even swim in the fucking sea, that's all. Then it's like a prison. You and I can be here, in a stranger's kitchen. I can make you a smoothie. But the instant I ask you to the beach for a swim, for a party, Fowler and his *fascistas* will be there with the handcuffs ready."

"Sounds kind of kinky."

Pietro snorted. She could see real anger bubbling beneath

his indignation now. He was tightly wound, this one. Maybe the island life was not for him.

"Now you are the one making fun."

She enjoyed the way he spoke, though. *Bloddy lovvly.* He had a softer voice than Carlo's had been, but the strange clumsiness of his English was very similar. Hell, was she really going to compare the poor guy to her ex-boyfriend all afternoon? Marla chuckled as she realized that was exactly what she'd be doing.

"No need to be so grumpy, I wasn't poking fun, honestly."

She beamed at him. Pietro tried his best to maintain his scowl. Eventually, the corners of his mouth cracked into a smile and they laughed out loud together.

Spontaneous laughter between two strangers can be a dangerous thing, thought Marla. In this case, it had led to Pietro inviting Marla to join him on the veranda. There, he had bewitched her with those hazel eyes of his and within minutes her Birkenstocks had been cast aside wantonly. And here she was, lying like a tart as he gave her the most incredible foot massage she'd ever experienced. In fact, it was the *only* foot massage she'd ever experienced. She giggled as his fingers skated the sensitive arch of her right foot, tickling her. Her giggle became an uncontrollable moan of pleasure as he applied pressure just beneath the ball of her foot. As his fingers and thumbs worked their magic, she relaxed into the springy cradle of the sun lounger.

Pietro had filled Marla in on the last few months of his life, the Consortium's job offer giving him the catalyst he needed to throw caution to the wind and do something different for a while. The monotony of tending bar night after night, followed by the bitter failure of his own business venture, had made coming to island impossible to resist. Marla detected a weariness similar to Jessie's when he spoke after that, however. Pietro was clearly bored as hell out here with hardly anyone to speak to, surrounded by an ocean he was forbidden from swimming in. His mood was too heavy, and her small talk wasn't enough to lift it. Their faltering conversation had switched to her reasons for coming to the island, and about her aspirations, her dreams. She'd avoided going into too much detail, but as she spoke,

Marla had realized just how much she needed to be on this island right now.

The afternoon sun flared across the azure sky and she closed her eyes tightly for a moment, imagining herself on some endless vacation on this sun-trap island with her personal masseuse-stroke-lover literally on hand to pleasure her whenever she so desired.

"You have very good hands for a barman."

The sigh that crept from her lips like dry ice made Pietro smile with pride at a job well done. His hands went to work on Marla's left foot.

"I took classes. There are two things most people want in this world. One is a well-mixed drink. The other, a fucking good massage."

Marla laughed dirtily, her own sound embarrassing her a little. Her calf muscles stiffened, their movement giving Pietro a clear signal to stop what he was doing. His fingertips felt and delivered the message and he gently ended the massage with two spiraling motions of his thumbs. Sitting erect, Marla raised her hands up to the sky yawning and stretching like a cat. The sun was dipping now, in a couple of hours it would be bedding down behind the treeline.

"It's getting late. I'd better get going. Thanks so much for the foot rub, Pietro."

"No problemo. Anytime."

She stole a look at his muscular arms as he crouched down by the pool and rinsed off his hands in the clear water. His skin really was flawless, save for a beauty spot punctuating the point where his right bicep ended. Suddenly, Pietro looked at her over his shoulder. Marla quickly pretended to be looking beyond the pool, into the skyline. She stood up and slipped her tingling feet back into the now rather harsh reality of her sandals. Pietro stood up, too, and leaned in to air kiss her goodbye, once on each cheek.

Marla didn't exhale until she reached the gate, turned and closed it. The breath seemed to shiver from her body. She'd felt sure Pietro had meant to kiss her full on the lips, but had decided against it at the last minute. Looking up to the house over the gate, she watched as Pietro ran his fingers through his thick, dark hair. He was gazing at his own reflection in the glass of the French windows. Then she remembered what Jessie had said about Pietro. *Totally loves himself, that one.* Her amusement at this lasted the entire journey back to her summerhouse. As she flopped down on the wicker furniture, she realized she hadn't given another thought to the lack of reading material on the island. Tomorrow she'd find a pen and some paper and write some damn reading material of her own. Marla hadn't felt this alive for months.

Chief of Security Fowler glared at his men. All these patrols, all this manpower and still they couldn't get it together to find Anders. He asked questions and his men recapped the answers. Last radio transmission? *Just before nightfall, sir.* Nobody thought to check in before daybreak? *Anders specified radio silence unless in the event of an emergency, sir.* Last known coordinates? *The dark side, sir.* I know he was on the goddamn dark side, where exactly on the dark side? *Don't know, sir. May as well get out there and do it your fucking self, sir.*

Imbeciles. *Sir, yes, sir!*

Fowler snapped his pencil angrily. They would now have to patrol the island in search of two targets—an unauthorized interloper and Anders, who could be injured and stranded somewhere. Anders, his best man. What a fucking mess. They'd better get some results or there'd be hell to pay. He dismissed his men, tossed the pencil in the trash. When they were gone, he headed for his private sanctuary. The Snug was where he needed to be right now. While his men scoured every inch of the island in search of Anders, he'd locate that bastard interloper. Even if he had to keep watch twenty-four-seven, he'd find him.

CHAPTER FOURTEEN

Finding a pen and paper in the main house had proven as fruitless as trying to locate a book and Marla had very nearly quit out of sheer frustration. Then she'd remembered the closet under the stairs, where a basket containing spare light bulbs had borne buried treasure in the form of a small jotter pad and a pencil. Only a few sheets had been torn from the pad, and Marla could just make out the indentations of what looked like a shopping list on the first page. She wondered who had made that list and when, imagining the house full of flowers and laughter—kids excited about a shopping trip to the mainland. Marla had the sudden urge to look over her shoulder into the hallway behind her and the kitchen beyond that. The house suddenly felt very cold and vast, swathes of gooseflesh erupting across her arms in agreement. Mansions were like mausoleums without the movement of their families to warm them, quiet as graves without the voices of children to give them life, to give them purpose. Marla shut the closet door and headed outside into the sunshine, escaping the chilly silence.

She spent the rest of the day on the porch of her little summerhouse, scribbling furiously in the notepad. Her hand ached from writing so much and more than once she had to duck inside to sharpen the pencil using a paring knife from the kitchen drawer. The knife's little wooden handle fit her fingers perfectly and the act of sharpening the pencil became just as satisfying as writing with it. Page after page she wrote, her handwriting becoming scruffier the more she accessed her thoughts. It was all there, her disastrous career as an au pair, her subsequent nosedive in London, and the unexpected providence that had brought her here to the island. Stream of consciousness reportage flowed out of her, and she even found herself noting down in minute detail the plants and insects she'd seen since her arrival. Only when the sun was setting was she spent. Her wrist ached from the repetitive strokes of pencil on paper and at the front of her head, the beginnings of an eyestrain headache. Marla looked up at the house, as if becoming aware of it for the first time. She had barely done any chores today. But they would still be there tomorrow, and who was really bothered if she'd mopped the floors, watered the plants? *No one* came the answer, in the gentle breeze that whistled through the tree branches and in the lilting songs of the birds that perched among them.

The stench woke Anders even before he heard the sounds. Candle wax and burnt fat, rusted metal, and a foul blocked drain smell. He gagged and opened his eyes. But his eyes weren't there. He tried to put his fingers to his face, to learn what atrocities had been committed there, but he was tightly bound to a hard metal surface. His fingertips brushed the cool surface and he felt sticky dampness there. He knew instantly it was his own blood—the same blood that was now clogging his throat, making it almost impossible to breathe. His gag reflex kicked in, and he coughed up a torrent of the hot sticky stuff, thick as a fur ball. Anders' senses then reeled at the impossible touch of his own blood spattering the pits of his raw eye sockets. His mouth formed words too painful to utter and then, only then, did he realize he was not alone.

Anders started, his body convulsing like a sleeping animal's at the proximity of a presence by his side. He could hear sharp, excited little breaths. The sound filled the darkness inside his head with terrors and he struggled against his bonds, every atom in his body wanting to be free of this place. The horrid breaths turned to songlike chuckles, and Anders felt sickly warm little hands on his thighs. The power behind those hands was immense, lifting and tilting his body to one side as far as his bonds would allow. Then, the touch of one of the hands left him momentarily, before being quickly replaced by a violent stinging sensation in his right buttock. His flesh remembered the sensation, distant memories of inoculations clouding his mind. It was a syringe, injecting him with something. Something to take the pain away. He clenched his teeth and waited for oblivion. But it did not come. His guts lurched at a new tingling, nauseating, sucking sensation. The sucking grew more intense and he felt the tissues in his buttock breaking up, giving way. The syringe in his ass was being used not to inject, but to extract. The pain was excruciating now, and Anders cried out in damaged tones, begging for it to stop. But when it did stop, any inkling of relief was stamped out by the dread of what was to come. Anders felt blood and spit cooling on his chin and his face as he listened hard to what was happening around him. Nearby, he heard those vile little breaths again and the icy tap-tap of a fingernail against a hypodermic syringe. A sharp breath, louder than the rest, then a sickly moan of pleasure.

All went silent, the rank air bloated with expectation. Then Anders felt a weight on his chest. Warm folds of fat flesh, straddling his own. He felt his bonds tighten. Something stubby and fat probing the mucous pool where his eye used to be. The warm thing thrust in and out of his eye socket, defiling him with a wet sucking sound. Eagerly burrowing deeper and deeper, searching out his brain matter. And Anders knew now he was to suffer long dark hours until oblivion would come. His lips could no longer make sense of words. If they could, he would surely beg for death.

The same song that had lulled Marla to sleep woke her at dawn. Then, a rapping at the door. Groggily, she prized herself out of her bed sheets, pulled on a robe and plodded over to the door. Yawning heavily, she could make out the shape of a dark-skinned man through the glass. *Oh shit*, it was Adam. Brilliant—Mister Handsome had deigned to pay her a visit, and here she was looking like crap in a crumpled bathrobe, vest, and shorts. She tried to straighten her hair, then thought better of it as the tangles threatened to trap her fingers. Brushing sleep residue from the corners of her eyes, she blinked rapidly to moisten them and opened the door.

"Oh, I woke you. Sorry 'bout that."

Marla made a sound that was meant to be *no problem* but came out more like a Japanese cartoon character—with no subtitles.

Mild confusion registered on Adam's face for a few seconds, like he'd forgotten why he was there. Then the weight of the cardboard box he was carrying reminded him.

"I have supplies for you. Some fresh food."

Intending to say *fantastic*, Marla let out a massive yawn instead and stepped back from the doorway beckoning him in with a barely alive gesture of her free hand.

Adam carried the box straight through to the kitchen, with Marla plodding behind him. He pulled out an unbranded packet of fresh ground coffee and waved it at her.

"Guess you need some of this? It's the good stuff, Colombian Dark."

"Oh, coffee, that'd be brilliant thanks." Wonderful, she'd regained the power of speech without yawning.

Adam filled the coffee filter and busied himself with the jug.

"I can do that, it's okay," offered Marla.

"I've got it." His eyes scanned Marla's sheet-indented face. "Why don't you take a quick shower and we can drink this outside? It'll take a little while to brew up."

Marla didn't need to be asked twice. Ten minutes later, she was showered and refreshed, wearing her least crumpled clothes. They sat together just outside the summerhouse. The coffee was gorgeous, with that particularly stimulating roasted smell only found when someone else makes the coffee for you. Adam had opened a pack of sweet biscuits and Marla took one, unashamedly dunking it beneath the deep black surface of her coffee. Sugar and caffeine rush. The stuff of dreams.

"This is lovely, thanks," she said through a mouthful of sweet, soggy biscuit.

"You're welcome. Don't know about you but I'm never fully awake until my second cup."

Marla smiled in agreement. "More like my third. Sorry I was so groggy back there, I don't normally sleep so deeply. Unless I've had a big night."

"No big nights here, unfortunately. It's probably the journey catching up with you. And the island is pretty sleepy in general compared to the city, I guess."

"You like working on the island?"

"Must admit, even working for the chief I find this place pretty relaxing. How about you? Settling in okay?"

"Oh, yes. I think I'm going to love it here. The silence is going to take a bit of getting used to. But if it's too quiet I'll just hang out with Jessie. She's the life and soul."

Adam smiled and nodded, took a sip of coffee. In the distance, the breeze quickened, lifting and rustling the leaves. Marla remembered the day she'd found Adam crouched among the trees.

"Did you mention the cat to Fowler?"

"The cat?"

"You remember, when you showed me the way to Jessie's place—the dead cat."

"Oh, yeah. It was pretty messed up, wasn't it? Sure, I told the boss. He said one of the owners must've left it behind."

"I thought there weren't any pets on the island?"

"Well, technically there aren't. Who knows, maybe the cat got away and the owners couldn't find it."

"I suppose. Poor thing."

He smiled her way again. He had a deep dimple on one side of his face. She began to blush.

"Animal lover, huh?"

Marla giggled, "Yes, yes, I am. More of a dog person than a cat person, though."

Adam finished his coffee. The small talk had run out, and the coffee with it. He took his empty cup back inside, then said his goodbyes. Marla wanted to invite him over for dinner. *What time do you finish work? Maybe we can go for a walk sometime?* But she felt awkward and just thanked him again for the coffee and supplies.

She was halfway through her chores before she realized just *how* awkward she'd felt speaking with Adam. Fixing a stray lock of hair behind her ear, she grinned to herself. Whenever she felt that about a guy, it generally meant she actually liked him. Marla suddenly felt a little sick. Blushing, she got on with her chores.

Sadly, the sick feeling proved itself to be the beginnings of

Marla's period rather than the tummy flutters of true love. Back at the summerhouse, restless, hot, and itchy, she'd tried reclining on the wicker furniture next to an open window. The breeze had begun to annoy her, however, and the furniture had become the focus of a series of violent fantasies involving kerosene and a large box of cook's matches. By the time the sun had gone down, she was already curled up in bed holding a pillow against her gut in the absence of a hot water bottle. Drifting off into a sticky sleep, Marla could see those flames raging in her dreams—vast towers of creaky wicker furniture blazing like idols in some bizarre pagan rite. Chairs and two-seater couches interlocked with hand- crafted coffee tables, forming cages inside which cats and dogs screeched and howled. Hundreds *(no, thousands)* of the creatures jostled against each other, tearing into their fellow inmates' fur and flesh as the kerosene flames billowed higher. A plume of dark crimson smoke rose over the scene, stinking of burnt coffee grounds and black metallic death.

When she awoke, Marla's bleeding had started and was heavier than ever before. She went to the bathroom to staunch the flow, clutching at her belly. The Consortium Inc. had kindly provided a box of tampons, unbranded of course, in with her toiletry supplies. She grabbed the box and was about to open it when the hollow gnawing pain inside her inverted, becoming a kind of kicking spasm. In agony, she began to feel afraid. Normally she'd have a day or two of increasing cramps and nausea before her flow began, and the discomfort would never be as bad as this. Her hands shook as she used the applicator to insert the tampon. Another painful spasm seared in her gut. Doubling up, she let the rest of the tampons fall to the bathroom floor in their box and limped back into the bedroom, head spinning. Collapsing on the bed, Marla watched the ghosts of her imagined wicker fires die behind her eyelids then promptly blacked out.

Morning birdsong rang out across the island. Marla, meanwhile, slept like a dead thing. Her breath was barely audible above the joyous chorus of birdsong outside on the roof. Gradually, the shrill orchestra penetrated through the layers of sleep, and Marla groaned herself awake, remembering the agonizing abdominal pains of the preceding night. She was already in the bathroom, taking a pee, when she realized the pain had gone. Not just gone, but disappeared entirely, as if it had never been there in the first place. In fact, she felt healthier than ever, rejuvenated somehow. Removing her tampon, Marla was stunned by its dryness. She had expected to see lots of blood, but there was very little. And what scant blood was there had already taken on that deep brown color, like autumnal leaves turned to rust. She was puzzled about how her flow could have diminished after such an aggressive bout of pain. She pressed some tissue paper between her legs and inspected it. Marla could now see that her menses hadn't just diminished, they had *stopped*. There was nothing on the tissue paper—not a trace of blood at all.

Beyond the green belt, towards the beach, Pietro lay in bed trying to masturbate to some memories of a blonde he'd fucked on the beach one night in Palermo. He couldn't remember her name, or where she was from—some Eurotrash from the East no doubt—but he had clear memories of seducing her back to the beach and doing her over the bank of a sand dune. He tried desperately to fixate on an image of her ass, pale and round as two full moons, but try as he might he just couldn't stay hard. He grunted in frustration as his dick went limp in his hand, vowing that he had to do something about this; he needed to feel alive again. Life on the damned island was sapping his virility. Pietro concentrated on a mental facsimile of Marla's face. Maybe this new blood could, well, give him some new blood. He traced the line of her mouth around the head of his cock with the digit he lovingly referred to as his "pussy finger." Oh, wait. There was a little stirring in his loins. It was a start.

Something else stirred on the island too, a presence that sensed its time was coming. A sudden shift in the seasons. It churned the waves in the sea like a great invisible oar. It rattled the branches of the trees and hissed through their leaves. The birds flapped their wings and stopped singing for a few moments, as if steeling themselves for changes yet to come.

CHAPTER FIFTEEN

As the days passed, Marla found herself becoming accustomed to her new life in paradise. Whenever Adam dropped by with a food parcel, she imagined herself the Lady of the Manor and he the faithful servant. They drank coffee together outside the summerhouse and got to know a little more about one another. Adam was a business school dropout, who had gotten into the security profession after a brief stint as a volunteer at summer camps. Gradually, Marla opened up to Adam, regaling him with tales of her wilder days and nights in London. At points the conversation became a little muted, whenever Marla began to dwell on the past. She made a mental note to avoid sounding too maudlin in future—nobody likes a Moaning Minnie after all. But there was lots of laughter, too, with Adam making fun of Marla's "posh English accent" whenever he could. She enjoyed his easy humor, and his company in general, but after a time she began to feel there was a downside (*isn't there always*). This was her thing; Marla was actually beginning to wonder if there was something "wrong" with her. Waiting for Adam to make a move was becoming something of a thankless task. She wasn't enjoying the way his visits had descended into a routine indiscernible from the systematic list of chores she had to perform daily up at the house. The initial relaxation of her first few days on the island had turned into a kind of breathless tension—a cycle of expectation and disappointment that left her feeling very much like a tightly coiled spring. Mopping the huge expanse of kitchen floor at the house became an act of aggression and perhaps most disturbingly, Marla had begun chattering to herself like some insane old washerwoman. This wasn't good, she'd decided, and so opted to visit Jessie in the hope of getting good and loaded on her secret stash—and to hell with the hangover.

"Ah, you've got cabin fever already," said Jessie with an evil twinkle in her eye, "Pietro's gonna be gloating, that bastard. He said you'd only last a week. I had you down for at least a month."

"You were running a book on me?" asked Marla, incredulous.

"We sure were. In case you hadn't noticed, which obviously you didn't, us old timers went *totally* cabin a few months back. Wait and see, you'll be placing bets on all kinds of things soon. One of the oldest forms of entertainment known to humanity, especially for sexy young human beings like us who are stuck on a rock without music, TV, or books to keep them occupied!"

"I see. Well, maybe there's an opportunity for me here. I'll write the bloody books, then you and the Italian Stallion can read them…"

"Awesome. I like that plan."

"For a fee."

"Not awesome. See? You're settling right in."

Marla laughed. Finally, some of the tension was dissipating. She had been taking herself far too seriously these past few days.

"Does it get any easier? The isolation, I mean." There was an upward curve to her voice as she mouthed the question. It ended on a hopeful note.

"No. Not really."

Marla's face fell again, hope shattered.

Jessie placed a comforting hand on her shoulder.

"Look, you just have to be creative about how you spend your time. That's all."

"I did have a long walk over to the beach, met Pietro at his place, it was really lovely."

"Yes, I saw him yesterday too. He said he'd met you. Listen, you're a big girl Marla, so I don't need to tell you to be careful of that one. Hey, was he complaining about not being allowed to go swimming in the sea again?"

Marla nodded.

"Oh, I wish he'd change the damn record."

"It's his passion, though, isn't it?"

Jessie scoffed. "One of them, maybe." Her smile shrank. "But anyway, the lovely island walks, they soon get old."

"I really can't imagine that."

"Oh, you can't imagine it *now*. Just like you couldn't imagine booking into the Cabin Fever Motel when you first arrived here—trust me, everything reaches boredom point here. The question is; what can we do about it? What can we possibly do to liven things up around here?"

She looked pointedly at Marla, who was now feeling like a school kid who'd been caught staring out of the window. Her mouth fell open, dumbly.

"Secret party. That's how."

"Beg your pardon?"

"That's how we liven things up. With a fucking party. And you, dear—well, I need your help to pull it off. How's your yoga?"

"My yoga?"

"Yeah. Ever indulged?"

"No, well, I went to a pilates class once, but…"

"Follow me, look and learn. Come on, the lawn awaits."

Marla plummeted towards the ground again, as her belly dipped causing her legs to give way. As her outstretched palms skidded across the grass, she tried to twist her head to one side and ended up rolling onto a garden sprinkler. Arching her back and sitting up painfully, Marla rubbed her lower back with one hand. It was very tender where she'd pivoted onto the sprinkler valve. Both her hands were stained green from the grass and began to sting furiously with friction burning. Yoga, it seemed, was not very relaxing.

The complicated move that Jessie had assured her was "beginner-level stuff" was called "Downward Dog". Marla honestly thought "Collapsing Cow" would be more apt a description. Jessie did too, clearly, as she spent the next five minutes rolling around with laughter on the lawn watching Marla fail. Her student gave up, lying back down on the soft grass breathless, remembering to avoid the sprinkler head this time round.

"Giving up already?" Jessie was still laughing.

"I'm glad to be the source of so much amusement," Marla said dryly as Jessie lay down next to her, shielding her eyes from the sun with a saluting hand.

"You'll get the hang of it. Takes practice, that's all. Just wait 'til I show you 'The Wheel.'"

Whatever "The Wheel" was, it sounded downright painful and Marla wanted no part of it. She rubbed at the tender spot in her back and quickly changed the subject.

"Are you serious about what you said earlier—about throwing a secret party?"

"Deadly serious."

"Who would we invite?"

Jessie gave her a stern look.

"Jesus, you're so transparent. You can invite Adam if you want, I think we can trust him. But none of the others, especially Anders—he's a total slime."

"Where would we have the party? The houses are off-limits right? And the rule about gatherings—Fowler was pretty adamant about that."

"The whole point of having a party is to stick it to The Man. And where there's a will, there's a way." Jessie lowered her voice. "There's a mansion on the other side of the island, around the coastline from Pietro's place but off the beaten track, surrounded by huge old trees. We call it The Big House."

"The Big House?"

"Damn straight. The place is fricking massive, and really cool, it looks like the oldest house on the island. Thing is, it's all locked up with shutters and shit. The security defenses are all computerized. I'd love to find out what's so precious they lock it up in there."

"So how are we going to get in?"

"Simple, I hack into the computer network and modify the house's security parameters. If I do it behind the scenes, the Chief and his boys won't notice a thing; it'll look like everything is functioning normally. Then we slip in through the back door."

"So, you're a computer hacker now?"

"Look. I could tell you but…"

"Yeah, yeah. But then you'd have to kill me, right?"

Jessie nodded sagely.

"But what about Fowler's rules, hey? What if we get caught?"

"Screw Fowler's rules. And we won't get caught. I have a plan, Marla, a very good plan."

"I don't doubt that. It's just… I can't afford to mess up my chances of getting paid."

"Don't worry your pretty head about it, toots. An integral part of my plan is that it is founded upon the bedrock principle of not messing up getting paid."

Jessie's words were doing nothing to reassure her. She had a fleeting vision of herself, Jessie, Pietro, and Adam standing in front of Fowler's desk stone drunk and wearing idiotic party hats, desperately trying desperately to explain themselves.

"Admit it, you want to stick to The Man, too. I see it in your eyes."

Marla was of two minds, but the idea of spending the night partying with Adam was tipping the balance a little.

"So, there was another reason I brought you out here, toots, apart from yoga practice, I mean…"

Jessie's voice had taken on a hushed, conspiratorial tone. Marla turned to her, placing a hand over her forehead to block out the sun. She was a mirror image of Jessie, partners in crime.

"Don't be too obvious, but I want you to lie back and look up at the trees to the right of the house. Make it look like you're just stretching out, relaxing."

"I don't understand…"

"Just. Do. It," Jessie whispered firmly.

Marla did as she was told. The trees to the right were away from the sun and as Marla's eyes adjusted, she could just make out a white bird perching high up in the topmost branches.

"What do you see?"

"A white bird."

"Look again."

"What the hell is this about, Jessie?"

"That's no bird. *Look again.*"

Marla squinted up at the trees once more. The white bird looked strangely still. No song emanated from its black beak.

"Marla, it's a security camera."

"No, it isn't…"

"Yes, it is. And they're all over this island, watching us night and day."

Marla's skin flushed cold.

Marla could see security cameras everywhere as she and Jessie walked through the trees towards her own summerhouse. She could see them in the white of the clouds peeking through branches and in the feathers of songbirds perched on the gatepost as they approached the house. Then they were part of the house itself, insinuating themselves into the neutral stucco background beneath the eaves. She felt herself becoming twitchy and nervous, watching for the glint of a lens, listening out for the whirring of tiny camera motors. *Shouldn't have smoked that joint*, thought Marla, *get a bloody grip. I mean it's not as though London was exactly short on security cameras. Paranoia, that's all this is. You've got The Fear…*

"You okay, toots?"

Jessie was part way up the path to the house. She looked back at Marla who had stopped at the gate, staring blankly up at the white stucco giant.

"Fine. I'm fine." She walked on, catching up. "Let's just get inside, shall we?"

She passed Jessie, who looked a little concerned by Marla's behavior, and headed for the summerhouse door. It was framed by late afternoon shadow, cool and inviting.

Inside, Jessie poured them both a stiff drink from a little stainless steel hipflask that she had hidden behind a throw cushion. Marla slugged back the drink, balancing out the effects of the smoke and the heat.

"Why didn't you tell me about them before? The cameras?"

"Look, you seemed so damned blissed out, I didn't want to lay any downers on you. I thought you'd spot them yourself soon enough anyway, city girl like you."

"Must be losing my touch, or my eyesight. Or both."

Marla felt positively myopic. How had she missed these spies in the skies, watching her as she walked up the path to the house, tracking her movements as she made her way to Jessie's and Pietro's? Why didn't she notice them zooming in on her as she chatted with Adam outside the summerhouse?

There's a thing, thought Marla, sighing with relief. *Maybe there isn't anything wrong with me after all. Adam didn't want to make a move because he knew the cameras were there!* Her sigh became a dry chuckle. Then her chuckling stopped—he should've told her about the cameras sooner, too. Whatever, she'd just have to drag him inside and jump him next time. Try zooming in on *that*, pesky cameras. Then a new flood of paranoia invaded her daydream—what if there were cameras inside the summerhouse? In the bedroom. The *shower*? She looked up at the ceiling, nervously peering into the corner shadows.

"Oh, don't worry girl, they're not inside," laughed Jessie, reading her mind.

"Yeah but...how do *you* know that?"

"First thing I checked. Fucked if I'm giving Fowler a free show of my ass."

Marla made a harrumphing sound, unconvinced. But, try as she might, she could see no cameras inside her little home.

"So, are you gonna help me? Get this party started?"

"Do I have a choice?"

"No. No, you don't."

"What do I have to do?"

"Easy. Go for a jog."

First yoga and now jogging? This was turning into a full-blown triathlon. Marla snatched the hipflask from Jessie's hand and drank from it defiantly.

Jessie's instructions seemed simple enough. Three days from now, Marla was to get up at seven o'clock, have a light breakfast of fruit and juice, then shower. She would then slip into a pair of shorts and a vest and start jogging at exactly eight o'clock. Her route was to take her away from the house, down the path she had first walked up on her arrival at the island, then down past the security building. Reaching the steps on her left, she was to jog down them and onto the jetty, where she would be required to perform a series of seductive stretches to distract Fowler's bored black-clad security drones.

And the purpose of this fool's errand? To divert interest, enabling Jessie to sneak round to The Big House and break in undetected. So they could have a secret bloody party.

Marla had decided she needed her head examined. She wasn't even sure if jogging that far was possible. The last time she had run, really run, was for the number 29 bus on Tottenham Court Road. Wishing she hadn't pointed this out to Jessie, she now faced the prospect of two "practice runs" leading up to the main event. Anyone watching on the cameras would get used to seeing Marla taking a morning jog. They would, in fact, think she was being a good girl and following Fowler's rulebook guidelines about daily exercise. Her change in route down to the jetty, though, coupled with the sexy stretches, would create enough of a stir to prevent them from noticing Jessie skulking through the trees towards The Big House.

With a resigned sigh, Marla pulled on her sneakers and jogged out the door. Truth was, she needed a party just as much as the others did, even if it meant exercising. And if Adam was around—well, a little interest from his cohorts might provoke him to finally make a move next time he and Marla were alone.

Closing the blinds in her little room, Jessie carefully slid the laptop from out of its hiding place. The plastic casing actually creaked as she opened up the lid and wiped dust from the grubby screen. She hit the power button and the battered old machine's hard drive made an alarming grinding sound as it booted up. She should have gotten used to the noise by now, of course, but the skittering growl, like that of an ancient pet cat, never failed to give her the willies. It was a deeply unsettling sound to her, the sound of the island's only unauthorized laptop threatening to die horribly, taking with it her only hope of hacking into the network. She felt nervous, twitchy, and gnawed on one of her fingernails. Jessie hoped she'd been convincing enough about the party, that Marla wouldn't suspect anything. Getting inside the Big House, all that was true of course, but merely a by-product of what was really at stake here. The machine's tiny screen flickered into glorious life (if slightly burned out through the layer of grime)—the expanse of pixels lighting up her face with the red glow of the Consortium Inc. corporate logo. She'd been tempted to grab a different desktop wallpaper off the net, a picture of the New York skyline, civilization, anything—heck, even a picture of The Hoff in his Speedos would do. But to do so would be too high a risk; she needed to stay within the intranet parameters wherever possible, only straying outside at the last moment. She remembered the thrill of first hacking the communications protocols and finding the island's satellite uplink. It had taken a week of solid decoding—all so Vera could make a call home. What a mistake that had turned out to be. Jessie tried to put such bitter regrets to the back of her mind and focus on with the job in hand. Even after months away from the mainland, her grasp of operating code had not diminished. In fact, on an archaic machine like this, which forced her to learn everything all over again, she could genuinely say her coding had improved. She involuntarily crossed her fingers, willing herself to be lucky when the time came. She would only have a few minutes to hack in and she'd better be ready. The laptop had better be ready, too. Jessie hissed through her teeth as the dirty glow of the screen dipped suddenly. She had almost forgotten to plug the power cable into the wall socket to charge the baby up. Quickly rectifying the problem, she flicked on the wall power. The laptop's little yellow light came on, just below the border of the screen, to tell Jessie the battery was charging. She kicked back tensely and smoked a cigarette, waiting for the light to turn green.

Chief of Security Fowler wrestled the pistachio nut from its shell and bit into it, never once taking his eyes off of the bank of monitor screens in front of him. The observation room, affectionately known as "The Snug," was both his sanctuary and the nerve center of his entire security operation. He had as many eyes as a fly in this place, one screen giving him a view of sandy coastline, another floating high above the jetty. Dozens of cameras, dotted around the island, constantly feeding him visual intelligence about what the hell these goddamn Lamplighters (not to mention his own work-shy grunts) were up to. Still no goddamned sign of Anders. Fowler was beginning to suspect the worst. His best guy, washed out to sea or worse. What a waste.

Flicking the pistachio shell into the wastepaper basket, he selected another nut without looking away from the screens for one second. *Fucking blink and you'll fucking miss it,* the foul-mouthed Senior Prison Warden used to say to him. His old boss was a man with a sense of humor so dry you needed to take a glass of water with every joke. Fowler marveled at the clockwork precision with which the screens clicked from one scene to the next, on a never-ending cycle of pan and track back, pan and track back. Looking at the screens, the Chief was reminded of the three-sixty-degree view of the watchtower at the Prison— Bentham's Panopticon, a favorite invention of Fowler's from the nineteenth century. It featured a central watchtower around which prison cells were situated. The effect was such that the inmates began to police themselves, as they were unsure when they were being watched—either by the guards or by each other. Rather like the Panopticon, the cameras not only served to monitor, but to subtly discipline the island's inhabitants. The Snug was his very own watchtower, and he was so very pleased whenever he saw the fruits of his labors being projected onto the screens in front of him. Like right now, for instance.

The Neuborn girl had surprised him by beginning a morning jogging routine, lasting exactly thirty minutes and therefore burning at least two hundred fifty calories. Give them a rulebook and they will learn self-discipline, it is in the nature of the subservient. He switched camera views, watching the girl working her way along the coast path, perspiration forming dark patches on her vest. He'd always liked to watch, to look. His eyes had done so from an early age—right from when he was a young boy. He recalled the time he'd been watching his mother from the garden, seeing her brushing her long black hair, unaware of his inquisitive gaze. His father had beaten him later that day with a thick leather belt. Fowler felt his cock stiffen as he watched Marla and leaned closer to the screen, biting into the pistachio nut. An unpleasantly sour taste filled his mouth like bile and, cursing, he spat the bad nut out into the waste paper basket. Wiping his mouth on a handkerchief he turned his attention back to the screen, which reflected the light of the room's single light bulb. Marla was now a dark indistinct shape, like a trapped fly buzzing on the other side of his window onto the world. He reached out and touched the screen, a little frisson of static crackling against his fingers. Look, but don't touch.

As she ran, Marla found herself thinking of London again. Taking a deep breath of fresh sea air (*in through the nose, out through the mouth*), she remembered the stink of the city. Subway air had been her least favorite aspect of metropolitan life, the strangely metallic smell and stagnant closeness was overbearing especially during the summer months. Up on street level it hadn't been much better. Even on her walks through the park she could still taste the fumes from the millions of car exhausts clogging up the arterial city streets. Whenever summer came, albeit briefly, Marla had enjoyed the sun but dreaded seeing the dense menstrual smog hanging over the tower blocks in her neighborhood. Then when the rain came to wash the last rays away, the streets felt like they were disintegrating into a mass of slime. Rotting garbage and leaf matter pounded by relentless acid rain became an indistinct gloopy mess. This in turn was replaced by the grim black and brown sludge that passed for snow during a London winter. Running past a palm tree, Marla glanced up at it and recalled a holiday poster campaign that had, for what seemed like an eternity, adorned every bus shelter and every billboard in town. "Who would live in the city?" the caption asked, emblazoned in bold letters over a split screen view of a polluted industrial cityscape giving way to a deserted island beach. *Weren't they always deserted and yours only, in the ads?* Jogging here now on Meditrine Island in the middle of nowhere, Marla smiled to herself, realizing she had found that very place the adverts always promised but never delivered. Deserted, and hers only. If your average city dweller even got a taste of the clean air here, they'd probably go into a kind of reverse toxic shock. And the peacefulness, the soothing, lulling quiet of it all might drive them to hurl themselves into the sea—thrashing wildly in the water just to make some noise, desperate to make some city-sense of the place. Marla's ears tuned in on the little sounds that when combined, formed the subtle background noise of the island. The insects chirping and clicking like tiny watch mechanisms, birds singing to one another, their chorus an agreement that this was indeed paradise. In the distance, the shushing lullaby of ocean waves massaged the shore. No, this wasn't background noise, thought Marla. This was background *atmos*—the very sound a masseuse or aromatherapist might try to recreate using a crummy recording. This was the real thing. As Marla finally came to halt, panting from her exertions, she wondered if she could ever live in the city again after this place. Stretching out the burn from her leg muscles, she looked out to sea. Perhaps there was something out there for her on the mainland, but what it was she didn't know right now. Maybe she had to come here first, to the island, in order to find it. Wiping a bead of sweat from her forehead, she prepared herself for the jog back to the summerhouse—her temporary home here in paradise.

CHAPTER SIXTEEN

Practice runs over, it was time for the real thing. Marla wriggled into her shortest shorts and tightest vest, recalling Jessie's school ma'am-ish instructions to look as hot as possible on the day of The Run. Arranging her hair in a loose ponytail, Marla checked herself in the mirror. She wasn't looking bad at all, she had to admit. The dark circles under her eyes had been eradicated by a few days' sunshine, and a few nights' sound sleep. Her skin had begun to tan slightly and a rosy glow had sprung up where once there was only the pallor of a city girl who rarely saw daylight. *If you are confident about yourself, you will be confident about the mission.* This was the mantra Jessie had her repeat for what felt like a thousand times. She checked out her ass in the tiny jogging shorts. *Hot damn.* Yes, she was feeling confident about the mission all right, the clock was ticking and it was time to run.

Marla was already short of breath by the time she reached the halfway point; it was an oppressively hot morning, with the sun beating down on her back and shoulders. She kept going, pushing herself through the dizziness towards the security outpost and the jetty that lay beyond it. Glancing up from her shadow on the path and into the trees she caught the glint of a security camera, panning with her movement as she passed it. Gasping for breath and feeling the beginnings of a stitch in her right side, Marla thought about Jessie sneaking through the trees on the other side of the island. Strangely, the thought amused her, and she cracked a smile as she ran towards the finish line.

Breezing past a couple of surprised security guards, Marla ran down the steps leading to the jetty. Her footfalls made satisfying echoing beats as she padded across the platform at speed. Slowing her pace as she neared the edge of the jetty, she looked out at the sunlight glistening across the waves. It was a beautiful sight, and it felt good to be so close to the water again. Stopping still and stretching out, Pietro's complaints about not being allowed to swim in those lush, inviting waves rang in her ears. She felt his pain, itching to dive in and feel the refreshing water enveloping her skin. But she had work to do. Bending over to give the guards a good view of her ass, Marla chuckled to herself; she was genuinely enjoying provoking them. Then, as she rose, the shouting started.

Raised voices from the guards telling her to *freeze, stand still, don't move, turn around slowly with your arms raised.* Marla was still laughing; surely, they were just making fun, joining in with her little gym-tease. One of the guards barked the order again. She was wrong, dead wrong, he was being serious. The perspiration on her neck and shoulders went cold, giving her gooseflesh and hardening her nipples. Her heart beat as she raised her hands and turned slowly, just like the nice man told her to. *Please be nice.*

Marla remembered her nightmare about the jetty as she turned around to find Adam pointing a gun at her. He was flanked by about a half dozen security guards. Not one of them was smiling.

The guards had been so rough with her, Marla felt almost relieved to be finally shoved into Fowler's office. As the door slammed shut, she rubbed her wrists and forearms where they had grabbed her and frog-marched her off the jetty. Her skin was already red and mottled with fingerprint patterns from the guards' rough hands; they would surely bruise; this was not cool. Then, seeing Fowler's face she realized just how uncool this whole thing was. His eyes blazed from beneath his gray-ing eyebrows and he looked for all the world like he wanted to murder, cook, and eat her. It was a long time before he spoke, and when he did his voice echoed the same carnivorous aspect of his eyes.

"The jetty is out of bounds."

"I'm sorry I…"

"You don't speak, Miss Neuborn. You listen."

Marla's voice became a croak, then merely breath.

"I don't know what you think you were doing down there, but let me tell you this, you are lucky my men didn't open fire. This could have been a messy incident today, very messy indeed. There are many places to run on this island, but the jetty, this compound—in fact anywhere the fuck near my security operatives and I—are out of bounds. Do I make myself clear, Miss Neuborn? Don't speak, just nod."

She nodded. *Security operatives and I.* Pompous bastard.

"Protocol dictates that I file a report on you, Miss Neuborn, send it back to the mainland and await further instruction from the Consortium Inc. I am going to do just that, because protocol is very important to me, and now it is of the utmost importance to you, too. I will be monitoring your progress from here on in, and if you fuck up again I'll make damn sure you're off this island before you can even pack your panties. Do not piss me off again. Do I make myself clear? You can speak this time but keep it very short."

"Crystal." She tried not to hiss at him.

"Good. I suggest you get back to your chores, and spend some downtime studying the manual I gave to you on your arrival. Protocol, Miss Neuborn. Learn to love it, learn to live it, or get the hell off my goddamned island."

My island? Marla's head began to spin with rage at the way he was talking to her, and at herself for being so green. Why had she agreed to run down to the jetty? Of course it was off limits. And why did Jessie ask her to do it if she knew Marla would get in so much trouble? *Oh, wait a minute…*

"Dismissed."

She didn't need to be asked twice. One thing was certain, she'd bloody well strangle Jessie when she saw her. Storming out of Fowler's office Marla threw a murderous look at Adam, who swallowed hard and absent-mindedly fingered his gun holster. With just one look, Marla had virtually pointed a gun straight back at him.

On the other side of the island, Jessie cursed at the laptop's hard drive, which was creaking and groaning like the timbers of some old beleaguered ghost ship.

"Come on come on come on, fucking stupid machine."

She could do without the threat of a motherboard crash; it had been stressful enough getting over here in the first place; she felt sure one or two of the cameras had caught her as she wriggled through the bushes. With her backpack, shades, and khakis on she'd felt like Lara Croft—but crouched here now with the Consortium Inc. logo taunting her from behind the progress bar she just felt like a klutz. Then, her breath stopped in her throat as the hard disc's disconcerting scraping sound picked up speed and the progress bar lurched towards the end zone. Something was happening, hopefully something good.

Jessie punched the air. *Tomb Raider.* She was in.

There was no time to lose, no time at all. Her fingers worked at the greasy track pad, tapped the keys, and began to unlock the floodgates to freedom.

The march back to the house hadn't cooled Marla's blood any and neither had her shower. It wasn't until she was on her hands and knees scrubbing the kitchen floor that her anger turned to shame and despondency. She always messed up, whatever job she'd had, even here on the island when all she really had to do was be a glorified cleaner for a few months. No, she couldn't even get that right. She remembered her foster mother hitting her with the hairbrush, hitting her so hard that she couldn't sit down for a while, yet sit she'd had to, while the crotchety woman angrily tore the spilled paint out of Marla's tangled hair. *Useless. Clumsy, useless girl.* Nothing had changed. Marla started to cry. Her tears fell onto the sterile white surface of the tiled floor, almost invisible. Inconsequential, just like she was.

She spent the rest of the morning curled up on the uncomfortable wicker sofa in her summerhouse, the discomfort of her seat acting as a kind of self-imposed penance. It was not long before her mind wandered back to thoughts of Jessie again. That stupid girl had ruined everything—sure, Marla shouldn't have agreed to such an idiotic plan, but Jessie had been on the island longer than her. Did she want Marla to get into trouble? Want her off the island for some reason? Maybe she'd gotten so bored on the island that fucking with Marla was the only form of entertainment left to her. She wondered bleakly what else Jessie had been up to; she'd probably told Fowler all about the clandestine drinking and smoking, too, making it all sound like Marla's idea. She punched the cushion in frustration and got up off the sofa. There was only one thing for it, and Jessie's place wasn't such a long walk away. She might even bloody well jog over there, and when she did, she was going to get some answers.

Carried on her wave of defiance, Marla made light work of the walk to Jessie's place. Her stomach was growling by the time she got to the halfway mark and she realized she'd missed lunch. The acid in her empty belly frothed at the thought of all the food back at the summerhouse. Then, passing the place where she and Adam had seen the mutilated cat, her hunger quickly turned to queasiness. Her belly seemed to wince, writhing in its own juices as she recalled the animal's ruined skull, fragments of bone jutting through the blood-slicked fur like dead fingers. Gritting her teeth, she pushed on towards Jessie's summerhouse.

Approaching the little path that ran through the garden, giving access to the main house, Marla stopped for a moment hearing Jessie's unmistakable laugh. Scowling at the sound, she changed her route and headed round back. *Giggling about me no doubt*, Marla thought bitterly, *and I'd like to know who's in on the bloody joke.* Passing through the shadows of the trees that towered over the house, Marla peered in at large dark windows realizing Jessie wasn't inside the main building after all; the place was deserted. Then, a dark shape against the shutters near the patio door caught her eye. Creeping closer to investigate, Marla was horrified and puzzled in equal amounts by what she had stumbled across. A dead bird was pinned out with its back against the wooden shutter, wings splayed wide open. The aspect gave the odd impression that the creature had flown backwards in terror into the wall, killing itself. Flown in terror from what? It was clear someone had gone to some trouble to do this to the poor animal, as long metal nails had been driven through each wingtip to hold it in place. The nails had begun to turn the same angry rust color of the bird's innards, which were visible through a puncture in its body the size of a small fist. Who could have done this to the poor little thing? And why? She peered at the bird's blank, expressionless glassy black eyes. Whatever secrets it had witnessed, it wasn't about to give them up now. Marla felt unease pricking at the fine hairs on the nape of her neck and startled at the sound of another distant shrill giggle. She welcomed the distraction from the horrid find and made a quick about-turn. Marla made her way back through the trees and ended up back on the little winding path to the summerhouse. She crept around the treeline and caught sight of Jessie through the window. Adam was inside with Jessie, tickling her playfully. Marla stood silently watching as the tickling gave way to passionate kissing. She stood, shocked, for a few moments then stepped backwards into the trees. She turned and ran into the anonymity of dark foliage, tears welling up in her eyes.

As Marla ran, a cloud drifted across the sun, gray and heavy with the promise of rain. Close by, cold, watchful eyes turned their attention away from Marla, Jessie, and Adam and looked skywards. A storm would be coming to the island soon…

CHAPTER SEVENTEEN

The very air she breathed seemed to cool as Marla moved through it, stomping past the house where she'd been dutifully scrubbing earlier, across the track she'd jogged along in the morning and on towards the sea. She still felt disturbed by the sight of the dead bird, pinned out like that against the wall of the house. Perhaps more so, she also felt deeply resentful about Jessie and Adam's tryst, and foolish at the same time for feeling that strongly about it. Recalling the quiet times she'd enjoyed with Adam these last few days, drinking coffee outside the summerhouse, she did feel she had good reason to feel betrayed, however. Well, perhaps *betrayed* was too strong a way of putting it, but she certainly felt she'd been made a fool of. Rejection she could take, that was one thing, but to be humiliated like this was more than she could bear. Walking on, her foul mood clinging to her like the cold clammy shower curtain from her bed-sit, Marla found herself approaching familiar ground. The path wound its way down the rough terraces of the headland and on towards the beachfront, which lay beyond the white stucco giant and its gardens up ahead—Pietro's place.

She'd found him in the garden sunbathing half naked beside a large palm tree, the shadow of a huge leaf creating a dark tribal tattoo on his olive skin. He'd invited her inside for a drink, and a few more drinks later (*no smoothies this time, the real stuff*) saw them *both* half naked, rolling around tipsily on the huge bed in the main house. She bit his lip drunkenly as they kissed and dug her fingernails a little too hard into the muscular flesh of his back. *He knows what this is*, Marla thought mischievously as she straddled him and began pulling at his shorts, *he knows this is revenge sex. But he doesn't care and neither do I.* Her aggression was doing nothing to pacify him and she could feel his arousal through the drunken haze. Marla had not had sex for quite some time, and Pietro's enforced abstinence had gone on for even longer it seemed. She kissed him and bit him again, a little bit harder this time. To her delight, he began to fight back with passion more than equal to hers, as the rest of their clothing fell away. The rest was an alcoholic blur.

A sick feeling in her stomach woke her—that and the violent need to pee. She lurched from the bed, head swimming, still under the influence of all the alcohol she'd knocked back. *Never mix your drinks, idiot.* But Marla had already begun to blame Pietro, wishing upon him the worst hangover Bacchus could visit. The room smelled stale. Afternoon sunlight bled into the room from gaps in the blinds like a sick breath. Glancing back at the bed, she saw Pietro lying there face down, one arm dangling over the side of the bed like a broken wing as he snored softly. A used condom lay on the floor near his fingers, giving the impression that a vile worm had shed its skin there. Marla's face wrinkled in disgust at the sight. She looked back at Pietro coldly—he looked like a corpse lying on a mortuary slab, dust motes swirling around him aimlessly in the queasy yellow light. Fighting her bladder's desire to open up the floodgates right there on the bedroom floor, Marla quickly gathered her clothes and clutched them to herself tightly, concealing her nakedness. Stealing down the hallway as quietly as possible, she closed the bathroom door behind her and relieved herself. She was about to get dressed when she suddenly smelled Pietro's scent all over her. With the smell came memories, indecent flashes of their aggressive coupling before she'd passed out from the alcohol. Dreadful suspicions about what he may have done to her while she was unconscious sprang into her mind, but she reminded herself he had been as wasted as she was. Unless he was feigning inebriation. She felt suddenly dirty, sullied by what she'd done in anger, ashamed of making such a scene. Moments later she was scrubbing herself clean in the shower, muttering under her breath that she shouldn't have come here, that she certainly shouldn't have slept with him. Her tears mixed with the hot water and trickled away with it down the plughole and into the silence and black of the sewage system.

Pietro awoke at what sounded like a clap of thunder but was in reality the main door to the house slamming shut. He stretched and yawned dryly, wondering where he'd left his cigarettes before he'd gone to bed with Marla. She'd spared him from the boredom of small talk, he'd known why she had come the instant he saw her, but he hoped to God she hadn't taken his fucking cigarettes with her. Frustration and shame wound a tight knot in his stomach as he remembered losing his erection moments before Marla had passed out on the bed. He recalled flipping her unconscious form over and trying again from behind before he, too, passed out from the excess of alcohol. He reached over the side of the bed and grabbed the used condom off the floor, checking it to be sure. It was devoid of semen, a sad, pathetic thing shriveling up in its own spermicidal lubricated juices. What the hell was wrong with him? He'd never had this kind of problem before. Not before coming to this godforsaken island, anyhow. He pictured the island now as a great sponge, slurping up all his energies greedily, leaving nothing for him except a list of tedious chores to do and long dull hours staring out at an ocean he was forbidden to swim in. Where the hell were his damn cigarettes?

"I thought you said this cruise would be relaxing," Brett said as he peeled his umpteenth potato. Scott just looked at him, blankly.
"It is."
Brett hissed through his teeth. Cooking, cleaning, hoist the sail, drop the sail—none of it was relaxing.
"It's so fucking not! I was having a great time at the resort, picking up girls, partying every night. Where's the bloody party on this tub, eh?"
Scott rolled his eyes. If he looked like he'd heard this from Brett a thousand times before, it was because he had. All the dude did was complain about something or other. If you gave him a beer, he wanted a glass of champagne—if you passed around a joint, he wanted a damn bong hit instead. There was just no pleasing the guy. Throw him overboard, toss him a lifesaver and be done with him. Scott fought not to lose his temper, an

argument was probably what Brett wanted, a pathetic way to ease his boredom.

"Look, we have to earn our keep here, this is the real deal not some package tour. We're crewmembers and we have to do our share, mate, fair and square."

Crewmembers. Brett scoffed at this. It had been Scott's wet dream to work on a boat like this since they'd met at school. Only he wasn't allowed to refer to it as a boat, it was a yacht. Just like he wasn't allowed to bring any dope or pills along with him. In case The Skip found out and made them swim home. Who the fuck called himself "The Skip" anyhow? Fucking asshole. Brett snarled with amusement at the memory of a kid's TV show from his youth, *Skippy the Bush Kangaroo*. Oh, wait a minute though, Scott hadn't quite finished.

"There's just no pleasing you, is there?"

"What the hell does that mean?"

But Scott was leaving the galley now, he'd said his piece, leaving Brett to bitch and whine in there all on his lonesome. Best place for him.

Brett threw the peeling knife into the sink in disgust. The only reason he'd gone along with Scott's idea of a pleasure cruise anyway was so he could get to know Idoya a little better. She was a ripper—beautiful tanned skin, long dark hair, deep hazel eyes. She'd given him all the signals, too, back at the marina over cocktails, but since boarding she'd developed a kind of superiority complex, as if she knew that she could have any guy on the yacht whenever she wanted. Which was probably the truth of it, of course, but if so, then why on earth give him the come-on? Wasn't bloody fair. Now he was stuck on this shitty fucking boat for the best part of a week when he could be living it up on the mainland. Frustrated, he decided to go topside for some air. Maybe she'd be up there in her bikini— at least his eyes could get lucky today, even if none of his other organs could.

He arrived on deck to find everyone crowded around the cabin. A fair bit of commotion, too—what the heck were they all so excited about? He ambled over, his steps slowing as he spotted Idoya's ass. The supine curves of her butt cheeks framed the dark line of her G-string and he felt himself salivating at the sight, then getting hard at the thoughts it was provoking. He reached into his shorts to try and adjust his erection, make it less obvious. Right on cue, a couple of the crew turned and caught him in the act, hand down his pants tugging at his penis. He flushed as Idoya turned and looked, fixing him with an indifferent look that made him feel all of ten years old.

"What's going on?" his voice squeaked involuntarily as his heavy Australian accent made a steep curving ascent of the question.

"Distress call," The Skipper said (sorry! "The Skip"—asshole). "Gonna have to change course, check it out."

"Looks like you're in some distress there yourself, mate," Scott bellowed, pointing at Brett's crotch. The others fell about laughing.

A pleasure cruise. Relaxing. What a fucking joke. Brett felt his face burning red as he retreated back to the galley to peel some more bloody bastard potatoes.

Self-loathing was closing in on Marla like the clouds that gathered high above her. She'd fled the scene of the crime while her hair was still wet from the shower, unable to face him after their ill-advised tryst. She traced her shitty day backwards in her mind's eye, through the drunken tumble with Pietro, past seeing Jessie and Adam together in the summerhouse, and back to her impromptu disciplinary in Fowler's office. Yes, a shit-tastic day. She cursed herself for not having the presence of mind to steal Pietro's cigarettes. As her pace slowed to a brisk walk, her mind drifted grumpily to the handbook Fowler had been so determined she read and digest. He could shove it up his ass. She'd only been on the island a few days and she'd already screwed everything up. Better to just go jogging on the jetty again, and let Fowler's "security operatives" assist her gently to the floor, guns pointed at her head.

But what then? Her prospects looked pretty dire; go back to a city where she couldn't get a job with her record, or start over in another country without a single penny in the bank. No, she'd have to stick it out here, do her chores up at the white stucco house every day and keep the hell to herself the rest of the time. What she needed, what she *really* needed was a place to clear her head—somewhere to think where there weren't security cameras prying at her every move, where no other Lamplighters could lure her in with drinks, drugs, kisses. As the landscape turned from sandy soil and wild grass to jutting rocks and steep drops, Marla realized she'd found such a place.

A rocky promontory unwound in front of her, its spiny ridges like the backbone of some giant fossilized beast, and there at the end stood the high tower of a lighthouse. Crosswinds opened up and licked at her, invisible tongues sent by the sea to push and pull her into the depths below. She folded her arms tightly against them and walked carefully across the rocks, on towards the lighthouse. The structure seemed to multiply in size as she neared it, towering over her now. It looked drastically older than any of the other buildings she'd seen so far on the island. Patches of leprous lichen crept from the rock beneath her feet and up the peeling walls. Layer upon layer of white paint had peeled back like dead skin flaking from a corpse to reveal the skeleton of stonework beneath. She climbed up a couple of feet onto its foundation, which had been hewn from massive slabs of native rock, and began circling the base in search of a way inside. A door presented itself halfway around the building, loose on its rusty hinges and banging against its frame in the ocean wind, unlocked. Rickety metal steps stained with browning rust lead up to the door and they gave a metallic groan as she walked up them. Grasping the equally rusty door handle, rough and cold against the palm of her hand, she pulled the door open and peered into the gloom.

A spiral staircase, dimly lit by tiny portholes in the exterior wall, curved upwards and into the darkness out of view. At the foot of the staircase was a wide puddle of water, green-tinged from the algae that straddled its surface. Marla stepped inside, curiosity fueling her deep desire to take shelter from the bitter snap of the wind. As she neared the puddle of water, a strong stench of stagnant seawater hit her nostrils. Her stomach heaved as her senses tried to adjust to the stink. To one side of the puddle beneath the curve of the stairs, a pair of wooden doors were set into the wall. It looked like a closet might be behind them. Marla walked over to the doors and her heart leapt with fright as the rusty metal outer door slammed shut, forced into the act by a strong gust of wind. Turning nervously, her composure still rattled from the shock of the noise, Marla muttered some colorful words under her breath in the general direction of the door. Returning her attention to the closet, she stooped slightly and reached down to try the wooden doors. They opened, revealing a complex spaghetti of tangled wires and cables, looping out of the great metal racks that filled the closet space. Faded electrical warning decals hung peeling off the inside of the doors—they looked ancient, as did the wiring. A blinking light deep inside the confusion of multicolored strands caught Marla's eye and she leaned deeper into the closet to get a closer look. Her heart froze once again, but not at the door banging this time, but at the hand which grabbed her shoulder. A strong, manly hand with one hell of a grip. She whirled round in terror, reflexes already pushing her hands up in front of her face to protect her from the intruder. Losing her balance, she clattered backwards into the closet doors. Tense moments passed as she righted herself and awaited her fate.

The old man was looking at her with surprise in his eyes. He had a leathery face, with deep-set wrinkles etched around his eyes like a relief map of the rocks outside. But his eyes were somehow younger, bright, alive, and thankfully completely non-threatening. Marla wasn't quite ready to trust him yet, though.

"Who the hell are you?" she said, her voice wavering despite her best efforts to sound in control, authoritative. Gone was the voice of the city girl, the one she used to use on cab drivers when she'd had too much to drink, back in the day. "What do you want?"

At this, he chuckled dryly, then said in a soft wheezing voice, "I might ask you the very same, young lady. I guess you can tell me over coffee. Just brewing up a fresh pot when I heard the damn door banging again. Needs fixing. Everything needs fixing round here."

He adjusted his oil-stained blue overalls and started climbing the stairs, beckoning for her to follow.

"Come on up. It's warmer upstairs. It's no problem."

With that, he was on his way up the stairs—sprightly as a young lad, taking two steps at a time and whistling a jolly tune as he ascended to god-knows-where. Marla sighed heavily, her system exorcising the last remnants of the scare from her frazzled nerves. Hearing the howling wind outside, she decided upstairs where it was warmer didn't sound like too bad a place to be. Following him up the stairs, Marla was greeted by the faint aroma of real coffee. It was a welcome smell after the rank stench of the seawater puddle, not to mention after the kind of day she'd had.

The old timer told her his name was Vincent. She watched as he busied himself with the promised pot of coffee, although it was less a pot and more of a can, an old catering tin filled with dark bubbling liquid atop a little gas stove that spluttered angrily with blue flame. She glanced around his quaint abode, engrossed in its many little details. Seashells and pebbles lay everywhere there would have been bare space, and driftwood, nets, and other beach debris gave the impression the tide had recently come in and gone back out again—inside the room. The room itself was surprisingly large. It was the control room for the lighthouse, but it looked as though it had not been used as such for quite some time. Ragged blankets hung over portions of the three-sixty-degree windows that encircled them, moving slightly in drafts as they struggled to keep the elements at bay. Beyond the windows, Marla could see the remnants of a flag fluttering pathetically outside in the growing wind. The flagpole was attached to a gantry, accessible via a metal door—or would have been accessible if not for the huge stack of books leaning up against it. She crossed to the books and scanned some of the spines, many of which were torn, moldy, and ruined. Vincent's library was in a poor state of repair, but contained everything from old encyclopedias to pulp fiction, literary classics, and well-thumbed puzzle books. Marla felt like a child in an Aladdin's cave up here, peering out beyond the treasures at the dark clouds that danced dramatically above the high seas.

"Got another mug around here somewhere," Vincent muttered, half to himself, as he clattered around in the cupboards.

Marla watched him reflected in an exposed section of glass as he located a second mug and gave it a good scrub at the sink. She remembered the night she'd watched Jessie making coffee for her in the summerhouse kitchen, the same night she'd seen those cold, hollow eyes watching her through the window. Marla shivered.

"Soon warm up. Have a seat."

Vincent gestured to a beat-up chair next the stove. He placed the steaming mug on an upturned tea chest that served as a coffee table. Next to it was a plate of dry crackers. Marla sat down and picked up the mug with both hands, enjoying the heat as it throbbed into her icy hands.

"Thanks."

He took a cracker from the plate, bit into it, and created a little shower of crumbs.

"Help yourself."

"I'm okay, thanks, coffee will do me fine."

She looked around the room again. It was a stark contrast from the mansions of the rich on the other side of the island, even from her "servant's quarters" with their sturdy shutters and home comforts. The dilapidated chair she was sitting in now was much more comfortable than her crappy wicker furniture, though, she had to admit. Overall, this place had an earthy charm that appealed to Marla perhaps more than any opulent mansion house ever could.

"Cozy place you have here," she ventured.

"Ain't much, but she's home," he said, blowing vapor from the surface of his coffee. "Wouldn't much know how to live anywhere else."

"How long have you lived here?"

"My whole adult life, feels like. Stayed on as lighthouse keeper after my wife died. She died young. Figured I could get my head clear in a place like this."

"I'm sorry."

"No need. Ancient history now, all that. Kept my boy out here with me for a spell. Good place for a kid to be I figured, all that fresh air."

"Your son? He's on the island?"

The old man snorted. It was a bitter, unhappy sound. "Nope, he left long ago."

"Back to the mainland, you mean?"

His eyes twinkled, as fluid as the puddle downstairs. "He died, too, here on the island. Turns out I was wrong. No place at all for a young lad."

Marla stiffened and took a gulp of coffee, not knowing what else to say or do. The liquid was darker than freshly dug earth and stronger than anything she had ever tasted before. She took another gulp.

"Took his dog out for a walk. Damn thing ran into the ocean, chasing lord only knows what. My boy ran after him, caught hold of the beast, but then they got swallowed up by the waves. Both drowned."

"How awful. I'm so sorry to hear that."

The old man sighed. He took a sip of his coffee and blinked the memories from his watery eyes. "No matter."

"What was his name? Your boy?"

"No matter," he replied.

Awkward silence clouded the space in the room. Marla looked over to the exposed glass as a shaft of light cut through it. The clouds were breaking.

"Looks like it's brightening up a little. I'd better get going."

She stood up and took another gulp of coffee before replacing the mug in the sink.

"I'm really sorry for intruding."

"Intruding? Not at all. Don't get visitors up here much, not the polite conversation kind anyway. Just the goddamn uniforms, poking around."

"Don't you get lonely, up here by yourself all the time?"

"Sometimes. But you're never *really* alone on an island this small."

"Maybe I can visit another time, read some of your books?"

"Welcome anytime…"

She realized she hadn't told him her name. "Marla, I'm Marla. Very pleased to meet you, Vincent, and thanks for the coffee."

Vincent stood politely up and Marla shook his leathery

hand. She gave him a warm smile, then turned and headed down the spiral stairs.

Listening out for the familiar metallic clang of the door as it slammed shut, Vincent looked out to sea. He found himself hoping young Marla would head back to the mainland before the storms came. You could never really be alone on an island this small and it was no place, *no place at all,* for the young.

CHAPTER EIGHTEEN

Pietro lit up a cigarette and strode out onto the porch to watch the sky. As the clouds rolled by, he realized this was the first time in months he'd seen so many. Weather rarely visited Meditrine Island, and so when it did, it became as much a grand spectacle as a fireworks display. He blew smoke through his nostrils, watching the little gray wisps as they appeared to mingle with the heavy cumulous in the sky. Becoming bored of the sight already his thoughts returned to Marla, in particular her smooth skin, pert breasts and firm buttocks. How on earth had he lost his erection with material like that? He wondered how long it would be before she came back to visit him, and how long after that before she ended up in his bed again so he could try again. Not long, he wagered, but even as he thought it he realized how disinterested he already felt towards her. Towards sex in general. Pietro felt more passion for his beloved A.C. Milano than he did for any female. It was true what they said about any lover, absence makes the heart grow fonder. He made a disapproving smacking sound with his teeth as he remembered asking her who had won the European soccer championship. Outrageously, she hadn't even known who'd played in the final. He'd quizzed her on his other great passion and she'd failed spectacularly on that one, too. *No, I don't know if U2 have an album out*, she'd said mockingly, *why do you even care about that?*

"Why do I even *care* about that? Bitch."

He was speaking aloud to himself now. He spat into the swimming pool defiantly, and then flicked the cigarette in after it. The stub made a satisfying hiss as it hit the water. Fuck it, he'd be cleaning the pool again soon anyway, and again soon after that, and on and on until his dick truly shriveled up and he died. Jessie had been telling him for weeks now to be patient, but he really was all out of patience. Jessie pissed him off anyway, a victim of that dreaded condition he called "Golden Pussy Syndrome"—swanning around the island like she owned the place just because she had a cunt between her legs. He kidded himself for a while that he didn't fancy her after all, that she wasn't his type, but what really pissed him off was knowing she was giving blowjobs to the security guards in return for smokes, booze, and a bit of substandard weed. When he'd offered Jess his own personal services in return for some cigarettes, she'd given him a few packs, but in return for *not* sleeping with her. *Golden Pussy Syndrome*. His lips smacked again. At least Marla had seen sense, although it had cost him most of his booze stash to get her panties off. Fat lot of good it had done him. Maybe he should start offering the security guards some mouth-to-cock action in return for some reliable information about A.C. Milano? He reckoned at least a couple of the boys in black were shirt lifters. Hell, even if they weren't, any hole was a goal, right? He groaned and stretched, feeling stiffness and tension in his muscles where there should've been post-coital numbness. What he really needed was a swim. *Oh, for the love of all that's holy, a swim.* He looked back at the pool, seeing the cigarette butt floating there atop the chemically treated waters, doing backstroke. The clouds suddenly parted, bathing the surface of the pool in sunlight. Shimmering ripples danced across his vision, reminding him the ocean back home. Yes, what he really needed was a swim in the *sea*. Pietro spat into the pool again, and as he watched his phlegm float on the sparkling water, he felt himself descending into a funk. *Fuck Fowler and his rules*, he thought, *fuck Golden Pussy Syndrome and her rules, too.* And with that, he headed back inside to find his swim trunks.

Thankfully, the wind had died down a little, and Marla decided to take a different route back from the lighthouse. She felt warmed right through by the heat of the strong coffee Vincent had given to her. She didn't want to waste the opportunity of exploring this new part of the island before heading back to do more chores, knowing full well she'd only mope around at the summerhouse anyway. The path across the rocks presented her with two new routes. One was a pebble-strewn path that thinned out in the distance around the headland. The other was a steeply tiered craggy outcrop leading down to the sea, its twists and turns making it seem almost like a natural spiral staircase. Feeling adventurous, she chose the latter and carefully began her descent down the rocky steps. It was slow going, especially when she reached the sharp turns, bending down then clinging onto lichen-covered fissures in the rock. Slowly she lowered herself bit by bit down towards the sea, which she could see lapping and swirling at a sandy cove far below.

Turning another corner and sliding down onto a particularly huge boulder, Marla could now see that the cove was actually quite large. Much of it had been hidden by the gradient on the way down but now she could see it in all its glory, a wide expanse of virgin sand sheltered from the wind by the huge rock face that bordered it like a gigantic windcheater. At the far end of the cove was an inlet, a cave, with a spiky overhang of blackened stone. Marla took a cursory look around the outcrop on which she stood. It seemed the only way down to this quiet paradise was a ledge some five or six feet below, maybe even further. Crouching down to look for a handhold, Marla awkwardly swung her legs out from under her and pivoted around so she was now facing the surface of the boulder. Gingerly, she slid her legs downwards whilst hanging onto the rocky outcrop above. A slight slick of perspiration had begun to form on her forehead. Taking a deep breath, she let go of the handhold first with one hand then the other and trusted in gravity to do its thing. She slid alarmingly fast, her clothing dragging against the rock so that she felt the cool alien surface of the boulder against her belly and legs. Then, with a thankful gasp, she hit the ledge and steadied herself before turning around. The drop had cut off the last of the wind current and she felt a palpable sense of calm in the still air. Smiling to herself, she continued climbing down to the cove, hopping over the last of the rocks with the ease of a mountain goat.

Kicking off her Birkenstocks, Marla sighed at the cool

comfort of the white sand beneath her feet. She walked down to the sea and watched the waves for a while, mesmerized by the beautiful simplicity of white foam gently buffeting a driftwood branch. The waves undulated like a soothing breath and they whispered to her, the sound folding in on itself in the strange acoustics of the rock walled cove. Making her way to a sheltered spot from where she could still see the ocean, Marla lay back on the sand for a while and listened to the waves. The distant song of a seagull echoed around her, conspiring with the other sounds to lull her to sleep.

Just as her eyes were about to give in to the lullaby, Marla saw a shape in the distance. She squinted at it, thinking at first that it was a dog or some other animal making its way across the beach towards the cave at the other end. Sitting up and wiping the drowsiness from her eyes, Marla looked again and saw that the distant figure was a small child. Confused, she stood up and started walking towards it, her strides quickening as the child built up speed. She could now see clearly that it was a little boy of no more than ten years of age. A dark, tangled mop of hair jostled on top of his head as his little legs carried him over the sand toward the cave opening.

"Hey!" she cried out, but the child pressed on either ignoring her or just not hearing. "Hey, stop!"

The boy was now at the cave entrance, where he stopped suddenly. He threw Marla a glance over his shoulder and his deep-set eyes made contact with hers. There was a melancholy in those eyes that even from this distance chilled her to the marrow of her bones. His face was deathly pale, starkly contrasting the crow black bird's nest of hair framing it. Her steps faltered, and she was about to cry out to him again when all of a sudden he turned and ran into the darkness of the cave.

Marla chewed her bottom lip, pondering for an instant what to do next. Her feet decided, following the boy's path into the cave and risking the darkness that lay within. As she rounded the curve created by the thick rock cave entrance, the cool damp atmosphere hit her. Blinking away the daylight and willing her irises to widen so she could see in the darkness, Marla craned her head backwards and saw the ceiling of the cave arching over her like that of a prehistoric cathedral. Stepping inside, slowly now, she inched her way inside—her footfalls accompanied by the echoing drip-drip-drips of water on stone. Carefully avoiding a chunky cluster of coppery yellow stalagmites, she was headed for what looked like a turning at the back of the cave. *Mites go up and tights come down,* she told herself, remembering a seaside field trip from orphanage days long ago. A small child back then, she had looked on in wonder as her teacher described how the rock and mineral formations had formed over generations and would continue to do so long after their lifetimes. Marla found herself wondering why the little boy she had followed was on his own out here, and felt a bleak chill pass over the surface of her skin. Her eyes now adjusting to the dark, she reached the wall at the rear of the cave and felt the source of the chill. A cool breeze emanated from a smaller passage that joined the main cave forming a sharp bend. She peered inside and whispered, "Hello? Hello? I just want to say hi, make sure you're okay... Are you in there?"

The drip-drip-drips of the water grew louder, accentuated by the lack of any human response from the gloom of the passage. If the boy was here, he was quiet as a mouse and hiding in the dark. Marla's skin prickled at the thought of walking into the passage alone but she also began to worry that the child had come to some harm in the cave. Newspaper headlines about potholers getting stuck underground in damp tombs like this one flashed by her mind's eye like microfiche projections. She called out to the boy one last time and, hearing only the echo of her own strained voice, she backed out of the passageway and into the cave. The high ceiling was an instant comfort to her after the stifling claustrophobic black of the mysterious corridor. Turning toward the light, Marla made her way back to the beach and its soft carpet of sand. As she turned the corner out of the cave, she saw a figure silhouetted against the glare of the sunlit ocean waves. She squinted, her eyes struggling to make out the detail of the figure. The unexpected sight was accompanied by an unexpected droning sound, rather like that of a huge sluggish bee heavy with pollen in the last days of summer. Marla felt dizzy. A faint crosswind bent the sound waves in her ears and the refracting sunlight made the silhouetted figure shimmer before her eyes. She tripped through the deep sand, now more of an obstacle than a comfort, and moved toward the figure, squinting as she went. Beyond the figure was another shape, small and hard on the horizon of her vision. It was moving, and seemed to be the source of the droning sound.

Then the brightness was briefly diffused as a cloud enveloped the sun and Marla saw the figure turn to face her. It was Jessie. And far behind her in the distant ocean bobbing on the waves was a large pleasure yacht. Jessie glanced back at the boat, then to Marla.

"We need to talk," she said dryly.

"Yes, we do," Marla agreed.

A moment passed between them. The boat's engine sputtered like a spectator clearing its throat then droned on louder than before.

"You found the cove then? Quietest place on the island. The most private, too. No spy cameras, well, none that I'm aware of."

Jessie was looking out to sea, holding her hand flat above her squinting eyes so she could see better. Marla didn't answer.

"Hey, I guess I owe you an apology. Fowler wasn't too harsh on you, was he?"

Marla felt her blood beginning to boil. "Oh, of course he wasn't. Invited me in for tea and muffins right after his grunts shoved their guns in my face."

Lowering her hand, Jessie turned back and looked Marla in the eye a little sheepishly.

"Look, for what it's worth I'm real sorry, Marla, but there wasn't any other way for me to get into the computer system. I would have been caught. And if that happened…well we can wave goodbye to our party at the big house."

Her eyes darted to one side as she said her piece. Marla knew that Jessie was lying to her. Bile rose in her stomach and she felt new urgency to extract what Jessie was hiding from her, not to mention an apology for allowing her to make a complete fool of herself over Adam. Leaning in close to Jessie's face, she spoke slowly and clearly, her voice just an octave away from real anger.

"For what it's worth, Jessie, I think you're full of shit. This has nothing to do with any bloody house party; you just wanted me to fall spectacularly on my backside. And thanks, by the way, for rubbing my nose in it with Adam, that was a nice touch."

"Oh…"

Jessie's mouth fell open, wide. Then, to Marla's further distaste, she chuckled. Her dry laughter sounded like cockroaches in a drain.

"You really think this is about Adam, don't you?" More chuckles came with the realization. "Dammit, Marla, I knew you were green but… Jesus, there's more at stake here than some security jock!"

"Like what, for instance?"

Jessie just pointed, out to sea. Marla looked, her teeth fixed in a grimace. There was a shape on the horizon, a boat.

"I used the computer network to get a message to the outside world. Y'know, invite some friends along to our little party? You have no idea what it's been like, stranded here on this fucking island."

Disbelief swirled like an ocean fog in Marla's brain.

"We're hardly stranded. How could you be so stupid? Fowler will crucify us for this! I don't care how bored you are; you've sent us all home with no pay. I can't believe you did this…"

"Can't believe I did it, eh?" Jessie shook her head, bitterness creeping across her face. "You'll thank me one day, Marla, trust me you will. There's only one way off this island and it ain't on Fowler's boat with your pockets stuffed with cash."

Marla felt her skin prickle with gooseflesh, yet the air was still warm.

"What do you mean?"

But Jessie didn't answer, instead looking over Marla's shoulder at something high up on the rocks above the cave entrance. Her mouth seemed to mouth the words, *what the hell?*

Following her eyeline, Marla turned and looked upwards. High on the rocks stood a figure, muscled and erect against the blue sky. Pietro. He was standing perfectly still on the very edge of the rocks adjacent to those overhanging the cave mouth. Far below him, the sea swelled and foamed against the craggy rock face that sloped into the water like the roots of some gigantic tree. With a swift movement, Pietro raised his hands into the sky making a spearhead with his body and propelled himself off the rock face, headfirst into space.

Jessie cried out, the shocked sound echoing off the cove's walls like a dog's bark in the city. Marla stepped back and gasped, her hand rising to her mouth. The moment seemed frozen in time, and all the while, Marla's racing mind cycled through every possible scenario. Each one ended with the image of Pietro slamming against the rocks in a confusion of ruined muscle and battered flesh to the nightmare soundtrack of Jessie's screams.

Pietro hit the water, just missing the rocks, breaking the spell. Both girls let out a sigh of relief, cut short by the sudden realization that Pietro had gone under the waves but had not yet resurfaced. Marla's eyes darted this way and that, looking for Pietro's head to break through the rush and swell of the water. Her mind's eye conjured a memory of his sweaty head as it lay on his pillow after she'd woken up at his place. Her fear subverted the memory; showing Pietro's head cracked open and spilling blood across foam white waves. She blinked the image from her eyes, willing it away, and continued scanning the surface of the sea for signs of life.

"There!"

It was Jessie, shouting and pointing at a sleek form powering through the water toward the pleasure boat—Pietro. He'd survived the dive after all.

Marla felt relief that he was safe, but utter confusion at all that was happening around her, all that she'd heard. *Only one way off this island,* Jessie had said. What the hell did she mean by that?

She turned to ask but saw that Jessie was engrossed in watching Pietro swimming to the boat, willing him on with half-muttered encouragements like a parent at a child's sports day. Marla saw Pietro stop and tread water for a few moments, judging the distance, before kicking out into the last few meters that lay between him and the sleek white vessel.

Seconds ticked by as Marla watched Pietro nearing his

goal. Then there was only fire and noise, black smoke and a ball of searing orange flame as the huge yacht exploded. Debris rained down into the undulating water while, unbelievably, the onboard motor still droned on.

As the thick black cloud began to clear, Marla realized she was hearing an altogether different engine. She saw the same realization on Jessie's face, too, as a carrion black vessel broke through the dissipating smoke and circled around the flaming wreck where the pleasure boat used to be.

Marla saw the name painted on the hull. *Sentry Maiden*. Fowler's men.

She and Jessie turned and ran, their hearts beating in their throats. They ran faster than either of them had ever run before.

CHAPTER NINETEEN

Brett was below decks when he heard the commotion. Excited voices were raised above the sound of the onboard motors and the ceaseless splashing of the waves against the hull of the vessel. He'd been soul-searching down in the galley and had decided he had no choice but to try and make the best of things, stuck as he was on the yacht. Maybe Scott had been right, they were crewmembers like the next man, and they had to do their bit. No point pining for the mainland while he was out there on the waves. He liked Scott, even though he bugged the shit out of him all too often, they were still mates since college and that had to stand for something. Brett was mentally preparing a little speech intended to placate Scott and smooth things over with him, when he heard the voices and the noise above reach new levels. The engine noise had dipped and the movement of the yacht slowed suddenly. Putting aside all thoughts of his peacemaking with Scott for a moment, Brett seized the rails of the metal steps leading up to the deck above and began to climb. He peered out over the hatch, watching animated yachters darting to the port side of the vessel. One of them, a girl cried out, "Over there! Over there!" and all eyes followed the tip of her finger out across the waves to the distant shape of a landmass. Brett was up on deck now, walking over to join the others by the observation deck. Where the hell had they ended up, back at the mainland? Maybe someone had made a navigational error. No such luck, he discovered, realizing the landmass was an island out in the middle of nowhere. Ocean still surrounded them as far as the eye could see. He looked over to the control room where The Skip (still an asshole, for the record) was talking rapidly over and over into the handset of a radio. His First Mate (less of an asshole, but still high in the charts) was muttering something about the island and how could there be an island out here, GPS was showing a whole bunch of nothing. The Skip looked puzzled at this, but kept on repeating his transmission into the little radio handset, working its coiled wire around his fingers as he spoke.

"There in the water! In the water!"

The same girl was shouting again and more deckhands rushed to her side of the yacht to see what she was caterwauling about. Brett went with the flow and joined the group, peering out over the surf in the vague direction the girl was looking. Then he saw it—a small, powerful figure ploughing through the waves with swimming strokes as regular and machinelike as an automaton's. The swimmer was heading straight for the yacht, his arms rising and cutting into the water like twin metronomes keeping a beat. Brett could almost feel the sheer physical effort of the swimmer. If he'd come from that island, he'd swum one heck of a long way already.

"Someone get him a life preserver!"

The cry echoed Brett's thoughts. He looked up at the girl who'd shouted and found himself staring into Idoya's eyes. He began to blush, remembering how his lower decks had betrayed him when he looked at her earlier. But her eyes were urgent and she seemed to have forgotten the incident for now. Something rose inside Brett's chest—it was purpose. This might be his chance to do his bit, to make a difference, to be accepted as a *bona fide* member of the crew. He fixed the Ibizan beauty with a serious gaze, nodded his head as if to say *I'm on it*, then turned and dashed off to find a life preserver.

There. The life preserver's bright circle was a beacon glowing striped orange at him from its mount next to the cabin entrance. He reached out for it, hearing Idoya calling for him to hurry up somewhere behind him. But he did not hurry. In fact, he stood frozen to the spot as a new shape entered his field of vision. He moved to the other side of the boat now, ignoring the life preserver, and looked out over the rail. A huge, sleek black boat was gunning through the ocean towards them. He could see black-clad figures on deck, holding onto the safety rails as their mighty boat powered through the waves, spewing spray in huge arcs from beneath its nose.

"Help him on board! Someone help him up!"

His crewmembers' cries were muffled static to Brett. All he could look at was the black boat, and the men onboard who were armed to the teeth. All his brain could process was the speed of the vessel and the fact that those who piloted it were pointing something decidedly large and weapon-like right at the yacht. There was a flash, a spark of flame and a sound like the world ending. Fear clutched at every tendon in Brett's legs as he launched himself arms, hands, head first over the safety rail and into the ocean. Submerged, his whole world went silent for a few seconds as he swam down beneath the waves, powered on by the force of his dive. Then there was a sound like a house collapsing in on itself, and Brett felt the aftershock of the explosion above him as it ripped the boat, and all of his crewmembers, to pieces. He opened his mouth in shock as he neared the surface, gagging on salt water as something heavy plummeted from the sky and struck him between his shoulders. He blacked out.

"What just happened?"

Marla struggled to keep herself from vomiting, retching at the acid tang of stomach bile hitting the back of her throat. She leaned against the cool damp surface of the cave wall and shivered, her body all at once aroused by the adrenaline rush of the frantic run and shaken to its core by fear. Jessie stood nearby, panting heavily from her exertion and rummaging through a small tie-dyed cotton shoulder bag.

Blind panic had driven them both into the cave, all the way round to the dark passageway where Marla had given up on her search for the young boy earlier. She was no longer afraid of its coal blackness, now more wary of Fowler's men in their boat outside. Her heartbeat quickened as she pictured them dropping the *Sentry Maiden*'s anchor and storming the beach like a SWAT team in a movie.

"We should be safe in here, although I have no idea where this tunnel leads, I'm afraid," Jessie said as she pulled an object from her bag. "Though last time I was in here I didn't have this."

Triumphantly, she twisted the head of a small metallic Maglite flashlight and pointed its beam down the passageway— it stretched on way past the extent of the beam, myriad tiny droplets of cave water cutting through the light like summer rain.

"I said what just happened?" Marla repeated, trying to make out Jessie's face beyond the flashlight's glare.

"Plenty of time to talk about that while we find out where this goes," Jessie replied. "If it goes anywhere, that is."

From somewhere behind them in the main body of the cave, they heard a sharp *chink-chink* sound. Marla's nerves, such as they were, drove her back further into the dark passageway. Jessie nodded grimly and started walking, too, keeping the flashlight beam low in front of her.

They walked for several minutes in strained silence. Every *drip-drip* of water, every *chink-chink* of stone, set their teeth on edge and renewed the fear they'd both felt when running from the aftermath of the explosion. Only when they'd followed a series of sharp turns in the tunnel did Marla dare speak again, in a hushed whisper, as the atmosphere transformed into quiet stillness far away from the entrance to the echoing cave chamber.

"I wish you'd tell me what the bloody hell is going on…"

"Okay, toots, don't freak out. I just wanted to put some distance between Fowler's cronies and us first. I hope to God they didn't see us run in here. Chances are they didn't, what with the smoke and all. But we can't be too sure…"

"Who was on that boat? Friends of yours, you said?"

"Just a figure of speech, girlfriend. I honestly don't know who was on that boat—and I guess we'll never find out now, will we?"

"But you said you'd *invited* them to the island. How is that even possible? I mean there's no way of communicating with the outside world, is there?"

"That's what I thought, at first. Look, I'm pretty good with computers, so it didn't take me long to figure out a way of hacking into the island's comms network. After that it was just a case of pushing the right buttons, if you get my meaning. I used the uplink to put out a digitally cloaked beacon. Only problem is I had to include a subroutine to keep randomizing the target range of the beacon to help disguise it for longer. So I had no idea if anyone would actually pick it up, it might just seem like background noise, radar interference. I think those poor bastards on that boat must've stumbled across it for sure and come for a look-see. But Fowler's goons got to them before I could."

"But how did you..." Marla voiced her confusion. "You were doing all this while I was..."

"Creating a diversion, yeah."

"Thanks a bunch. Why did you lie to me?"

"I'm sorry I lied, really I am. But I had to make sure, *damn sure*, you weren't a plant."

"A plant? What the hell do you mean by that?"

Jessie stopped walking and moved closer to Marla, hushing her voice until it was barely audible even in the womblike silence of the tunnel.

"Listen, this island is fucked up, Marla. Something very bad is going down here and I'm scared. I've been scared for a very long time now."

The urgency in Jessie's eyes told Marla she was being honest. "Go on."

"Before you came here, there was another Lamplighter. German girl, name of Vera. She was going stir crazy, seeing things at night and not sleeping, all that jazz. Anyhow, she straightened herself out gradually with the help of some yoga and a little smoke, but she was desperate to have some contact with the outside world."

Jessie paused, guilt flooding her eyes.

"I'd gotten friendly with Adam and he managed to smuggle a decommissioned laptop out to me. My first experiment was to get the uplink working and I needed to test it out, so I arranged a three-minute window for poor Vera to make a quick phone call. Took a few attempts to get it right but it worked. She made a couple more calls, but I never even got the chance to find out who she'd called because after the last one she was gone."

"What do you mean, gone?"

"I mean gone! Just disappeared. I told Pietro but he was too pussy to do anything about it…so I went to see Fowler myself."

"What did he say?"

"He told me Vera's contract had been terminated. When I asked why, he said she'd breached the rules of the island and that if I asked any more questions, I'd be next."

"Jesus, you were lucky. At least he didn't find out you were hacking in, or whatever it was you said you were doing?"

"Oh yeah, I'm so goddamned lucky." Jessie had to fight to keep her voice down. She trembled with frustration and a tear fell from her eye.

"Why do you want to get off the island so bad, Jessie? I mean, don't you care about the money? Once your contract is done?"

Jessie took deep breaths, fighting back tears with sheer effort of will.

"Why are you so afraid?" Marla asked. She was beginning to feel very afraid herself, standing in a tiny pool of light partway down a tunnel to God only knew where.

"I'll tell you why I'm so afraid," Jessie spat wetly. "I've already worked my contract and there's no cash payout, nothing. It's all B.S."

Marla's ears did not want to believe.

"How long did they tell you that you had to work here, Marla?"

"Um, twelve months."

"Here's a newsflash. I've been here for a year and a half. No payment, nothing."

Marla's head swam. "You're kidding me?"

"It gets worse, Marla, so buckle up."

The look in Jessie's eyes was the most disturbing thing Marla had ever seen.

"I think there's someone else on the island with us. I think whoever they are, they killed Vera and I'm pretty damn sure that we're next."

"Hey, that's enough, you're scaring me now."

"Good. You should be scared. Who knows you're here, Marla?"

Jessie's words chilled like ice.

"On the island—who knows you're even here?"

Marla felt so cold. The truth was no one knew she'd come here, no one at all.

"Thought so," said Jessie darkly.

Marla shivered, remembering broken glass and the acid taste of fear in her mouth. *Hollow eyes, watching from the trees.*

CHAPTER TWENTY

The flashlight beam dipped slightly and Jessie rattled it in an attempt to revive the ailing batteries.

"Come on," she said, moving off down the passageway. "We'd better get going before this runs out."

Marla followed quietly behind, trying to absorb all Jessie had told her. For a moment back there, her paranoia and fear had begun to take a hold of her, too, but now Marla wasn't so sure. Jessie hadn't been able to tell her who might have killed the German girl, only that it was "just a feeling" she'd had. What if Vera had simply been dismissed from the island for breaking Fowler's precious rules? It was certainly in keeping with what she'd seen of him so far. And all that stuff about hacking into computers, which Marla had to admit was beyond her, just sounded like paranoid stoner ramblings. Marla was bitterly disappointed with herself. She'd hoped to turn over a new leaf by coming to the island, but all she'd done so far was get wasted on smoke and drink, not to mention her bleak one-afternoon stand with Pietro. Regret flooded through like a virus and she could almost feel it thicken and slow her blood, making her limbs feel dense as mercury. She stopped walking and sighed heavily.

The fading flashlight beam, now a sepia color, skated around the passageway wall as Jessie stopped to see what was wrong.

"Why did you lie to me about the party, at the Big House?" Marla asked. Her tone made it more of an accusation than a question.

"Marla, we have to keep going. I don't wanna walk through here in the dark…"

"Me neither, so why not explain it to me as we walk?"

Jessie exhaled loudly in frustration. "I told you already I needed to find out if you were a plant. I wanted to make sure you weren't sent here to spy on me. You arrived so soon after Vera left, I just couldn't be sure. Her disappearing like that, gave me the jitters. I needed to nix the security cameras—that was no word of a lie, I promise you, toots. And getting access to the Big House was part of the deal, too. But not for a party..."

"What for then?"

"As a place to hole up if things got rougher, after I'd set the SOS beacon. Figure if I can hack in, unlock the place and fuck with the spy cams then I can lock it down again, too. It's the perfect defensive position. I was going to tell you all of this, I totally was, but I had to make sure you weren't one of Fowler's cronies first. That's why Adam made sure he was on duty when you ran down to the jetty, so he could see if you'd go through with it—or go tell Fowler."

"So now you know I'm just another *loser* after all, is that it?"

"Oh, we're all losers in this game, Marla. Nobody knows I'm here on this island either. Way I see it is, we're expendable. Maybe that's why they brought us here."

"If you really think someone wants to kill us, then why didn't they just shoot me on the jetty? Why go to all the trouble of job interviews and business class flights and security details? Answer me that."

Jessie wasn't listening. She'd seen something up ahead. Her pace quickened and Marla fought to catch up to her as she rounded a slight curve in the tunnel. They had to stoop inside the passageway as it funneled inwards. There in the distance, like a pinprick in a curtain, was a tiny speck of daylight.

"Look, Marla, a way out. But we're gonna have to crawl to reach it. Are you game?"

"I'll bloody well crawl out of here," Marla said. She'd had enough of the cloying subterranean dark but felt a dread sense of claustrophobia at the prospect of dragging her sorry backside through the narrow tunnel.

"Follow my lead and keep your breathing steady. In through your nose, out through your mouth. We'll be there in no time."

Marla cringed. Jessie was beginning to sound like a

motivational coach. A motivational coach who was clearly suffering from paranoid delusions. True to her own words, Jessie had indeed gone "totally cabin." *What a joker, dragging me in here*, thought Marla as she felt gravel scraping painfully against her leg. As the walls closed in tighter and tighter, she had to crush her limbs inwards then force them out again in a wriggling motion to move herself forwards. Jessie was some way ahead now, giving it her all, and Marla's sense of dread began to mutate into cold white panic. *What if I get stuck? Jessie's not going to be able to turn around and help me. Jesus, what if the roof falls in—I'll be buried alive, trapped down here until I suffocate. In through your nose. Out through your mouth.* Marla had stopped still in the tunnel, hyperventilating now. Fear entered her mouth like dust, drying her tongue and clutching at her throat. In the distance she saw Jessie's wriggling form surrounded by a thin halo of light, like an iris in the eye of a dark and distant storm. Then she felt something brush against her foot. As it slid along her ankle and up her leg, she tried to scream.

The scream died in Marla's windpipe and her body lurched forwards in panic at the cold clammy *thing* gripping her ankle. Dust motes flew up in front of her eyes looking like hazy baubles against the still distant shaft of daylight up ahead. Scrabbling like a mad thing to rid herself of the chilling grip, she clawed at the rough rocky surface of the wall. She felt a jolt of pain as one of her fingernails bent back and tore away from the tender flesh hidden beneath it. Tears flooded her eyes and pain-fuelled anger shot through her system conspiring with the adrenaline already there, causing her to lash out violently with her free foot. Contact. Whatever she'd hit felt heavy and fleshy and hard and clearly had feelings, judging by the muffled cry it made when she kicked it. She kicked again, only harder, then shuffled for all her life was worth up the tunnel. Her breath sounded like an alternator inside her head as she pushed and slid, and pushed and slid, her way toward the light. *In through your nose. Out through your mouth. In through your nose. Out through your mouth.*

She could sense the thing still following in the tunnel behind her. She heard its rasping breath, guttural and hideous, beyond the pounding of her own head. Her brain felt like an extension of her heart, throbbing and pumping as blood rushed around its vascular expressway, threatening to burst out of her skull any moment. Marla felt her pursuer's dread touch at her heel again and this was all her shattered nervous system needed to push herself the last few feet to the lip of the tunnel. As she erupted from the hole like a stopper from a champagne bottle, she saw Jessie's shocked face looking at what must be the thing behind her.

Jessie grabbed Marla's hands and pulled her free, the two of them tumbling into sand and stones and dirt. They rolled over and tried not to fall as they stood to face the mouth of the tunnel.

"What is it?" Jessie's voice, a hot-wired alarm.

"Something...something in the tunnel. It grabbed me."

They stood, watching and waiting for some dread thing to come scurrying after them over the sand. But nothing came. Jessie looked at Marla quizzically.

"There was something in there with me. I swear."

"Let's go," Jessie said and marched away. Marla took one last look into the gloom of the tunnel mouth and followed.

Chief of Security Fowler cursed as he shook droplets of scalding hot coffee from his fingers before shoving the raw digits into his mouth. Sucking the still-steaming fluid away, he removed his fingers from his mouth and surveyed the damage. Little pink welts were already forming on his skin—a visual representation of the shooting pain he was feeling as the heat penetrated the sensitive epidermal layers. *Sonofabitch.*

He placed the coffee cup back on the desk, then thought better of it and hurled the whole sorry mess into the trash can. Returning his attention to the bank of glass-screened monitors in front of him, he replayed the footage of the pleasure boat's last moments one more time. The image was annoyingly grainy. In fact, "grainy" was being far too kind; there was so much digital noise on the footage it looked like it had been captured on an island in the Antarctic—during a blizzard. Data from *Sentry*

Maiden would no doubt prove more revealing, but for that he'd have to wait for his men to complete their maneuvers around the island.

The screen told pretty much the whole story, however degraded the image. A pleasure boat had somehow made its way unnoticed to the far side of the island. No proximity alarms had been tripped, no radar alerts forthcoming. Visual contact had been confirmed by a lookout. *Thank Christ someone was doing his goddamned job,* he thought. He'd dispatched *Sentry Maiden* immediately and had followed protocol to the letter. In this instance, "protocol" denoted blowing the fucking thing right out of the water. Despite this efficiency, Fowler very much doubted his superiors would be happy with the situation. Far from it. How could a yacht get past all the safeguards and end up that close to the island? That's what they'd want to know and Fowler would be lacking the answers. *They'll be pissed as all hell and I'm damned if I'm gonna take the fall.* He glanced down at the spilled coffee in the trash can. *What a mess.*

Switching the screens to display current views of the island compounds, Fowler placed his stinging coffee-singed fingers against the cold glass of a monitor. A pair of exotic birds fluttered by the great eaves of the Big House. Palm trees swayed gently in the wind, casting fingerlike shadows across summerhouses and swimming pools alike. No doubt the Lamplighters were slumbering behind shuttered windows, oblivious to the clean-up operation being undertaken just a few scant nautical miles away. *All quiet on the Western front.* Good, long may it remain that way. Sighing heavily, he balled his other, good, hand into a fist and left The Snug. Once outside, he'd begin the search for someone to blame for this mess.

Marla and Jessie were working their way across the rocky ledge towards the lighthouse when they saw him. A near-naked figure, lying there on the lowest rocks where the waves churned with foam. Pietro. His body looked broken, his once-perfect skin battered and bleeding. From up here, Marla could not tell if he was breathing. They looked to one another and, without speaking, knew what they must do.

Jessie went first, taking care not to slip on the sheer surface of the rocks as she made her descent. Marla followed at a cautious distance. Climbing down to the treacherous waters was the last thing she wanted to do, but it would take both of them to haul him up to safety—if he was still alive.

CHAPTER TWENTY-ONE

High above the rocks, in the control room, Vincent took a dirty rag from his pocket and spat on it. Wiping at a patch of dark green mold on the windowpane, he peered out at the three figures approaching his lighthouse.

At first, he'd thought they must be Fowler's boys, come to check up on him again. He hated their little visits, always picking and pecking and messing with his stuff. *No business of yours*, he always said, *best left alone*, but it always fell on deaf ears with Fowler's mob. *Bunch of bastards*. No matter; this wasn't the goon squad anyhow, it was young Marla and she'd brought some friends. He hadn't expected her to come back so soon, certainly not with company. Vincent frowned at the three of them, then tore his gaze away from the window. Rifling through drawers and cupboards, he eventually found his rusty old telescope beneath the fat *Sudoku* puzzle book that had helped him while away many long evenings of late.

He returned to the window and peered out through the 'scope at the three figures as they stumbled over the headland and onto the rocks leading to his door. The one in the middle looked in pretty bad shape. He was all cut up and bloodied like roadkill and Marla and another girl were doing their best to carry him, shouldering an arm each. It looked like thirsty work that was for sure. Sliding the little telescope shut with a click, Vincent made his way over to the kitchen area to get a pot of strong coffee on the boil.

He paused for a moment as the wind rose up outside and rattled the windows. *An ill wind brings an ill guest*, he thought. Then, *no matter*, as the coffee began to bubble its welcome in anticipation of the familiar clatter and bang of the door downstairs.

Pietro weighed a good deal heavier than he looked. Marla remembered his weight, his heat, bearing down on her during their brief drunken tryst just hours ago. Then, his movements had been controlled and supported by contacting muscles, yet here on the wind-blasted lighthouse steps he was hanging from her shoulder like a dead weight. She shifted her own weight onto first one leg, then the other, praying the whole time for Jessie to get the bloody door open. A rusty metallic grinding sound told her Jessie had done just that.

"Come on, let's get him inside," Jessie said.

They dragged Pietro's ragged and bleeding body over the threshold and heard him murmur indistinctly as his feet slid from the cool winds outdoors into an even colder puddle of water at the foot of the stairs. He was alive, but only barely.

"Shit, get him onto the steps," Marla said, really struggling to bear his weight now they'd reached their destination.

His murmurs became agonized groans as they laid him out on the cold hard steps. Marla stretched and rotated her arm in its shoulder socket in an attempt to alleviate the stiffness and pain caused by carrying a grown lad what felt like halfway across the island. Pietro looked terrible. As Marla placed her palm on his burning forehead, his eyes rolled back. He looked, for all the world, like he was going to pass out any moment, which was possibly a good thing. Marla could only guess at the extent of his injuries, but however concussed his brain and broken his insides they had to get him up the stairs to warmth and a bed. Jessie, it seemed, had other plans. No sooner than Pietro's damaged body had hit the steps, she turned and headed back down to the entrance. Carelessly splashing her way through the puddle, she pulled open the closet doors and wriggled inside frantically.

"Hey, I could do with some help up here."

No answer, save for Jessie cussing as she bumped her head on something. Marla had no choice but to leave Pietro alone on the steps, and went down to see what Jessie was up to. Peering inside the closet, Marla saw the source of the blinking lights she'd noticed on her first visit to the lighthouse. A beaten-up old laptop was connected to a nightmare of wires and cables, its little lights blinking like some ancient prop straight out of a retro sci-fi movie. Jessie was typing and clicking furiously at the laptop's keyboard and trackpad, her face a mask of pure concentration. Droplets of sweat fell from her brow and sizzled on the laptop's hot plastic casing like raindrops on a barbeque. Jessie chewed anxiously on her lip as she worked. Marla felt almost scared to disturb her.

"What are you doing?"

"What does it look like?"

"It looks like you're playing *Tetris* in a broom closet to be brutally honest," Marla retorted.

"Well, I'm not. I'm actually trying to get us rescued," Jessie said sharply.

"Where'd you get that computer from, anyway? I thought they were forbidden on the island?"

Jessie tutted. "I told you that already, got it from Adam."

"Handy. That your dealer also dabbles in electrical goods…"

"It'd be a damned sight handier if he'd gotten me a computer from *this* century," Jessie hissed. She winced as the hard drive made a threatening grinding noise. "Hell's teeth, hang in there, old gal. Almost there…"

Marla watched as Jessie made her final calculations and clicks. Whatever she was doing, she'd better get a move on. Pietro was looking to be in a pretty bad way. They had to get him upstairs, and fast. Marla chewed her lip, wondering if Vincent had anything in the way of a first aid kit. A startling yelp from Jessie broke Marla's train of thought. The grin on Jessie's face told her she'd managed to make the ancient laptop work in their favor.

"I've widened the beacon, put it on a shifting loop, like a distress signal. Now all we have to do is hole up for a while and wait."

"Wait? What for?" Marla was dumbfounded by Jessie's technobabble.

"For help. From the outside world. Someone's gonna come and help us get off this rock, Marla, you'll see. Fowler can't blow everyone who answers our call out of the water."

"There's a casualty up there needs our help first."

Jessie nodded and clambered out of the closet, untangling her arms from the electronic entrails and closing the doors behind her carefully. She marched over to Pietro and gestured for Marla to grab his ankles. As Marla did so, Jessie reached under Pietro's arms and hoisted him aloft. Together they heaved his dead weight into the air and began the difficult climb up the stairs. Pietro groaned loudly in protest. The painful, melancholy sound echoed Marla's own dread. *Fowler can't blow everyone who answers our call out of the water,* Jessie had said. Marla wasn't so sure.

Once upstairs, the heady smell of boiling coffee hit Marla's nostrils. It was a welcome scent after the cold dank of the tunnel and the metallic sourness of Pietro's bloodied skin. She and Jessie shuffled inside the control room, stooping with his weight and sweating from their exertion. Vincent regarded them with a curious raising of the eyebrow and set his coffee down on the little table.

"Boy looks in a bad way. Set him down over there. In back."

He gestured at an unkempt cot bed that lay partially hidden behind a vast pile of books and almanacs. The girls wasted no time, heaving Pietro's bulk across the room and onto the mess of blankets that covered the bed. For a moment Marla was concerned about getting blood on Vincent's sheets, but as she drew closer to them she began to wonder if they'd been washed this century—if at all.

"D'you have a first aid kit up here?" Marla asked hopefully.

"Got some bandages and stuff in one of them drawers somewhere," said Vincent matter-of-factly. "Take a look and see if you can't find 'em, while I clean this here feller up."

Marla got to work and rifled through the kitchen drawers. Most were littered with sand and dust and contained a random series of utensils, broken crockery, and other bric-a-brac. Eventually she located a faded cardboard carton containing bandages, gauze, and a couple of bottles of antiseptic fluid. Turning one of the bottles in her hand, she saw from the label that the use by date had long since expired. She sighed and looked around the lighthouse room with its tidal wave of rotting books and molding furniture. *Pretty much everything is past its use by date in here,* she thought as she made her way over to the cot bed.

Jessie had filled a chipped ceramic bowl with lukewarm water at the behest of Vincent, who was now mopping congealed blood and dark matter from Pietro's once olive-perfect skin. The act of cleaning revealed the true extent of the young man's injuries. Deep lacerations ran almost the full width of his chest, giving him the appearance of a shark attack victim. Blood oozed from a wound in his left side, just below the rib cage. Marla gulped down nausea as she caught sight of pale yellow bone protruding from the wound—the flesh had been torn down to Pietro's ribs. As Vincent continued his work Pietro let out a gurgling rattle, which sounded almost as traumatized as he looked.

"Here, I'll have to pack this wound the best I can. Soak a coupla those bandages in some of that antiseptic," Vincent said. "What the hell happened to this boy anyhow? Looks like he went fifteen rounds with Orca the Killer Whale."

"Fowler's men," Jessie said.

Her speech was clipped and bitter, as she replayed the horrific scene in her mind. The pleasure boat, floating on the water. Pietro's lithe form swimming for all he was worth towards it. Then the shock of smoke and flames and the dreadful sight of the Sentry Maiden's black form, patrolling the water like a carrion bird. She blinked the memory away, feeling suddenly cold.

"They did this to him? Why?"

"There was a…a yacht, just offshore. One minute he was swimming towards it and the next, *FOOM,* they just blew it out of the water."

Vincent frowned and shook his head grimly as Pietro bucked violently beneath him at the touch of the antiseptic-drenched bandages.

"Will he be all right?" Marla asked.

"Hard to tell. Depends how much is plain shock and how much blood he lost from these wounds. Bleeding's subsided, but he needs more than vinegar and brown paper that's for sure."

"We have to get him to the other side of the island. They'll be able to give him proper medical attention over there, maybe even ferry him off the island to a hospital."

Jessie glared at Marla. "Take him to Fowler's compound? Are you nuts? Those are the same people who just blew him out of the damned water. They won't be in the slightest bit interested in ferrying him to a hospital. God, we are so royally fucked."

At this, Vincent nodded sagely. "She's right, Marla. Only one way off this rock—and this poor bastard damn near swam himself right into it."

"What do you mean?" Marla asked. She looked over to Jessie pointedly, recalling her exact same words in the cave tunnel. She saw the grim despair etched into Jessie's face, a sight that only furthered her own rising panic. "Only one way off? What's that supposed to mean?"

"I mean," Vincent said firmly as he packed yet more bandages around Pietro's ribs. "If you want off of Meditrine Island you'd better not have any unfinished business is all."

Marla looked from him back to Jessie, her mouth sucking air and her eyes searching for answers.

"You mean death, don't you?" Marla knew she was right. "The only way off this island is if you die?"

The old man's eyes seemed to glitter wetly as he looked up at them both.

"Better get the stove burning again," he said quietly.

A piercing chill had descended on the room, like a sharp winter fog.

It was getting dark outside, the dying sun a thin vein of crimson bleeding into the sea. Marla sat watching Pietro sleep fitfully as she listened to the wind whistling by the lighthouse windows. He hadn't so much fallen asleep but rather blacked out, the shock of his injuries and the stress of being dragged to the lighthouse finally getting the better of him. She glanced over at Jessie, who had bedded down on a pile of old magazines and was finally getting some shut-eye beneath a thick woolen blanket. She had made a compelling argument; Fowler's men were the very same people who'd mercilessly blown Pietro out of the water in the first place—but had they actually seen him before the boat blew? Perhaps it wasn't an attack but an accident, a gas explosion or the like. Whatever the reason, the reality of Pietro's injuries was undeniable. Looking at Pietro's clammy skin and the bloodstained bandages barely holding him together, Marla felt sure Vincent was right. He'd lost too much blood to survive without proper medical attention. Marla was certain Jessie's paranoia and fears were preventing her from thinking straight. Hopefully a few hours' sleep would see her right and they could discuss their options in the clear light of morning. Too wired to sleep, Marla mopped Pietro's brow with a damp rag and felt his flesh burning angrily with the beginnings of a fever. Her fingertips were dry and flaky and her hands bore mystery cuts that she couldn't remember acquiring. She thought of her cozy summerhouse on the other side of the island with its hot shower, moisturizer, well-stocked larder, and fragrant garden. Then she imagined Adam and the security patrols, their flashlights cutting through the gloom of the night to find her and Jessie's beds empty. Spy cameras would show no lights on in the main houses, nor any sign of life at Pietro's place, no chores being done. Then Fowler's men would come looking for them. It was just a matter of time. She grew frightened, Vincent's disturbing mantra looping inside her head like an old stuck record, *only one way off this rock…only one way*. With these fears weighing heavy on her already troubled mind, Marla fought to keep her eyes from closing and giving in to sleep. She imagined those awful hollow black eyes staring at her through Jessie's kitchen window again, and tumbled into their depths.

Her own loud yelp woke her and she sat bolt upright, opening her eyes. Marla shivered and looked down at Pietro, still sweating in Vincent's old cot bed. His eyes were closed and his mouth clamped tightly shut behind dry lips. He looked awful; sleep was the best place for him. The crick in her neck told Marla she had drifted off with her head hanging over him. Massaging her neck with a cold hand she got up carefully, not wishing to disturb their patient.

Crossing to the window, Marla saw the first moments of morning and the sky she'd fallen asleep beneath was in reverse.

This time the sun's rays were spiking upwards, creating watercolor blurs of yellow, green, and muddy reds where they met the sky's vapors. For a moment, the surreal quality of her situation struck her—here she was taking shelter in a lighthouse on the other side of the world under an alien sky.

"Strange, the light this time of morning."

It was Vincent. Marla hadn't even noticed him, sat in his chair with his feet propped up on a rickety wooden stool.

"It's beautiful," she replied before crossing to sit in the chair opposite him. "You must have seen so many mornings like this one."

"Oh, I've seen 'em, all right. Winter sun is best, sharp and cold as a shark's tooth out here. But the seasons drag. Seen too many mornings and far too many nights."

"How long have you lived out here, Vincent? What brought you?"

Vincent reached over and picked up a pipe, filling it with coarse, dry tobacco as he gathered his thoughts.

"Truth is, in a way I was the first of the Lamplighters."

Marla listened intently as Vincent went on to describe arriving at Meditrine Island as a young man in his early twenties, to take up the post of lighthouse keeper. The island was then, as now, owned and operated by the Consortium Inc. on the mainland. The great white stucco mansion houses had just been built back then, and soon enough The Lamplighters had arrived to look after them. Fairest of these was a girl called Susanna, pink in complexion with flowing blonde hair and a Nordic lilt to her accent. Marla found herself smiling wistfully as Vincent described falling in love with Susanna on first sight of her as she gathered seashells in the cove near the lighthouse. She'd fallen pregnant not long after they began their courtship, her visits becoming more frequent as they conspired about their future together. They were both happy on the island and so approached the Master of the Watch, Chief of Security Fowler's predecessor, to ask the Consortium's permission for them to live in the lighthouse together with their child. After she gave birth, however, Vincent never saw Susanna again. The Watchman told him she'd been sent back to the mainland, never to return to the island again, as punishment for breaking her code of conduct as a Lamplighter. Vincent's own punishment was to raise their child, a boy, alone in the lighthouse until he was old enough to replace his father as lighthouse keeper.

One night, Vincent took a boat from the island, determined that he and his boy should return to the mainland together and find the boy's mother, his beloved Susanna. The Watchmen used his own lighthouse against him. By its light, they pursued him through the waves in a skiff and ran him and his son to ground. Their discipline was harsh, and Vincent was told he and his son were confined to the lighthouse, their only contact with others being the sporadic food drops made by the security staff on their rounds. One or two of the men were decent enough types and showed some pity in the reading material they smuggled out for Vincent and his boy. With each box of canned food and powdered milk came a puzzle book, comic book, or novel—the foundations of the mildewed library that helped keep the draft out in the control room today. The years passed and as Vincent's son grew, so too did his desire to see beyond the lighthouse windows, to run across the beaches and explore the island's coves. Vincent woke one morning to find his boy had snuck out during the night. He heard barking from outside and from the window saw the lad tearing across the sand in hot pursuit of a black dog. The animal was ragged and skinny and, as is often the case with such black dogs, proved to be a portent of doom. For as the beast was swept away by an almighty wave, as big as a house, so too was Vincent's son. The waves crashed down on the rocks like heaven's thunder, drowning out Vincent's cries as he battled his way through the wind and spray. Upon his next delivery of supplies, he sent solemn word to the Master of the Watch that he would remain at the lighthouse as agreed, but that his son would no longer be able to replace him. And here he had stayed for over forty years, amassing the books and periodicals his kind jailers bestowed on him month after month, year after year.

"I like puzzle books the most. Their solutions are always the simplest."

He sighed dryly and Marla blinked a tear from her eye. The old man's story had touched her more than she'd realized.

Vincent stood, breaking the spell conjured by his oration, and busied himself making the now customary fresh pot of coffee. Only then did Marla realize Jessie had gone.

It hadn't taken Marla long, about a nanosecond, to figure out where Jessie had gotten to. Walking down the lighthouse's winding stairs, she could hear faint sounds emanating from the service closet down below. Avoiding the pool of stagnating water, Marla approached the service hatch and sure enough found Jessie squatting inside working intently at the old laptop.

"Sleep well?" Jessie asked. Her voice had a "just another day at the office" tone to it. Maybe it was the laptop. *Computers have that effect on some people,* thought Marla, *turn them into robots.*

"Kind of. How long have you been down here?"

"Dunno, toots, maybe a coupla hours. Had to try another subroutine, had to dig deeper, see if I could boost our signal some."

"Did it work?"

"We'll only find that out if someone comes to save our sorry asses."

"Speak for yourself. My ass is toned—I went *jogging,* remember?"

Jessie sidestepped her remark.

"So, you're on side now you've had some time to think?"

"How do you mean?"

"Well, you were looking at me like I was crazy or something when I told you we had to get off the island. I know I can come across as a bit…paranoid sometimes, but it's not like I don't have my reasons."

"Jessie, I'm sorry I doubted you, it's just—it's all been a bit of a whirlwind since I got here and I can't take things at face value, you know. But for what it's worth, I do believe you that Fowler and the Consortium are up to something. After what Vincent just told me well I…"

"That old looney? What'd he tell you?"

Marla recounted his account of how he arrived on the island, his lover's disappearance, and the tragedy of their young son. Jessie listened intently, her eyes darkening as Marla described the Consortium's betrayal of Vincent's basic human rights, his imprisonment on the island.

"Hate to say I told you so," Jessie said bitterly after Marla was done. Marla smiled in spite of herself.

"There's more," Jessie continued. "When I said I had to dig deep, I meant *real* deep. I found something."

She moved the laptop around on her lap so Marla could see the screen. Several windows were open on the display, running complex background programs that looked like something from a science fiction movie to Marla's eyes. Then she saw a window that looked different from all the others, a spreadsheet of some kind with dozens of rows and columns of data.

"What am I looking at?"

"The Consortium Inc.," Jessie said triumphantly, "More specifically some of their employee records. Look, on that line you can see the German girl I told you about, Vera. See?"

Marla leaned in closer to the screen, peering at the data entry.

"How did you get this?"

Jessie grinned, "I sure can dig, can't I? Do you see the line or not?"

"Yes, I see it. Name, date of birth…termination date?"

"That's the date Fowler said she'd left for breaking contract."

"Oh, okay, that makes sense…"

"Now look a little further down."

Marla's eyes traced across and down the next line.

Pietro's listing.

"Look at his termination date, Marla."

It was yesterday, the day of the explosion.

"Now the next line."

"I don't…"

"Read the next line, Marla."

Marla's eyes found Jessie's listing.

"And the next one. Go on."

A chill began to clog Marla's throat as she read her own listing. It, too, had a termination date.

The date was the same as Jessie's. Today's.

No one knows we're here. Expendable, Jessie had said. Marla felt her skin prickle.

Then Marla jumped at a sudden loud fizzing sound from deep within the wiring inside the service closet, the shock making her cry out. The security light above the door blanked out. The stairwell lights flickered violently in tandem with the electrical cacophony, then died. The laptop made a painful grinding noise, its screen the only light inside the cramped space. The battery indicator popped up on the screen counting down its forty-five-minute lifespan.

Jessie took a sharp breath.

"We haven't got much time."

A sudden, violent piercing sound, like that of a kettle's whistle began to ring out in Brett's ears and he opened his eyes. A troubled sky was far above him, and for a moment he imagined himself stranded on his back, high up in the branches of some vast tree. Then he felt the waves lapping gently at his face and he realized he was on his back all right, but still in the bloody ocean. And it *was* bloody. He rolled over painfully and began to tread water and as he did so, saw the carnage all around him. Debris from the yacht was floating all around him on the waves, which were stained blood red. He spat out water as his disbelieving eyes took in the horror of the severed limbs and other body parts of his crewmembers as they bobbed horribly on the undulating surface of the red water. Perversely, a section of arm drifted past him, its elbow hooked over a life preserver. Salt-water bile churned in Brett's stomach as he screamed and splashed, desperate to find a way out of this fleshy minefield. The waves moved all around him, churning up the soup of dead bodies and pieces of broken yacht. His screams died in his throat as he saw Idoya's beautiful hazel eyes looking right at him. She'd made it, she was a survivor, too, and together they could…. Then the waves barreled and churned again, and the girl's head capsized in the water revealing a mess of shredded flesh and tube-like innards at the place where her neck and shoulders used to be. Brett could feel blood pulsing from his wounds now. If there were sharks in these waters, they'd be along soon enough. Brett tried to swallow his tears and began to swim, his fevered imagination feeding his mortal burning terror—of swift black predators snapping at his heels.

CHAPTER TWENTY-TWO

They met Vincent when they were only halfway up the stairs. As they stopped to talk urgently to each other, Marla thought of her foster mother's old superstition. *Should never cross anyone on the stairs—it's unlucky. Oh well*, thought Marla, *bit late for worrying about that now.*

"Generator's down," said Vincent. "Have to get it going again."

"Okay, we'll keep an eye on our patient," Marla replied.

Vincent looked perplexed for a moment. "No, I can't leave the lighthouse. More than my life is worth, which ain't much, I admit, but there you go. No, I meant *you* have to go down and restart the genny—don't worry none, it's easy. I'll tell you how…"

"Where is it, old man?" asked Jessie.

"It's in an outbuilding at the foot of the steps below."

She and Marla listened intently as Vincent described the procedure to restart the genny. It sounded simple enough, but Marla repeated the instructions aloud to Vincent, just to be sure.

"Turn off, turn on, pull lever out then press 'restart'. If it fails, thump it. If it still fails, start over."

Then, a question struck her.

"And what do you usually do in situations like this? When you're alone, I mean, if you can't go out?"

Vincent looked at Jessie like she was a dozen kinds of stupid. "Well, I wait of course. I light a damn candle and wait. Here, take this…"

He tossed a flashlight to Marla. As he turned and headed back upstairs to look after Pietro, Jessie gave Marla a wide-eyed, sarcastic look behind his back.

They both stepped outside, Marla repeating Vincent's

instructions over and over to herself and Jessie cussing under her breath. As the buffeting wind enveloped them, their voices were silenced like the cries of drowning children.

The term "outbuilding" was something of a stretch. The rickety structure was seemingly held together by a random series of coincidences involving masonry and timber. When Jessie pulled open the door, she thought she'd fly away with it—all the way to Oz. As Marla helped her inside, she swung the flashlight beam around, looking for the generator. It was hard to miss. The rusty old metal contraption was mottled and stained with age and the ghosts of past oil leaks. Jessie crouched down to survey the damage, tutting and cursing. She reminded Marla of an old tugboat engineer she'd seen in some movie back in London. Marla couldn't help but snigger when Jessie hit her head on a metal support poking out of the generator housing, giving rise to further colorful language.

"I'm glad you find this so amusing. Here, point the flashlight over there, will you? Can't see a damn thing..."

Marla stifled her giggles and held the flashlight as steady as she could. Only then did they see the root of the problem—a large puddle of oil on the floor beneath a sepia-stained pipe that dangled uselessly from the tail end of the genny.

"Jee-zus. Main line's cut, look..." Jessie said, now wriggling on her hands and knees beneath the generator's bulk. She grabbed the pipe and studied it carefully, noticing a jagged tear right through it.

"Looks almost like it's been cut on purpose..." Marla said.

"Damn right, that's exactly what it looks like," Jessie replied, looking up at Marla with a worried expression on her face.

"Could've been a wild animal, I suppose?"

"Out here?" Jessie shook her head. "Why don't you take a look around, see if we can't patch it up with something..."

"Like what?"

"Like anything."

From Jessie's antsy tone, Marla thought it best to do as she was told and started rooting around on dust-covered shelves and in rotting storage boxes for anything useful. To her surprise, she found some duct tape and an old box of bandages—they'd have to do. Then, she jumped out of her skin at a sharp cry coming from beneath the generator.

Stumbling across the debris-strewn floor, Marla called out to see if Jessie was okay. Hearing more cursing, she guessed that whatever had happened, Jessie would live to tell the tale. She found her sitting with her back against the genny and sucking on her thumb, which was bleeding profusely.

"Let me take a look at that."

"It's fine, really," Jessie mumbled. "Saliva, best antiseptic known to man. And woman."

Ignoring Jessie's protests, Marla took a closer look at the injured thumb. A sliver of rusted metal was poking out of the deep cut in Jessie's flesh.

"Might need stitches," Marla said.

"Screw that. We seem to have left Doctor George Clooney on the mainland anyway—how careless of us. What you got there?"

After removing the offending piece of metal, Marla got to work fashioning a crude dressing for the wound using a length of bandage and some tape. Jessie rattled on, suggesting Marla head back to the lighthouse and load up with whatever supplies Vincent could spare them. The repair job on the genny could take quite some time.

"We need this fucker up and running or the laptop will zone out…and our signal will stop," she said delicately. "I don't know who in the hell would want to cut the fuel line on purpose…. I don't really *want* to know."

Marla shivered, suddenly feeling very cold.

"Leave the flashlight here, toots, I'll catch up to you when I'm done."

After fighting her way through the wind, Marla closed the heavy metal door and trudged back upstairs to Vincent's control room prison. The scent of oil and Jessie's skin was gone. She was preoccupied with the problem posed by having to move Pietro again.

At his bedside, she could see his normally olive skin had taken on a deathly pale hue. He shivered and groaned on the cot bed, physically burning up and freezing at the same time, a torrent of cold sweat pasting his obsidian locks to his clammy forehead. Mentally, thank heaven, he was in another place, his injuries short-circuiting his consciousness and muddying his head with fever.

"You'll have to leave him here."

Vincent had read Marla's mind; there was simply no way they could risk moving Pietro without distressing him further, or maybe even causing him additional harm.

"We can't just offload him onto you…" she said.

"Be glad of the company. Such as it is," deadpanned Vincent as he scanned the horizon beyond the filthy windows.

"Will he be okay?"

"No way of telling, 'til he gets to a doctor. That bastard Fowler will know what to do with him. We've done all we can to patch him up, make him comfortable, that's for sure. Damn fool thing your friend did, swimming out in the ocean like that."

"He spoke so fondly of swimming in the sea. I imagine when he saw the boat, he just couldn't control himself."

"Yeah, well. He should've learned to control himself by now, especially on this rock," Vincent grumbled. "Too many goddamn sharks in that sea. And *Sentry Maiden*'s the biggest damn shark of them all."

Just then a flicker, like the sepia wings of butterfly, caught Marla's eye. It was the meager light from a grubby emergency light above the hatch leading out onto the lighthouse walkway. Vincent looked at the flickering light as it faded then returned to unsteady life inside its housing. He nodded to Marla with a wry look of approval plastered across his face. Jessie must have got the generator running again.

Minutes later, the door below opened and shut with a loud clang and Jessie bolted up the stairs and into the control room. Breathless, she gasped for air, her hair wet with oil and perspiration.

"Vincent suggested Pietro might be better off if we leave him here," Marla said as she filled the flannel with cold water and mopped Pietro's brow.

"Damn right we will," Jessie said.

Then, tossing the flashlight back to Vincent, she asked him how long it had been since the lighthouse lamps had been activated. Vincent looked dumbfounded for a few seconds, as if Jessie was speaking in tongues like a woman possessed. He honestly couldn't remember that last time the lighthouse had been operational.

"I did you a favor, old man, I got the genny running," Jessie said firmly. "Now you have to do us a favor. Light the lamps, one last time. We have to go right now, so as soon as we're gone, get them running."

Marla spoke up. Jessie's action heroine persona was beginning to grate a little. "What's this?"

"We have to get to the Big House before Fowler figures out I've hacked into the computer system."

"But...won't they just come and get us, once they've figured out where we've gone?"

"Of course they will. I've included the location of the Big House in the SOS subroutine. Anyone who answers our call will know where we are. The trade-off is that Fowler and his mob will know, too."

"That's mental."

"Yes, yes, it is." Jessie looked like she was enjoying herself. "But I've also triggered an automatic lockdown in the Big House's security system. We should have enough time to get there if we quit standing around here chatting. And once we're in," she made a dramatic "shunking" noise, "down come the shutters, leaving Fowler locked outside and us safe inside."

"And then what?"

"We sit tight, wait, and pray someone picks up the SOS beacon before Fowler can shut it down."

"Or see the lights," Vincent said.

"Exactly," Jessie replied triumphantly.

"Light the lamps, one more time," Vincent whispered under his breath. His voice sounded like a distant sea shanty, dying on the surface of the waves outside. "That's if they're still even working."

Marla shuddered. They were both as insane as each other. And so was she for going along with a plan like Jessie's.

"Grab whatever food and water you can carry, we have less than an hour to quick march over there."

Actually, the action heroine thing suits her rather well, thought Marla as she did exactly as she was told, shoveling supplies into a backpack.

"That cool with you, old man?" Jessie asked.

Vincent didn't turn from the window, but just nodded and replied, "You'd better hurry. They're coming."

Heart in her mouth, Marla ditched the backpack and rushed over to the window.

She saw the black-clad men approaching over the headland like soldier ants.

Fowler's men.

CHAPTER TWENTY-THREE

Fowler was livid. His tired heart pounded out a fast drumbeat in his chest, a tribal call to arms, an invitation to fuck with whoever was fucking with him. His duty officer had spotted it, while routinely scanning the monitor screens in The Snug. How he hadn't noticed it himself was beyond Fowler's comprehension. Was he losing his touch, finally? Had he been on this godforsaken rock for so long that he'd let his standards slip so badly? No, it wasn't that. Whoever was responsible for duping him was going to pay, and pay dearly. Their manipulation of the image had been so well executed he could perhaps excuse himself for missing it after all. The subtlety with which the surveillance footage of the Big House had been copied and looped was almost admirable. But the eagle eye of his duty officer had proven more than a match for any such digital trickery. A subtle detail had revealed the ruse for what it was, two long-tailed parakeets, launching their sleek bodies from a branch and across the screen, only to miraculously reappear and repeat the exact same movement some time later. Darkness falling would have alerted them to the deception, of course; the Big House stuck in a daylight loop while the rest of the island hunkered down into lengthening shadows. But nightfall was still a way off, and so Fowler felt grateful for the providence of this head start. Then they'd discovered many more of the camera feeds had been tampered with, too. His technicians had traced the source of the bogus camera loops to a networked drive hidden behind a series of firewalls. Someone had actually had the audacity, and hardware, to hack into his security network under his nose. Once he found the hardware, Fowler was sure he'd find the hacker, and his retribution would be swift and merciless. The culprit was certainly tricky and had made it very difficult for his boys to trace, then decrypt the source of the network breach. Fowler found it difficult to wait for such tiresome tasks to be completed, urging his men to cut the technobabble crap and give him something he could sniff out and *arrest,* for Christ's sake.

And eventually, after an agonizing wait that felt like hours, they did. The network breach was sourced at the lighthouse.

The lighthouse. A barnacle on the ordered surface of Fowler's empire. Home to a useless, senile old busybody who was now proving himself to be a threat—just as he'd predicted. Fowler had requested the Consortium allow him to carry out a termination order but, for reasons unclear to him, they had rejected the request. Never one to question the chain of command, Fowler now felt anger on his very breath. If they'd just allowed him to do his job, to take the old man out of the picture, then this security breach would never have happened. He knew his men had a soft spot for the old man's stories, for his lies. That's how he'd compromised the island's security, right under their noses. The old timer had something to do with Anders' disappearance and Fowler knew it. He was sure the wrinkly bastard was the one who had broken curfew. How else to explain the unauthorized figure skulking past the security cameras at night? When questioned, the old fool had blinked those narrow bloodshot eyes of his and played the innocent. But he was guilty, and he'd been out wandering despite the rules laid down for him year-in, year-out. It ended here.

Wiping the sweat from his brow, Fowler pushed on towards the rocks. He was flanked by his men and had the reassurance of cool gunmetal beneath his fingers. He was an unstoppable force, and the old lighthouse keeper was far from being an immovable object. He'd get to the bottom of all this once they reached the lighthouse, and when he did Vincent would wish he'd drowned himself a long, long time ago.

Looking out across the landscape that had become his world, Vincent was fixated by the long shadows of the approaching men. He'd seen them before in dreams, coming to him en masse like a fleet of black ships with hard uncaring hulls, their only cargo a deep unerring woe.

Pietro's coughing whimpers of pain caused him to turn from the window, even though he knew the terrible sight that would greet him. Sure enough, rivulets of blood trickled from the boy's mouth, pooling in the craters formed in his neck by tightened and agonized tendons. Grotesque little bubbles of blood formed around his nostrils, popping wetly. Pietro coughed again and the smell of metallic bile tore away Vincent's brief olfactory memory of sweet, powdery candy wrappers. Casting a shadow over Pietro's face as he stood there blankly looking at him, Vincent saw the fear burning in the lad's eyes. Tears streamed down the injured boy's face, expressing the intricate, deeper pains that his cries could not find sounds for. His throat sounded like it was splitting as he emitted a single, massive, cracking cough. An eruption of hot blood, like lava from shattered rock, spat from the boy's lips. Vincent took the spare pillow from his chair, knowing now what he had to do, what he must do.

Pietro struggled at first, but as Vincent pressed the pillow harder and harder into his face he seemed at once to relax into his fate. His arms and legs thrashed and trembled wildly as his windpipe clogged with blood from his ruptured organs. The boy clung to his shoulder with one hand and Vincent pressed with all his might. He was at sea again, in the rage of a storm, clinging to his young son with all his might. As the waves crashed into him over and over until they broke his grip and took his little boy from him again, Vincent let go. Then he realized two things; he'd let go of his hold on the pillow and Pietro was serenely still, and he had a gun pressed to the back of his head.

The men's voices were just sounds to him. Background noise as if from a television set he'd forgotten was there for all these years. He knew not, nor cared, what the voices were saying. He got the gist soon enough anyhow as they punched and kicked him to the floor. At the sharp impact of a gun butt against his lips, the taste of his own blood was like salt water rushing into his mouth. He savored the flavor of an eternal ocean he was ready to slip into, ready to sleep forever until the waves delivered him to his boy. His child would be waiting for him, cold in the currents with his little arms floating limp like a puppet's awaiting their strings, the strong, comforting arms of his father. He wanted it more than anything, but a dark shape battered against his eyelids. He recognized the shape, spiteful and ugly as a wolf fish—Chief of Security Fowler. The security man was older and heavier, tired somehow. Sure, the hair was thinning and wrinkles were etching their testimony into the flesh around his eyes, but this was unmistakably his jailer. The very same man who had been keeping him prisoner all these years. He heard Fowler's voice through the fog of violence in his ears, every syllable a month spent in exile, every word a year apart from his beloved Susanna, a year in mourning for his dead son. Fowler barked loudly and a heavy blow knocked him unconscious taking the very light from his eyes.

Questions. So many questions. Vincent had been very confused when he woke from his dream to find himself tied to his chair. It was a lot less comfortable in this position. And with the lumpy old cushion taken away, now it was just a chair. They'd found the American girl's computer gizmo behind the service hatch below, of course, and Fowler was busily rattling off a tedious list of idiotic questions about it. What the hell did he know about computers, an old man like him? They could see he only had books and papers here, and most of those had turned greener than envy. A "canker" Fowler had called it, Jessie's laptop. A canker in a hedgerow of wires, ready to be pulled out. Vincent laughed and spat saltwater from his teeth and said *whatever, I don't know a damned single thing you're asking me and probably never will neither. All I have is this godforsaken lighthouse and the ghost ships that circle it. Which is still a darn sight more than you'll ever have, you petrified, grizzled little bastard.* At that, Fowler had shrieked like a horse and flew back downstairs to give his men some grief while they toiled over the damn fool computer like it was a hot griddle. Vincent laughed and laughed, then looked down at what they'd done to his fingernails, all peeled back like petals. *She loves me, she loves me not.*

Little petals on the floor. *Oh, where did you go my sweet, beautiful Susanna?* Hot red petals hanging by a thread from his fingertips. *Did you see our boy, did he brush pass you in the hallway? Did you feel his seaweed skin? Help me, daddy.* And then he passed out again with his brain all filled with blood. *Help me, son.*

It wasn't like he was asking the impossible, Fowler merely wanted the laptop disconnected from his network and he wanted it disconnected now. He could hear the logic in his tech guy's warnings that simply ripping the thing out could leave them open to all kinds of risks. Viruses, Trojans, the dreaded "blue screen of death," fuck-fuckety-fuck. But not even the prospect of a full security meltdown could temper Fowler. The old man had left him riled that was for sure, stubborn lips clamped shut despite their very best efforts to break through them and loosen his tongue. Even worse, his patrols had now confirmed the Lamplighters missing from their posts. With the Italian boy, or what was left of him, here at the lighthouse, he could only assume the kid had helped Vincent rig the laptop. This left the American girl and the new arrival, Miss Neuborn, to be accounted for. It didn't take a great leap to figure out where they had gone to. Fowler flinched, a facial tic that spasmed across his furrowed brow as he pictured the twin parakeets flapping across his security monitors, bright as fucking day. Swallowing down the beginnings of a bout of acid reflux, Fowler instructed one of his men to get on the radio and find out what the fuck was going on with Adam's patrol over at the Big House. This was the perfect opportunity for Adam to show what he was made of. *Made of shit, and he'll mess up—if my lousy day thus far is anything to go by,* thought Fowler bitterly. He instructed his tech team to get a goddamn frigging move on and stomped back upstairs with his head full of new questions for the lighthouse keeper. He was all out of fingernails, so he'd have no choice but to start on the toes next. *All ten of them.*

High up in the trees, a vivid green form rose up from a branch. It spread itself wide and embraced the gentle crosswind, gliding into an expanse of blue. Moments later, it was followed by its twin. The beautiful green birds soared high then weaved in and out of each other's flight path, lovers and nest-fellows entwined in an invisible trajectory above the dense foliage.

Far below, Marla and Jessie sweated and struggled on. Marla paused and rotated her shoulders in a circular shrugging motion, giving herself a moment's blessed reprieve from the clammy patch of sweat forming between the backpack and her spine. She cursed as Jessie, a few steps ahead, pushed past a branch that swung back and almost took her eye out. *All fun and games 'til someone loses an eye*, Marla thought darkly. Oblivious to the swinging branch, Jessie pushed on and Marla had no choice to but to follow. She had no idea how long they'd been marching like this, like conscripts plucked from the city and thrust into the jungles of some far-flung conflict they had no desire to fight. Cursing under her breath as she almost lost her footing in some brambles for the umpteenth time, Marla found herself missing the city. London. She pictured herself in her bed-sit, filling out the personality test again. The person who'd done that seemed distant to her now, even after just a short time on the island. She wondered if she'd have been so eager to sign her name on the dotted line if she'd known what she'd put herself in line for. Exploding boats, scrambling through tunnels listening to conspiracy theories from a whacked out American hippy chick and, worst of all, leaving poor injured Pietro behind. Not only that, but with only an apparently senile lighthouse keeper to tend his wounds. It didn't seem decent, or fair. If her legs didn't hurt so much she'd probably laugh, or cry, or both.

Just then, she noticed a dark form lying in the foliage just inches from her feet. She stopped to take a look, peering down at the shape to make out what it was.

The bird lay flat on its back, one eye completely closed—the other open. A tiny fly skated across the black ice surface of the eyeball. Both the bird's wings were tightly closed around its brown body like formal dress—a tailcoat of funereal finery. There it lay, looking to Marla like it was sleeping. Before she knew what she was doing, she'd crouched down and was gently cradling it in her cupped hands. She lifted it from the leaves and studied it more closely—she could see no sign of trauma. Most of all, she felt surprise at its lightness, its fragility in her hands.

She placed it back into its shroud of leaves. There was nothing she could do for the bird now. It looked as though it had simply fallen out of the sky, and Marla found this unfathomably sad. Even the skies around this godforsaken island, it seemed, were filled with death. Inescapable.

Then a shadow fell over her, and she looked up to see Jessie, clearly displeased at having to retrace her steps. As Jessie grumpily hauled her to her feet and dragged her on, Marla's ears were filled with the sound of her own breath, a heavy sound like that of a dog panting on a hot day.

"Quiet," Jessie hissed, her voice loaded with warning.

"Okay…" Marla said, panting, "I'll gasp…for air…as quietly as…I bloody well can."

Jessie scowled, doing her best not to begin an argument. Instead she pushed on ahead and then, seeing something, reached out and parted the web of branches that lay ahead of them. Marla could now see the source of Jessie's sudden caution, a massive sprawling structure with rows of glinting windows. The Big House.

"We made it. Now all we have to do is get inside," Jessie whispered. "And get a shift on, girl, there isn't much time."

Marla didn't need a second invitation, her clammy skin aching to fold into the cool shadows of the house. As they crept closer to the structure, she found it taking what was left of her breath away. It was *huge*, really massive, and much larger than the London town houses near the park where she used to walk—and those were vast. They pushed on through the barrier of dense undergrowth encircling the house, great leaves brushing them while the roots concealed beneath conspired to trip them up as trespassers.

Something crunched beneath Marla's foot, and she looked down to see another dead bird. This one had decomposed so much that it was merely a skeleton sheathed in scraggy feathers.

"Gross."

Marla lifted her foot and took a couple of steps away from the bird.

Scrunch.

Jessie had halted in her tracks and turned back again, her

annoyed look turning to wide-eyed horror as she drew near enough to see what Marla had blundered into.

The carcasses of dead birds lined the forest floor beneath Marla's feet in a messy spiral that spread out over some ten feet in diameter. At the center of the spiral of little corpses stood the stump of a tree. Its wood was blackened, as though the thing had burned down alive and every inch of it was riddled with writhing maggots. More dead birds covered the ragged surface of the tree stump, their ruination apparently the source of the colony of maggots that had taken root there. It was as though a tree full of birds had perished along with it, struck down by lightning or a death curse. Looking down at the little burst balloon of a bird's stomach, Marla saw disgusting, fat worms the color of blood writhing there. She tried not to shriek, biting her fist in revulsion. She stepped back and moved towards Jessie, hearing that dreadful scrunching sound with every step, tiny skulls imploding beneath her feet.

"So many birds. What on earth could do that?"

Jessie's question hung futile in the air. Marla did not want to linger for fear of discovering the answer.

They reached the House. Emerging from the dense green, out into the shade of gigantic wild palms, Marla felt as though she'd stumbled onto a ludicrous stage set in the middle of an amphitheater. The creepers and palms surrounding it added to the effect, looking like huge ropes and pulleys with their leaves and branches forming an umbrella of curtains and living scenery. Looking back the way they'd traveled, she could now see the curvature of the land surrounding the house. It banked gradually upwards in all directions forming a bowl-like crater around the building, which sat castle-like at its center. From this vantage point, the house had the aspect of a great meteorite that had crash-landed just meters from where she was standing and eroded over decades. The building was much older than the others she'd seen on the island so far, eschewing the millionaire's white stucco and double-fronted windows for more traditional materials. Old gray stone, weathered to an almost turquoise hue, made up the bulk of the structure with old timbers framing each dark window.

Exquisitely crafted eaves supported the slate roof. Each length of timber had the undulating curves of driftwood and was carved with subtle designs evoking waves, night skies, and the surrounding forest. As Marla studied them, her eye delighted at the discovery of hidden details—a branch carved here, a driftwood parakeet perching there.

The snap of a branch and the spell was broken. Marla looked around for the source of the sound, and found Jessie standing dead still a few feet away from her and gazing into the treeline nervously.

"We have to get inside right now."

Then another sound, this time from behind them, coming from the house. This noise was different, man-made, like grinding gears and cogs of some ancient fairground ride. Turning to look, Marla could now see great metal shutters coming down slowly over every window frame—and in front of the door.

"Run, Marla…"

Jessie's voice was so laden with fear that Marla quickly broke into a run for the door. There'd be time for explanations later. Looking over her shoulder to make sure Jessie was following, Marla saw the source of her fear. Black clad figures were crashing through the undergrowth, heading straight for them.

Marla ran into the solid wooden door with a thud and wrenched at the exquisitely carved handle with both sweaty hands. The grinding metal shutter continued its steady descent above her. Marla's teeth ground together in time with the mechanism as she gripped and wrenched the handle as tight as she could and shouldered the door with all her might.

Nothing. The door just wouldn't budge.

Then Jessie was on her and together they repeated the action, two frantic little human battering rams shoving against the door for all they were worth.

The door gave, flinging itself wide open with a sharp crack as the two surprised interlopers tumbled inside onto the floor.

"Godammit!" cursed Jessie. The impact had taken the door off one of its hinges.

Wriggling to her feet, Marla crouched, peering out through the remaining gap at their pursuers as the shutter continued to descend. Fowler's men were almost at the house, with weapons at the ready. One of the men, realizing he was now in range, skidded to a halt and aimed his weapon at the gap where Marla and Jessie stood crouching.

There was only one thing to do. Jessie got to the shutter a fraction of a second before Marla, pulling down on it with all her remaining strength. Marla helped her, wincing at the loud squealing protests of the shutter as they aided its descent. The man fired his weapon and a small cluster of wires exploded from its tip—a taser gun. Just then, Jessie applied her foot to the metal lip at the bottom of the shutter, forcing it down. Something snapped inside the mechanism and Marla was lucky not to lose a couple of fingers as the shutter crashed into place, sealing them off from the outside world. The taser projectiles rattled off the metal shutter like hailstones, followed by a thud and several muffled voices.

Jessie rushed over to a wall-mounted box and flipped the cover open. She peered inside at what looked like a complex home security alarm. An array of tiny LED lights danced, reflected in her gleeful eyes.

"The lockdown worked. You check all the window shutters on this floor, make sure they are secure."

"Secure? How do you mean? Aren't they secure?"

"Just make sure there's no debris stopping the shutters from closing properly."

"Debris?"

"Like dead birds. Stuff like that."

"Dead birds?" Marla shuddered.

"Look, just check the damn windows okay? I'll check the back door and upstairs."

Jessie turned and quickly headed toward the rear of the house. Marla nodded, then counted her fingers, to make sure they were all still really there. Now for the windows. She'd feel reassured to know they were all sealed tight. Maybe Jessie had set her the task to achieve just that. Whatever, she didn't have to be so damn bossy about it. As she began to check off the windows one by one, Marla heard a scream rip through the dust and stillness of the house.

Jessie.

CHAPTER TWENTY-FOUR

Vincent tried hard to blink himself awake through the heavy red fog clouding his eyes. He listened to Fowler grunting an instruction to his men and seconds later felt the bitter kiss of cold water hitting his face. The empty bucket made a hollow metallic clang as one of Fowler's boys set it down on the floor. It sounded like a boxing ring bell. *Round Five and the old guy has had the fight knocked out of him, they oughtta put a stop to it now, that's a pretty bad cut over the old timer's eye, looks like he's popped a lip too by the amount of blood on him.* Vincent's eyes rolled back and his body tried desperately to fall off the chair, but to no avail. Tied up as he was, he'd have to take whatever Fowler and his cronies had in store for him next. *Ding ding, gotta come out fighting, the roar of the fight fans, then blackness.*

Running out of cruel ways to punish the old man was not an outcome Fowler could have predicted in a million years. But here he was, drenched in salt sweat, knuckles raw and bloody and still the old fucker was tongue-tied. Maybe he really had lost it after all the years up here alone, retreated into some dark cove within his thick skull unable, or simply unwilling, to come out and face the music. Fowler upturned the empty bucket, placed it rim side down and used it as a seat. Looking up at the bleeding old man, he shuffled forward as if at some routine progress meeting. Close enough to whisper, he spoke clearly and softly, pausing only to wipe a small fleck of crimson from his lapel.

"You've been out, old man. We know this, and you know this. Our cameras have seen you, skulking around the island in your oilskins. We can't have cameras everywhere though. You know that, too, don't you?"

Vincent's leathery skin gathered itself around the meat of his eyes and mouth and he half-coughed, half-cackled as he tried to speak. Some nonsense about his "child." Fowler was growing ever more impatient.

"Where's Anders? Where's the German girl? We know she visited you here, at this lighthouse. Brought you books."

Fowler recalled the day he filed his report with the Consortium about the missing girl. Accompanying the report were his concerns about the sightings of a man walking the island at night. All efforts to intercept the unauthorized intruder had been fruitless. The mystery man knew the island like the back of his hand—that much was certain. Fowler could only conclude it was the lighthouse keeper who was prowling the island after dark. It was a fair assumption he had something to do with the missing girl but he'd need authorization from the Consortium to carry out a full investigation. When this authorization was denied him, he'd followed his ensuing orders to the letter, of course; keep it hush-hush, forbid his men to mention the matter on or off the island, and induct the new recruit, Miss Neuborn. He knew ,he Consortium Inc. had to protect its interests and he was in no position to contradict its ruling. So, he went on, he knew his place. But now Anders was missing. His best fucking guy. Looking into the old man's eyes, Fowler was at absolute breaking point. His blood boiling, he stood up and poured vitriolic words like hot oil into the man's face.

"No more, you old fucker, d'you hear me!? No more, no more! You must think I'm a blind man. Walking around this island like you damn well own the place..."

Fowler glanced at Pietro's corpse, laying contorted like roadkill on the cot bed. Vague excitement throbbed in his crotch as he replayed the image of the boy twitching beneath the pillow while Vincent pushed down on him, hard.

"Just show me where Anders is, old man. Tell me what happened and I'll let you live. I'll turn you over to the Consortium on the mainland and..."

The old fellow's ears pricked up at that word, "mainland." Gurgling like a baby, his head fell forwards and he tried to speak. It was a grotesque sound, like maggots against the lid of a tin.

"In therrrrground…"

"What's that? Speak up, old man. Tell me where you take them."

"I dugahhole…in therrrrground… I'llshowyou…"

Fowler gave his men the nod. They untied the bleeding lighthouse keeper, hoisted him to his feet, and dragged him towards the stairs.

Now he was getting somewhere.

The stale air in the control room had been so thick with the scent of blood, sweat, and mildew that Fowler felt blessed to be outside, his nostrils gorged on fresh island air. Up ahead, two of his men had Vincent by one arm each. His wrists were still tied behind his back, to make things difficult for him should he try to break free and make a run for it. Fowler studied the old man in the same way a young child might study road kill on a country road. The old buzzard was staggering as they climbed the gentle slope beyond the outhouse. He looked the worse for wear after Fowler's interrogation, blood congealing around his ruined fingertips, bruises ripening like fruit in the afternoon sun. Fowler felt a pang of something in the deep heart space within his chest—remorse? Or concern that his superiors might question his methods? He slowed his pace until he was standing still for a few moments as he attempted to identify the strange feeling. He closed his eyes and reached out for it, nerve endings desperate to entwine and fuse with his consciousness. But just as he felt a glimmer, a flutter above his ribs, the sensation was gone and there was nothing left but the machine pulse of his heartbeat. The functional rhythm provoked him into walking again and he hurried his pace in order to catch up to his men and their bedraggled prisoner. No, Fowler was getting somewhere at least and that was all he really cared about. It felt good to be out of The Snug, marching in the fresh air, marching towards the truth of the matter. Whatever he found there would surely justify his methods and curry favor with his superiors at the Consortium Inc. Wiping perspiration from the terrace-like furrows in his forehead, Fowler squinted into the golden sunlight with what looked very much like a grin on his face.

Vincent was on the verge of collapse, delirious from torture and exhausted by the unexpected hike. Suddenly, he stopped dead still and leaned against his captors, pointing with a single outstretched trembling finger into the middle distance. Fowler and his men followed the line of the old man's arm and peered out into a ring of scrubby bushes on the headland. Shoving the twitching man forward, he staggered ahead before falling to his knees. He pointed again, twisting his neck painfully, and mumbling gibberish at Fowler through dry, cracked lips.

Ignoring Vincent's mad ravings, Fowler pushed past him and his personnel and peered over the low bushes. The headland gave way into a natural dip, green with grass and dotted with color here and there from wild fauna. Looking out to sea for a moment, Fowler began to realize the significance of the spot. Zigzagging down the slope, he proceeded to the edge of the headland, which afforded a clear view of a rocky cove below. To the west lay the lighthouse, which confirmed Fowler's suspicions—this land lay directly above the spot where Vincent's son had disappeared beneath the water all those years ago. Turning and looking up at Vincent at the top of the slope, Fowler saw the haunted look in the old man's eyes. Then he noticed something, a pile of branches and bracken strewn across the ground a short few meters away. What had the crazy old bastard been doing up here? Tearing the branches and bracken away, aided by one of his men who skidded down the slope in order to help, Fowler took a step back to better appreciate the old man's handiwork.

"An empty hole?" Fowler's voice was strained with exertion, or anger, or both. "So, you dug a fucking hole? What is the meaning of this?"

At a gesture from Fowler, the remaining guard shoved the old man roughly down the slope and onto his knees.

"Was this meant for the girl? For Anders? Speak up!"

Wide-eyed and ranting, Vincent looked up at the security chief imploringly, spitting the words out of the tunnel of his mouth.

"My grave. I...been...digging my grave."

Fowler looked on as his man removed more of the branches, revealing the true size of the lighthouse keeper's insane project. It was indeed a grave, around four feet by six and at least eight deep. A brief burning phantasm pierced Fowler's skull—the image of the German girl and at least a dozen livid others, all piled up together naked and dead in the hole. His penis twitched like a dying bird, tethered inside his underclothes. But then the image was gone and there was just the smell and the color of the earth and the pitiful sobs of the old man.

"Bury me here, I beg you. I can't…I can't do this anymore…"

The final disappointment crept into every fiber of Fowler's being like a wasting disease. Vincent had been sneaking out at night, this was certain, but for what? To dig a grave—his own deep, tragic grave—on a hill overlooking the place where his son drowned. There were no digging tools in sight, not a pick or a shovel. Fowler glanced at Vincent's hands, remembering how filthy his fingernails were before his men set to work on them. He must have carved out this sad little abyss with his bare hands, night after night, for year upon year. Fowler felt like crying, but not from pity, no not from that.

Fowler sighed and ordered his man to hand over his pistol. The boy looked wary, nervous even, as he unclipped the weapon and passed it to him. Opening the chamber to reveal the dead brass eyes of the bullets within, Fowler removed all but one of them. He snapped the weapon shut and gently handed the remaining bullets to the gun's owner.

The old man's sobs subsided at the sound of the gun's mechanism snapping shut. Fowler sneered down at Vincent, who peered out over the headland, listening to the sea. The old codger looked like he would welcome death's release. His face had taken on a serenity that defied the bludgeoning it had endured. Fowler didn't like that face.

With a sickening thud, Fowler knocked Vincent out using the butt of the gun and shoved him headlong into the open grave. He tossed the pistol in after him.

A single bullet. The old man can have his wish. He can bury himself for all I care, thought Fowler emptily; *I'm done with him.*

He'd send his men to fill the grave with earth later.

CHAPTER TWENTY-FIVE

While his body lay deep inside his dirty hole, Vincent's mind descended too, into a kind of coma dream enveloped entirely in the crashing of waves and the crackle of sediment and pebbles. The sounds were like a monstrous breath, an undulating tide intent on carrying him away from his physical self and further into freezing impenetrable black. As his mind drifted, he became aware of a separate force charging through these neural waters like the hulk of a great ship. The mass approached him, impossibly large and fast, sending him into a spin as it moved above silent and cloudlike. The churning waters lifted him in its wake, and as his head broke the surface he saw that shape was indeed a ship. The sensation of daylight was licking at his heavy eyelids and Vincent struggled to get them open. The light was that of a lighthouse; *his* lighthouse right there on the rocks high above the stormy sea. Then the light blanked out—the lighthouse becoming, rather, the *absence* of light—and the ship was heading straight for the rocks. Vincent tried to cry out in warning but his voice was lost. His brain was smoke and his eyes were mirrors as he watched the beautiful sleek shape of the ship explode onto the rocks. It was a horrifying, awesome sight. Rigging and masts fell like tall trees onto the shattered hull as deckhands clung onto the failing structure like ants caught in a flood. A red mist descended over the water like a sick crust and Vincent was swallowed utterly by the deep once more. His neural pathways became reeds that folded around him, mummifying him in their fronds and folding him into the ocean's depths.

Jessie's piercing scream echoed off the metal shutters and solid walls of the Big House like the wailing of a siren. Marla found herself a few steps from the kitchen at the back of the house. Instinct had led her to follow the clarion sound of Jessie's shrill voice and she pushed on through the kitchen, through a utility area and into a shuttered conservatory at the rear of the house. The large room was furnished with a couple of sun loungers and a rustic dining table surrounded by heavy wooden chairs. It was the kind of room she'd dreamed about breakfasting in as a young girl, on imaginary holidays with imaginary real parents. This would be the perfect venue for birds to flutter in, singing Disney-style as Mother laid out fresh malt loaf and soft-boiled eggs on the table. But this was no bright and airy conservatory, at least not now. Shutters had come down to smother the glass in an impenetrable metal skin, and the only light that came in was via natural gaps in the mechanism. Dust spiraled unsettlingly in the thin strips of light to reveal Jessie, who was backing away in terror from a dark figure standing with his back to the shutters—right where the rear door would have been a few moments ago. Heart pounding, Marla was about to shout or scream or something when the figure stepped forward into the scant light, urging them both to calm down. Adam.

Vincent drifted up through the dirt like the stem of a thought. His eyes opened noisily, bombarded by glum light. He had the taste of the grave in his mouth and a violent whining sound, like a tuning fork, ringing in his inner ear. Above him, the mouth of the hole framed the sky darkly as a cool breeze flooded over the edge like vapor and down over the surface of his skin. The graying hairs on his forearms stood on end at the touch of the chill breeze. They were joined by pinpricks of gooseflesh as Vincent saw the pale little face staring down at him. His pulse lurched into palpitations as he squinted up at the face and realized he was looking straight at his son—his own dead son looking right back at him from over the lip of the hole. The old man was on his feet in seconds, a malformed word dying a death in his dry throat as he dug his ruined fingernails into the clay walls of his grave and began a desperate ascent. His fingers lost their purchase on the treacherous surface several times and each time he attacked the wall with new determination. It didn't matter to him that he was leaving what was left of his fingernails embedded in the clay like fragmented communion wafers, he just had to get to the top and hold his son in his arms. They'd be warm together; there'd be a fire in the stove at the lighthouse for both of them and a pot of hot beef stock to warm their bellies. He still had the boy's favorite mug, the one with the painting of the ship's wheel and anchor on it, a crack in the handle with a ridge of dried superglue and twine holding it together. Sweat trickled down the old man's neck and back, feeling like an army of cold insects beneath his shirt. His hands were a mess of grave dirt and finger blood as he reached out and grabbed hold of rough fistfuls of wild grass, pulling himself up and over the crumbling edge with all his might. His lungs felt fit to explode as he scrambled onto the grass and rolled over on his back, gasping for air because he had nothing left. Looking around frantically for the little pale face of his boy, expecting any moment to feel the weight of him on his chest, Vincent saw only the sky and the distant shape of the lighthouse. The cool breeze had become a harsh wind, moaning and mocking through the tall grass that he had bent and broken in his battle to escape the hole of his own making. *Lost, lost, lost,* the wind seemed to whisper and he felt the dead weight of the gun Fowler had tossed to him heavy in his pocket. He was a ghost, back from the dead, and cast back into the limbo of existence without his son. Tears made ice in the hollows beneath his eyes as he folded his arms around his midriff and lumbered in the direction of the prison tower he knew as home.

"Damn it, Adam, you scared the living crap out of me!"

Jessie scowled at Adam as she picked herself up and dusted down her clothes. She glanced at Marla, unaware that she'd rushed in upon hearing her screams. Marla felt a hot blush coursing into her cheeks. She avoided his curious gaze and looked down at his sidearm. Flashes of her dream about him pointing his gun at her down on the jetty splintered into her head. Marla looked away as Jessie scowled on like a disgruntled school matron.

Finally, he spoke, apologizing quietly for startling Jessie and causing Marla any concern. He explained how Fowler was on the warpath with Anders missing. How he had sent Adam and his team up to the Big House to check it out as soon as Jessie's security camera ruse had been discovered. Knowing they'd be heading for the house, Adam made sure to approach the building from the rear. The conservatory shutters, which stood firm behind him as he spoke, would give him the opportunity he required to slip inside unseen by his colleagues. They'd figure out he was missing pretty quickly, and after that it would be a small leap of the imagination to discern where he'd gotten to. But the security system was state of the art, built to order, and designed to be nothing short of impenetrable. Jessie's failsafe would make it impossible to achieve a computer override of the lockdown mechanism. Fowler's crew would have no choice but to go back to the compound and pick up the cutting equipment stored there for emergency repair work. Then they'd have to lug it across rough open terrain and through dense foliage in order to use it to attack the house's defenses. And all that would take time; hopefully time enough for someone out there to come to their aid.

"But when…if help comes, won't Fowler blow them out of the water like he did those poor people on that yacht?" Marla asked.

The fear in her voice was unmistakable. Adam's sudden broad smile did nothing to calm her nerves. Was this a joke to him, playing at being a secret agent, a superhero?

"We just have to hope Jessie's computer routine diverts Fowler's resources. The more time he spends on us, the less he has to worry about keeping tabs on the ocean perimeter."

Marla was struck by how white his teeth looked, just like a shark's. They reminded her of Welland, looking for all the world like he might devour her as he'd questioned her in his office. *Your chariot awaits,* he'd said on the quay before she boarded the *Sentry Maiden,* the same boat that killed those innocent people and crippled poor Pietro. *The boat, of course, the bloody boat.*

"Why can't we just take the boat! Sail her away from the island?"

"We thought about it," Adam replied, "but the jetty is so heavily guarded that it would mean involving a couple more of the guys. And frankly…"

"Frankly, we'd be fucked over before we even pulled

anchor," finished Jessie. "Not a trustworthy bunch, Fowler's men. Present company excepted, of course."

Adam smiled again, eyes twinkling. Marla channeled thoughts of cold winter days in a desperate attempt to prevent herself from blushing. It didn't work.

Jessie smirked at her and said, "Trust me, Fowler's gonna be furious that we're locked up in here. While he tries to bust us out, hopefully a few vessels will pick up our distress call—the bigger the better."

With that, Jessie returned to the kitchen and began rifling through Marla's backpack in search of something edible.

"Anyone hungry? Come on lovers, we can't explore a big old house like this on empty stomachs."

The house was massive, with each room revealing another doorway and each hallway or landing giving access to yet more rooms. Twice now, Marla and Adam had to retrace their steps to avoid getting lost, such was the labyrinthine complexity of the structure. Jessie had set up shop in the kitchen, busily preparing a meal from the unbranded canned and dried goods Vincent had generously donated to their cause. *Enough food to feed a small army*, Jessie had remarked, and she wasn't wrong. At this, Marla felt a sudden pang of guilt somewhere between her heart and her windpipe, thinking now of Vincent. She'd abandoned him, left him in his lighthouse to fend for himself and Pietro. Surely that made her as bad as those who'd forced him to stay there all these years—and surely she could've found a way to bring the old man along with them. If the island was as much of a threat as Jessie made it out to be, then Vincent was in danger, too. As she clutched the cool hard surface of the carved wooden banister, Marla made a mental oath to help get Vincent away from this place just as soon as help reached them. Feeling invigorated from the newfound determination, she began another ascent up the stairs and into the uncharted reaches of the Big House.

When they reached the next landing, Adam stopped still. Marla assumed he was being gallant—her breathing was rather heavy as they scaled the stairs.

"You don't have to wait for me," she said breathlessly, "I'm right behind you."

His hazel eyes twinkled in the half-light. "Listen. I just wanted to apologize…"

Don't make me do this, not now, not here, thought Marla but the only words that would come were, "Apologize? For what? You don't have to…"

"We…I shouldn't have played you like that. I can tell you're pissed about it, and I don't blame you."

He winced a little, as if remembering the way she'd looked at him after her grilling in Fowler's office. That harsh dressing down with her eyes. He'd known she meant it. And now, even with his face part obscured by shadows, Marla could see how very carefully he was choosing his words.

"I just wanted to say I'm sorry, that's all. We just couldn't be sure…I mean the timing of your coming to the island; Jessie said we should play it careful-like."

She was impressed. He was doing well.

"And you do everything Jessie tells you to?"

Adam smiled goofily. The flush on Marla's neck and chest indicated she'd already forgiven him for whatever sins he'd visited upon her.

"Pretty much, yeah."

Their laughter broke the thin veil of remaining tension between them. Marla climbed the rest of the steps to the landing.

"I don't know, Adam. Think I'd prefer Fowler as a boss over Jessie any day. She's such a *bully.*"

Adam laughed again, an infectious sound, and nodded his agreement about Jessie, his harsh taskmistress.

Drawing level with him on the landing, Marla said, "Can I just ask one thing. About you and Jessie?"

His eyes darted from left to right as he re-read the question in his mind then found an answer.

"Oh, we're not together if that's what you mean…"

"No, nothing like that," Marla said matter-of-factly, giving him cause to flush this time. "I just wondered. Jessie's conspiracy theories about this place, about people going missing, about what happened to Pietro and the boat…"

"Yes?"

"Do you believe her?"

Those hazel eyes narrowed and Adam did not hesitate.

"Oh, I believe her. Implicitly. And so should you."

Marla felt a chill on the nape of her neck, then heard a distant banging noise echoing through the maze of nooks and crannies that made up the house. Jessie in the kitchen? No, that was on the other side of the building. This sound—and there it was again, bang, only louder this time—was coming from above. Fowler's men, come to gun them down and throw their bodies into the sea? Her brain conjured a series of weak points in the structure of the house; an unprotected skylight rotting in its frame, a dry rot-infested nesting hole beneath the eaves, just large enough for a man to wriggle through...

Peering up the stairs to see how high they'd climbed, Marla and Adam could see one last door ahead.

"The attic. It's coming from the attic," he said.

Slowly, and without further conversation, Marla followed Adam up the stairs, wincing painfully as the old wood of the steps near the top creaked loudly beneath their feet.

As the banging sound continued from behind the door, Adam carefully tried the door handle. Locked. He crouched down by the door to examine the mechanism; it was a sturdy security lock, with no keyhole for him to pick at in order to gain access. He weighed up the options; on the one hand if the banging noise was that of an intruder, this locked door provided a useful obstacle. On the other, if the banging were the result of a faulty shutter or unsecured part of the building, he'd be better off checking it out and remedying the problem. Relaying his thoughts to Marla in quiet whispers, they quickly agreed it would be better for them to find out either way. It was important to keep the door intact so they could barricade it safely after locating the source of the banging. Rather than kicking the door down, Adam took a penknife from his pocket and set to work on dismantling the door handle. Marla watched intently as he set about his work. Adam gritted his teeth as he tried to work the point of the blade into the rear of the door handle housing. The blade skidded away, almost snapping shut on his fingers. It was fiddly work and looked like it might take him all night.

His grunting escalated, echoing off the walls as the metal plate behind the door handle refused to yield to his advances. Then, Marla's breathing stopped as she heard the sharp creak of the step behind her. At the sudden touch of a hand on her shoulder she squealed in surprise, causing Adam to drop his knife and damn near jump right out of his skin.

"Jessie! Don't sneak on me like that, Christ!"

Panic over, Marla noticed the flecks of tomato sauce on Jessie's clothes and caught the first whiff of something edible from downstairs.

"Didn't mean to startle you, girl. Chill out. I called to you guys—you didn't hear me?"

Adam and Marla both shook their heads at Jessie, who stood looking matronly surrounded by the scent of hot food, which had followed her up the stairs and onto the landing.

"Well, I made some food if you're hungry. It's not much but it'll keep us going 'til some help arrives."

"You go ahead," Adam said, "I'll join you guys just as soon as I've figured out this damn lock."

Jessie looked puzzled, only now noticing that Adam was crouched by the door with a penknife in his hand.

"What's with the door?"

A sharp bang replied in place of Adam, coming from somewhere behind the door.

Jessie's face frowned a question. "What the hell is that?"

"That's what I'm trying to find out. Go on, get something to eat. I don't know how long this is going to take me."

"Okay. You holler if you need any help. And holler loud; this house seems to *eat* sounds," Jessie replied.

"Hey, just make sure it doesn't eat all the food. You save me some," Adam said, as the girls began their descent down the creaking stair.

Jessie winked at Marla in mock-conspiracy. Marla could barely hear the creaks of the old wood above the manic rumbling of her stomach. She was starving. Only Jessie could think of preparing food at a time like this, locked in a mansion house together while (she was sure of it) all hell was breaking loose outside. But as they approached the kitchen together,

Marla's saliva glands took over and her mouth flooded with the thankful expectation of her first hot meal in hours.

They sat in silence, wolfing down the food hungrily. The pasta was delicious, even though the spaghetti was overcooked and burned molasses-brown in places where it had escaped over the edge of the pan. Marla wiped a glob of orange-red sauce from the surface of the table next to her bowl, enjoying the feel of the smooth textured wood beneath her fingers. The table, like almost everything else in this vast house, gave the impression that it was constructed entirely from driftwood rescued from the sea. Wood paneling, formed of gnarled and mottled beams that looked like they'd been plundered from the deck of some ancient sailing ship, lined the walls all around them, adding to the strange nautical effect. Marla sucked the spilled sauce from her fingertips and returned her attention entirely to the last morsels of her meal.

"There's more in the pan if you want it," Jessie offered.

"Better save it for Adam," Marla replied. "That was great, though, thanks, just what the doctor ordered."

Jessie smiled, her eyes narrowing. "You Brits are so polite. It was awful, I know, but we had to eat something. Plenty of supplies with us. Good job, too, all things considered." She paused, slurping up a long strand of spaghetti through pursed lips. "Your turn to cook next time, toots."

"I wouldn't advise it. Not if you don't want food poisoning."

"That bad, huh?"

"That bad."

"Ah, well, I guess then we'll manage," Jessie rose from the table, chair legs rumbling across the kitchen's rust-red stone floor, "Let's go explore the rest of the house."

"Now?"

"Sure, no time like the present."

They started with the ground floor, opening door after door into room upon room. Each time Jessie swung a door open, Marla expected to be back in the kitchen conservatory where they'd started but the house seemed to go on forever. As far as her confused inner compass could decipher, Marla was traveling in a wide circle around the perimeter of the building. Each room in the house seemed to serve a particular purpose—here, for instance was a games room stocked with a billiard table, which was clad in a formidable armor of thick, padlocked wooden covers. The table was the centerpiece of the room, surrounded by huge, also padlocked, cupboards and chests presumably stocked with board games and decks of cards. A room filled with forbidden games. Marla shivered, remembering seemingly endless games of checkers with her foster parents on rainy holidays in damp and leaky vacation rentals. As she followed Jessie out of the room and into a connecting corridor, she caught a faint scent—of damp, of remembrance. Glancing back into the room as she closed the door behind them, Marla drew a quick breath as she glimpsed a small shape flitting behind the billiard table.

"What's up?" Jessie was like a dog straining at its leash, eager to move on and get to the heart of this vast house.

Marla blinked into the half-light, her quick eyes scanning the room. She took a couple of steps back inside to afford a better look beneath and behind the billiard table. Nothing there, save for shadows, and that smell. The scent was old and so musty she could almost taste it. It was the smell of wasting away on rainy spring evenings when you are trapped inside instead of being able to play outside. The odor was thick with the taint of boredom. Marla shuddered and quickly shut the door. She walked on without saying a word to Jessie.

They followed the corridor as it formed a sharp left turn, then another after only a short distance. Here, the corridor grew narrower and the ceiling lower, ending in a small door that occupied almost the entire meager expanse of wall up ahead.

Jessie slipped in front of Marla to try the door. She gripped the globe-shaped door handle and twisted it. The door creaked open revealing a darkened staircase descending into impenetrable blackness beneath. Jessie pointed her Maglite down the stairwell. The cool air from within played across her face like a whisper.

"Cellar," Jessie said, and started climbing down the steps.

"Shouldn't we let Adam know—" Marla began.

Jessie's muffled voice cut her off in mid-sentence, "Come on, toots. Rich folks and cellars. Almost always fine wine and hard liquor where there's rich folks and cellars." She was already several feet away, a black shape back-lit by the flashlight's halo as she descended.

Marla shot a look back into the corridor behind her then took her first step down into the basement of the house and into the unknown.

The stairwell opened up either side into a low-ceilinged cellar. Jessie swung her flashlight around slowly, revealing wooden beams lined with rusty copper pipes and casting cobweb shadows that seemed to dance on the walls as the beam of light moved across them. Marla followed tentatively behind, the damp cool air turning the skin on her arms to gooseflesh. Something caught Jessie's eye, revealed momentarily in her searchlight sweep, and she quickly pointed the light at it again. Holding the flashlight steady and creeping forward, Jessie could see a mattress, child-sized and strewn with loose bedding, lying in the far corner of the cellar. Marla saw it, too, and walked close behind Jessie. Taking in the visual information revealed by the flashlight beam, they found themselves standing in what looked like a makeshift bedroom. Ramshackle shelves formed a perimeter around the mattress, laden with old toys—threadbare teddy bears, rusty spinning tops, a tiny broken blackboard complete with crumbling colored chalks. A tangle of soiled linen was heaped atop the unmade bed, sheets and blankets that looked like they had never been washed, their surfaces encased in a crust of filth. The mattress itself was mildewed and stained in hues of livid green and autumnal brown. A faint smell, of urine accompanied by something sickly sweet like rotting fruit, hit Marla's nostrils suddenly and she gagged. Jessie, made of sterner stuff, seemed unfazed as she crouched down to study something lying next to the bed. Smiling, she grabbed it and held it up in the light so Marla could see. She looked at its once-bright red plastic surface and realized, bizarrely, that it was an old Fisher Price kids' cassette player. Jessie hit the play button and a nursery rhyme sang out from the tiny speaker. *"Old MacDonald had a farm, and on that farm he had some pigs."* Marla didn't like the sound, especially down here where the air was cold and foul. She jabbed the stop button with a loud click and looked nervously over her shoulder into the gloom.

"Don't be so jumpy, there's nobody here." Jessie smirked. "At least we have some party tunes now."

Marla ignored her, glancing at a mess of grubby melted stumps of candles lining the lower shelves nearest to the mattress. Behind them stood a couple of liter-sized bottles, one uncorked and empty but the other almost filled to the top with clear liquid, cork intact.

Jessie saw it too and grasped it, excitedly twisting at the cork stopper and taking a tentative sniff. A look of evil delight spread across her face like a gleeful shadow. She held the bottle out to Marla, inviting her to take a sniff.

Marla leaned forward to inhale, curious about what was inside the bottle. As she did so, she noticed a ream of tattered papers lurking on the dusty shelf behind the empty bottle. Breathing in alcoholic fumes from the mouth of the bottle, Marla's senses reeled at the sudden vapors of aniseed and pure booze that cut through her nostrils like some kind of nefarious cold remedy.

"Ouzo," Jessie said.

Peering into the space behind the empty bottle, Marla began to make out what lurked there on the shadowy pages. As the vapors insinuated their merry way up towards her brain, she realized she was looking at a section of thigh, a trio of folded breasts and a series of parted legs—the pages forming a lurid gynecological catalog for whatever deviant had occupied the corrupt sheets atop the stinking mattress. The printed pornography looked so incongruous amidst the children's toys that Marla grimaced suddenly. Jessie laughed, mistaking her look for one of distaste at the scent of the ouzo. In sympathy she corked the bottle again and, pausing only to pick up the kiddies' tape player, swung her flashlight in the direction of the stairs.

Words of bafflement and disgust stuck in Marla's throat, choking her like pollen on hot day. She followed Jessie dumbly, desperate to be away from the dank basement, the foul mattress, and the excretions of whoever, or whatever, used it as a bed. Marla almost stumbled on the stairs as a fathomless panic seized her. She climbed the last steps two at a time, all the better to be away from that subterranean nightmare.

The cellar air felt like a cold, clammy breath on the back of her neck as the door swung shut behind her. Only when she and Jessie had walked the narrow corridor back to the high-ceilinged space of the games room, could Marla breathe again. The sound of her exhalation joined the howling chorus of wind as it whistled around shutters and walls only inches thick, but miles away.

CHAPTER TWENTY-SIX

Through the trees surrounding the huge wood, metal, and glass structure, over the headland and toward the rocks, the same fearsome wind buffeted Vincent as he made his way to the lighthouse. The door banged and squealed as loud as a wild boar as he rounded the crumbling base of the tower and began his tenuous climb up the rust-mottled steps. He tumbled over the threshold, his insides straining against the confines of his ribcage, piercing pain shooting through his middle as he coughed into dirty bloodstained fists. The smell of the earth on his fingers confused him for a moment—was he adrift, dreaming again in the depths of the muddy hole he'd dug with his bare hands? But the sound of the wind rattling the windows in the moldy library above was too palpable, too true for this to be a dream. He gripped the handrail and, as he hauled his knackered old frame up the winding stairwell, the welcoming scents of rust, decay, and stale coffee told him he'd come home.

Home. That was the name he'd given to his prison long ago. Even so, he had to admit to himself he was glad to be back in the old place. He found himself longing to fold into the chair that had been sculpted to support him, chiseled as it was by his backbone, which was becoming as bent as the spines of his oldest books. Vincent felt wetness beneath his feet and looked down to see the overturned bucket Fowler and his cronies had left behind. Unwelcome memories of their tortures flashed in front of his eyes bright as fireflies, their inane questions ringing in his ears like dull bells pealing from across the dead ocean outside. The sensations caused his legs to buckle and the old man limped blindly to his chair, almost falling short of the mark as he sat down, clasping a clammy hand to his forehead.

A great shuddering tremor passed through his body from his gut to his head and the floodgates opened. Tears streamed down his face as the delayed shock from the last few hours was given full sway by the very act of coming home. Salt water leaked from his eyes and splashed onto the cold floor, mingling with gobbets of his own dried blood, and making dark islands around fragments of ruined fingernail and chipped tooth. He sat like this for an age, cycles of tears and remorse squeezing the very moisture from him, futile snot bubbling from his nose as he wept on and on. Into this vale of despair he fell, further still, until he was weeping in his sleep. Finally, his tears subsided, their tracks beginning to dry on his wrinkled face like shame.

Shadows moved across him as he woke and he peered out through stinging eyes to find what had disturbed him. He struggled into a seated position on the chair and scanned the room. Pietro's body had gone to God only knew where, the stained and crumpled blankets lining the cot bed the only evidence he'd ever even been there. Vincent's eyes followed the slow rhythmic dripping sound of the leaky faucet above the sink. There, a shadow! His heart pulsed into life at the sight of a small pale form crouching beside the sink cupboard.

"Son?" he murmured in confusion, for the face of the little white boy was awful familiar.

Then, with revulsion, Vincent saw the kid's grubby fist was clasped around its fat little penis, kneading it like a water balloon. The child's tongue flicked out across dry, cracked lips leaving a snail trail of slimy wetness on their scaly surface.

"Eric? My child—is that you?"

At the sound of his name the child hissed like a wildcat and, releasing his engorged member from his hand, lurched back into the shadows and scuttled beneath the panoramic mountain of books lining the windows.

Wide-eyed and shaking with fear, Vincent was about to stand up and go look for the boy when a great, light-canceling *shape* filled his vision. Trembling, the old man looked up to identify this new terror and saw a monolith of a man standing over him. Tall as a wave and dark as the night ocean, the shape carried

Pietro's limp body over one shoulder as though it were merely a sack of feathers. Foul sulfurous breath emanated from the impenetrable black depths where the giant's face should have been. Empty eyes bore down on Vincent like black light, causing him to clamp his eyes shut in denial of these phantoms come to visit him in his home. Agonizing, breathless seconds passed as the old man listened to the dull thud of great footsteps. The monster was coming for him, to snap his neck and put out his eyes, hollows ready for the aberration that looked like his child to penetrate them with filthy digits and hook out his brains. But the great booming footsteps were fading and then they were gone, echoing into nothing as the lighthouse door clanged shut far below. Vincent sat there, terrified, with his eyes clamped shut until he heard the obscene crablike scuttling of tiny wet feet moving across the room and down the stairs. When he finally summoned the courage to open his eyes, Vincent felt warm metal in his hand and realized he'd been clutching onto the pistol for dear life the whole time. Vowing not to let it go of it until his work was done, he rose and clambered over the books to try and locate the control panel. If, with God's good grace he could remember how, he'd make good on his promise and light the lamps.

Light the lamps one last time.

Chief of Security Fowler still felt as mad as a bear.

Unknown to him, Adam's predictions had panned out just as he'd described them to Marla and Jessie; the security detail faced a long and arduous task if Fowler wanted them to haul ass back to the Big House with the cutting gear in tow. And, true to form, that's exactly what he'd ordered them to do. Relying on his computer guys had been a mistake, Fowler understood that now. Whatever technical mojo the cocksucking hippie girl had worked in the guts of the island's network was far too complex for his team to undo without a careful review of the defenses she'd put in place. His best option was to bust the bitch out of the mansion house and put her to work on the problem she'd created, under pain of death if she resisted. Something stirred in his loins, partly a need for violence and partly a manifestation of his vitriol at being duped by a bunch of fucking subordinates.

The wind shifted in the clearing around him and Fowler looked up to see two parakeets flying to higher branches against the darkening sky. Their cries had a mocking quality, like the teasing voices of children engrossed in some playground power play. Gritting his teeth so hard that they scraped together, Fowler unclipped the holster on his belt and pulled out his sidearm. Using his left arm to support his shooting hand, he pointed the gun at one of the parakeets as it preened itself wantonly like a knocking shop window prostitute. The painted bird disgusted him with its colors and its cries, perched there so high above him. He wanted to blow it out of existence. In a shower of blood and explosion of feathers, the act would announce that he, Chief of Security Fowler, was in charge on this island.

No hippie hacker was going to get the better of him—how could she even think she'd get away with whatever damn fool plan she'd hatched? And the British girl? She had only been on the island a short while. She was either very naïve or she'd brought some of this bullshit rebellion to the island with her. He suspected the latter was the truth of it; even now she was eroding his order like a poisonous wave lapping against the very fabric of the island. The black kid was in on it, too. He was sure of that. His men had been very thorough and there was no other explanation—his own guy, *his own fucking guy*, had snuck into the house with them. He recalled the satisfying crunch the kid's walkie-talkie had made when Fowler had smashed it beneath his boot, grinding it into the dirt where they'd found it round back. Fowler made a solemn vow to himself—he'd grind the turncoat's skull into the ground just the same as soon as his men popped the lid on their metal hideout.

Then, raised voices and movement in the trees separated Fowler from his angry reverie, and he turned to see his men approaching with the cutting gear. Alerted by the noisy activity, the parakeets flapped from their branches, chattering excitedly. Slowly, the Chief lowered his weapon and pointed it at the ground. No blood and feathers today. For now, anyhow.

"You took your sweet fucking time. Put your goddamn backs into it!" Fowler yelled, "Set it up over there by the main door. Bitches inside can pay for the damage."

His men were sweat=drenched and flushed from their efforts, their tanks all but empty as they struggled on the last few meters to the house.

Now we can get this party started, thought Fowler as he finally, reluctantly, returned his pistol to its holster. His mouth craved coffee and his ass needed to be in the pile cushion atop the swivel chair in the warm confines of The Snug. But right now, his men needed supervision—even now, one of them had stopped work and was staring open- mouthed at the treeline.

"I said get it set up! What the fuck is wrong with you..." Fowler began, but then he saw several more pairs of wide eyes locked on the horizon behind him. The Chief followed their gaze and saw what they saw. Streaks of light, rotating like great searchlights across the clouds in the glooming sky. Unbelievable. Someone had activated the goddamn lighthouse. Fucker would be seen for miles around, another nail in the coffin of his regime, another flagrant disregard for the rules.

"Get back to work, all of you!" he hollered, "I want that shitbox open by the time I get back!" Then, selecting three men at random he barked, "You, you, and you. Come with me. Keep up!"

As he marched off in the direction of the lights, Fowler pulled out his gun. He made a new vow to himself not to holster it again until he'd restored order to this godforsaken rock.

STRATUM GRANULOSUM

The condition of the boy infuriated him. It was a far from perfect specimen. No matter, this one would enrich the stockpot ahead of the main ingredient. He took the lad's body from the hook where it hung limp and heavy beneath the cold, unkind beams of the work lights, lifted it onto his shoulder and laid it down on the gurney.

Taking a fresh scalpel from the bench, he made the primary incision from the tip of the acromion down, being careful to use the belly of the knife not the tip. His wrist remembered the act from countless times before and gave its signature twist around the umbilicus as he sliced. He wiped the scalpel on his apron and put it aside, picking up the heaviest of his cartilage knives. Time to begin reflecting the tissues. A world of interest on the inside, so much more than the drab outer layers, slave to the tyranny of facial expression and superficial physique. He sawed with the knife, using its weight to help him pull the flesh back from the bone all the way up to and over the boy's chest. He wiped the knife and reverted to the scalpel. Now it was time to work on the abdomen, taking great care to slice layer by layer so as not to perforate the bowel. The silver kiss of the blade caused new lips to open expectantly in the boy's belly, which puckered open wetly like a flower. The peritoneum incised, he fingered the orifice, making a V-shape to raise the abdominal wall. Just as thousands of others had before, the organs fell away from the outer surface, crouching back as though they knew they mustn't be cut. He paused, taking in the saltwater bile stench of the lad's innards, then opened the abdomen fully. He grabbed the heaviest cartilage knife once more and got to work on the chest, cutting through the sternoclavicular joints, then sawing at the costal cartilages. The boy was in good shape, supple and young, easy work. Older cadavers could result in calcified costal cartilages, rigid structures like tombstones an epitaph to the specimen's age. Cutting and prizing against the posterior surface of the sternum, he lifted away the large elongated pyramid of flesh and bone and placed in a dish on the workbench. Adjusting the lamp, he peered into the deeper mystery of the chest cavity. He used the huge knife again, cutting close to the spine and then used his free hand as a scoop, dipping it into the thoracic cavity. Stringy adhesions stretched and snapped as he lifted the thoracic organs from out of their gory hole. He piled them up on the boy's neck then stepped back and admired his handiwork. He had usurped the superficial. He was looking at the boy's true face.

CHAPTER TWENTY-SEVEN

"Time for dessert."

"There's dessert?" Marla's face lit up as her sweet tooth kicked in at the mere mention of something sweet. Yes, the smell and the taste of something sweet would put paid to the bitter aftertaste of that horrible cellar.

Afters, that's what her adoptive parents had called dessert, or her favorite *pudding*—both terms betraying their Northern backgrounds. As she listened to Jessie clanking around out of sight in the larder, Marla imagined bowls brimming with apple pie with cream and custard, plate loads of fruitcake, immense trays buckling beneath the weight of crackers and cheeses. The sound of clinking glasses jolted her from her reverie, and she stared dumbstruck as Jessie proudly deposited the big bottle of ouzo on the table in front of her.

"Jessie, no way..."

"Dessert," came the characteristically wicked reply. "You pour."

Marla reached out and unscrewed the bottle cap, instantly feeling intoxicated at the heady smell of the anise-laden spirit. A flash of that dirty cellar with its stained mattress, broken toys, and tattered porno magazines pierced her brain, banishing all hope of sweetness. What the hell, she needed a drink—more than ever now. She poured a measure of the clear liquid into Jessie's glass.

"Any mixer for this?"

Jessie's lips curled slyly as she held out her glass. She clearly wanted it filled to the top. "Marla, please. After all we've been through together don't go all pussy on me now."

Marla sighed heavily and topped up Jessie's glass, then filled her own.

"So…what do we drink to?"

"To the Big House. And to getting off this damn rock in one piece, I guess," Jessie said after a brief moment's thought.

Good enough for me, nodded Marla as they each expelled a breath and gulped back their drinks. Marla coughed and spluttered as her natural gag reflex attempted to deny the harsh liquor from entering her body.

Neither of them could hear the banging sound from high up inside the house anymore, and both had forgotten about Adam working on the door lock up there. Outside, on the other side of the metal shutters that sealed them inside the sanctum of the Big House, a fierce wind picked up and propelled the clouds across the sky as if to make way for the sharp gloom of nightfall. Evening had fallen over the house like a shadow.

"Ladies, the DJ is *in*," Jessie said, reaching out for the toy tape player and switching it on.

Marla grimaced at both the sudden tinny blast of *Old MacDonald's Farm* and the sharp sensation of ouzo coursing down her throat. Trapped inside a maximum-security retirement home with a mad woman, drinking stolen liquor, and listening to nursery rhymes. It was going to be one of those long, long nights.

Jessie spun the bottle again, cackling that it was her turn—*her* turn—to spin, and not Marla's, despite the latter's protestations to the contrary. The booze was making her mean, spiteful even. Marla hated "spin the bottle" with a vengeance; she'd only agreed to play it in an attempt to placate Jessie for a while. Her alcohol-clouded brain accessed cringe-inducing memories of the last time she'd played this game. Never again, she'd sworn then—so typical to find herself succumbing to the game's dubious charms again. The rules were simple, spin the bottle and wait for it to stop rotating. If the neck of the bottle points your way, the person who went last (in this case Jessie, always Jessie) calls "truth" or "dare," then thinks up a humiliating question or even more humiliating dare. Refusal to answer the truth, or to act out the dare, might be the biggest humiliation and so often the case was.

Marla shuddered at the memory of her younger self, kissing a pimple-faced boy whose breath smelled strongly of onions. Maybe refusing to play wasn't such a humiliating prospect after all. But there again was the scraping sound of the bottle as it spun round and round on the hard surface of the floor. They sat cross-legged opposite one another, Jessie's face almost entirely occupied by her grin. The smirk on her face was accompanied by a high-pitched squeal of delight as the bottle slowed and came to a halt again, pointing right at Marla.

She groaned, her body lolling to one side until her shoulder was almost touching the floor. Marla wished to God that Adam had agreed to play this asinine game with them when he'd popped downstairs to eat earlier, at least that way some of the heat would be taken off of her. But she and Jessie had put away most of the ouzo by then and she'd seen the clear disapproval on Adam's face. The last thing he probably wanted to do was sit playing childish games with two half-soaked girls. The conversation had gone something like this:

"Where did you get the, um, nursery music?"

"From *Toys R Us*, stoopid." (Sniggers).

"Any food left?"

"Sure...and getch yershelf a glass...we're nearly out of ouzo."

"No thanks, just wanna grab a quick bite."

"Did you find out wasss behind the door?"

"Yeah. Another door."

And with that, he'd gone back upstairs taking a bowl of cold pasta with him. Strains of *Humpty Dumpty* echoed after him. His parting look had rattled Marla, and Jessie could see its after-effects on Marla's face.

"Truth," Jessie said mischievously.

Marla rolled her eyes, took an acid sip of ouzo and nodded in resignation to her fate.

"Did you do Pietro? You know, before he tried to jump the shark..."

Humpty Dumpty had a great fall...

Jessie's giggles echoed around the bare surfaces of the room. Marla looked around, studying her surroundings as if for the first time. What they hell was she doing locked in here, getting drunk with Jessie? She exhaled loudly—a tired, vaguely angry sound.

All the King's horses and all the King's men…

"You did! You did, you dirty girl, I just knew it!" Jessie's voice trailed off into high- pitched squeaking giggles, sounding more like hiccoughs than laughter. "At least you gave him a good send-off…"

Couldn't put Humpty together again…

That was the limit. How could Jessie be so insensitive? Marla stood up sharply, swaying slightly as the alcohol nausea hit her. She rocked forward on one foot then kicked out at the bottle as hard as she could with the other. The bottle spun past Jessie's shocked face and crashed against a cabinet, shattering on impact. *There, spin the fucking bottle now.*

"What the hell!?" Jessie spluttered.

"In answer to your question, I did sleep with Pietro. But only because I was drunk, and he couldn't get it up anyway. As I've been drinking again, with you *again*, I may as well see if Adam's up for it. If he is, maybe I should do him on the stairs right now. Anything, if it means I don't have to play your stupid games."

Her words chilled the stuffy air in the room. Before Jessie could reply, Marla moved through the space between them coolly and towards the door.

"What's gotten into you? I only wanted to blow off some steam."

Marla turned and looked back, hearing the hurt in Jessie's voice. She did look genuinely upset, and vaguely pathetic, like a child who knows it is way past bedtime. Garbled thoughts and emotions trampled over each other inside Marla's brain, fuelled by the alcohol and the aftertaste of her anger.

"I came to this island to turn my life around," she sighed. "But all I've done since I got here is repeat the same old fucking mistakes."

"This island can change you, Marla. Believe me, it can."

"Maybe it doesn't, maybe it just brings out the worst in you."

Now Jessie heard the bitter disappointment in Marla's voice. Something changed inside her tipsy brain and Marla could see she felt exactly the same, after months trapped on this island—this false paradise. Jessie blinked up at Marla and the surface of her eyes glistened wetly.

Marla thought of the jetty and the gunmen aiming right at her. She thought of Adam and how she'd secretly burned for him in her bed at the summerhouse. She thought of Pietro and his broken body, lying bleeding in the lighthouse, impotent and spent. All of it was so far away from the dream she'd been sold at those shiny offices in London—a fantasy to which she had so willingly subscribed. She tried to find the words that might articulate all her hopes and fears, struggling to show Jessie for once and for all that she was no mere plaything sent to the island for her own personal amusement. But no words came, only a cold, empty feeling. She felt hollow and useless, adrift like the dust in the house and at the same time tethered to its cobwebs.

Marla became quickly aware that Jessie's expression had changed from one of dismay to a shock of disbelief.

"What is it? Jessie?"

Trembling, Jessie raised a hand and pointed to the space beyond Marla, her eyes fixed on something there. From behind her, in the subdued half-light of the hallway, Marla heard a voice.

"What are you doing in my daddy's house?" the voice said, quietly.

God help her, it was a child's whisper.

Marla turned slowly, chilled to the bone at the sound of the child's voice. Standing in the gloom of the doorway was the little boy she'd seen running across the beach and into the cove. He looked ready to run again, already backing up as she instinctively took a step towards him—her arms held out like an offer of motherly care.

"How did you get in here?" she asked, then glancing at Jessie. "Don't be afraid, we're not going to hurt you..."

"Speak for yourself," Jessie muttered. "Creepy little bastard, sneaking up on us like that, I nearly had a heart attack..."

Marla quickly shushed her before she could do any more damage with her ouzo-sodden tongue, then fixed the boy with as open and calm an expression as she could muster.

"It's all right…. How did you get in here?"

The boy put a dirty finger to his mouth, chewed on it childishly.

"Were you in here already, is that it? Before the shutters came down? Poor thing, you must have been so frightened."

At this, the lad's attitude changed, his physicality shifting into a posture of defiance. He raised one bare foot off the floorboards and stamped it down, making a dull slapping sound.

Then he spoke.

"What the fuck are you two doing in my house?"

Marla's jaw dropped. Whatever she was expecting him to say, it certainly wasn't this. The profanity was utterly at odds with the boy's age, yet somehow suited his disheveled demeanor. Jessie cracked up with laughter, clutching her belly as she did so. Then the boy spoke again and her giggles began to subside.

"You made a big mistake coming here and locking yourselves in."

"We're waiting for some…for some friends," Marla tried to explain. "And when they get here, the shutters will open again."

"HE will know you are here. HE will be coming," the boy replied.

Something in his tone unsettled Marla. She tried to rub some warmth into the gooseflesh pricking at her arms, peering into the gloomy doorway to get a better look at the boy's face.

"Don't worry, kid, it's like the lady says, Fowler and his cronies can't get to us in here—they're stuck outside. You're perfectly safe with us…"

The boy snorted. "Not Fowler. Not outside."

"What…what do you mean?"

"HIM. HE'S inside with us."

Flushed, Marla looked over to Jessie, who just shook her head.

"Little bastard's just trying to scare us. There's no one in this museum except us two and Adam."

Marla turned back to the boy, crouched slightly to better meet his eye level.

"Who? Who's inside with us?"

Then, just as suddenly as he'd appeared, the boy turned on his heels and ran.

Incensed, Jessie took off after him first, knocking a surprised Marla to the kitchen floor. There was no time to dither, nobody spoke to her like that and got away with it, least of all a snotty kid. Marla would be okay. The boy was agile, and fast, darting this way and that through the halls and rooms of the house as though their layout was imprinted in his brain matter. A couple of times, she almost lost him in the shadows— only to pick up his trail again at the sound of his dull little footsteps on the floorboards. As she followed him through the glum interior of the games room, Jessie got an inkling of where he was headed. The cellar must be his bedroom. At this, she felt a sudden pang of pity for her quarry. What kind of life must this kid be living in such squalor, she could only guess. For him to even be in this house alone when all the families on the island were away just didn't tally. Had he been abandoned, she wondered as she ran, left behind by mistake when everyone set sail to the mainland for the season? She recalled the stagnant mattress and the ripe stink of the cellar and shuddered. She'd get him away from here, get him cleaned up, and make him talk—just as soon as she could catch him. Easier said than done when he was so damned fleet of foot.

"Get back here!"

She skidded around a corner and careered into the facing wall of the narrow passage she and Marla had walked down earlier. Steeling herself for a moment, Jessie filled her lungs with air and continued her pursuit to the basement door, which was open. Just as she'd suspected, the boy was headed to his sorry little hideout all along. Damp air smothered her respiratory system as she descended the steps into the gloom. Reaching the foot of the stairs, she did a one-eighty, looking and listening for signs of the boy.

"Hey? No need to be frightened, I just wanna talk with you."

At the sound of her voice, there was a movement, slight and rat-like from the corner of the room. There he was, a tiny phantom in this hellish little underworld, crawling towards a large flap of mildewed wallpaper that hung from the wall like skin from a wound. She started towards him, but knew the folly of her actions even as she did so. The flap of wallpaper gave access to a hole in the wall, through which the boy was wriggling even now as she took clumsy adult-sized steps towards him. The boy grunted with difficulty as he worked his distended little belly through the tight gap. Jessie remembered a picture book from her youth and almost chuckled out loud at the memory—*Pooh Bear* stuck in a hole in a tree, looking for honey. Looking for honey. Was the child suffering from the effects of malnutrition? Had he truly been forgotten—left here like some lost boy to fend for himself? Her eyes alighted on the pornography lurking on the shelves near the filthy nest-bed just a few feet from the hole in the wall. A dark kaleidoscope of images rushed at Jessie— abuses all too awful to consider, yet imminently possible given the implications of this dreadful scene.

"Don't run, come back, I won't hurt you."

Just his feet now, disappearing through the hole into the crawlspace beyond, or God only knows where. Jessie covered the final distance and dropped to her knees, intent on catching a glimpse of where the frightened, abandoned little lad was going to. As she kneeled there prostrate, peering into the gap, the air seemed to cool around her. A shadow fell, monstrously large, engulfing her. Something large was blocking out the scant light, turning the basement world into that of a photographic negative. Jessie felt suddenly so vulnerable and afraid that she inadvertently whimpered. Blind panic gripped every nerve ending, fear flooding every pore in her skin like coolant. Her eyes searched the filth for something to grab onto, some weapon or totem of defense. But there were no such amulets here, only the piss-stinking rags and tattered detritus of a childhood denied that increased the burden of her despair.

"M... Marla?" The sound of her own voice was hopeful as it rang in her ears. All hope was gone when she finally turned her head to see what was standing over her.

Marla picked herself up off the kitchen floor and dusted herself down. Damn Jessie, damn her all to hell. She'd done the worst thing possible in chasing the boy like that—he was already frightened enough. As she followed the distant clatter of footsteps through the house, Marla recalled seeing the child on the beach. He'd looked like a ghost then. But here he was a real flesh and blood thing, trapped in a big dark house and being chased by a mental American hippy chick half-soaked on ouzo. Marla picked up the pace—it would be better for everyone if she could do the talking.

Reaching the basement, Marla fancied that she heard Jessie's voice. Not the usual cocky, wisecracking tone, but rather a— whimper? Had she injured herself? Perhaps she'd fallen over on the stairs or tripped in the mess of the cellar. Marla headed down the steps to the basement, taking care not to tumble down them herself, her nose wrinkling at the stagnant cocktail of smells emanating from the depths.

Marla's eyes adjusted from the gloom of the stairwell to the dark of the basement, pupils widening to admit the scantest extreme of the spectrum. Another whimper. She turned to spy out its source. What she saw there shook her to the core. Jessie was, impossibly, levitating a full two feet off the floor. Her face was horribly contorted and streaked with dark shadows. Marla stood dumbstruck at the sight of her and tried to focus on what she was seeing, her eyes struggling to make sense of the details in the dim light. In what seemed like slow motion, her panicked brain pieced together the jigsaw. The dark streaks on Jessie's face were rivulets of blood, held in their course by great fingers. Fingers that penetrated the flesh covering Jessie's skull so Marla could not tell where the fingertips ended and where Jessie began. Even as the horror of the scene dawned on her, Marla saw that Jessie was not floating above the floor as she'd first imagined. The hideous fat fingers that had burrowed their way into her soft face were connected to great hands—as big as shovels— and these in turn were extensions of massive arms, like those of a circus strongman. The hulking form anchoring the weight of Jessie's helpless body loomed darkly, becoming clearer to Marla's eyes as it shifted its bulk in the shadows. Jessie looked like a doll in its massive hands. She made a pitiful whimpering, gurgling sound as the red lines of blood quickened from her face into the sinewy network of fleshy guttering that was the man's hand. Marla took a step back, bile rising in her throat as she did so, and heard her foot scrape noisily against some hard object. *A brick? Did he hear it, too?* Eyes, black and shiny as an insect's, burned their answer at her from the shadows. She felt them on her. The hulking thing had seen her and mortal panic took her breath away. Then, a sickening crack as the shape twisted Jessie's head in mid-air, snapping her neck as casually as a snap of the fingers. Marla turned and fled, desperate to be rid of the sight of this horror, feeling the sensation of her revulsion at the cellar and its secrets creep through every fiber of her body.

She clambered up the steps and wondered breathlessly how many—no, how *few* seconds would pass until she felt the grip of those foul butcher's hands on her body.

CHAPTER TWENTY-EIGHT

Thud. Thud. Thud. Marla's heart pounded inside her body, fit to burst. She'd battered and bruised herself clambering out of the basement in a white panic, bouncing off the walls of the narrow corridor like a pinball before clattering her way back through the games room. She felt no pain from her little injuries, the tidal wave of adrenaline coursing through her body saw to that. All she had was a kind of focus, like someone undergoing hypnosis keeping his or her gaze fixed on a pinpoint of light. *Don't turn around, don't turn around, don't...*was the mantra pulsing in her brain like a drumbeat. And she did not turn around. How could she? Knowing that hulking thing was there in the shadows behind her, probably taking one giant step for every four or five of hers, closing in on her in the darkness with those great hands outstretched. Those hands—she remembered how they looked in the dark, like thick twigs growing out of twisted tree branches—slicked with Jessie's blood. She pushed through a door into another corridor and it rebounded against the wall making a sharp cracking sound, like that of Jessie's neck when he—that thing—snapped it so casually. *Don't turn around! Don't...*

Bang. Bang. Bang. Was that the sound of her heart? Ready to split like a plum and sputter from her chest, utterly spent out of fear and terror and things that go bump in the basement. No, this was a new sound, joining the thudding of her heart in sympathy. Louder now. Bang! Bang! She turned her head towards the perimeter of the room through which she was tumbling and caught sight of the huge metal shutters there. The shutters—that was it. Fowler's men were trying to break through the shutters! Marla's face grimaced into what only a madman would recognize as a laugh at this new banging sound—this artificial mockery of her plight. In her mind's eye she could see them, the men, outside. Under the watchful scorn-filled eye of Chief of Security Fowler they'd be hard at it, chiseling away for all their lives were worth, trying to gain access to the house through its cloak of impenetrable steel. And she'd wanted to keep them *out*. Jessie had put the same fear into her mind, the same paranoia that had warped her all these long months on the island—and for what? To be locked in with the very thing they should have feared most. Whatever that she'd seen in the basement, it was more terrifying than a thousand Fowlers, more awful than a million of his security guards pointing guns at her head. She'd wanted to keep them out. *Idiot!* Now she'd do anything for them to break through the damned shutters and rush in to cuff her and take her away. All the better to be away from this house, to be away from that thing.

Bang! Bang! Bang! What the hell was keeping them? Didn't they know this house? Know all about its weaknesses? Couldn't they find that chink in the armor and take advantage of it, peel open the protective skin keeping her from making good her escape. Bang! Bang! Marla skidded to a halt as she reached the foot of the stairs, damp oxygen raw in her throat. *Please don't turn around*, she thought, but of course she did. She had to know if the monstrous shadow shape was there, ready to finish her before she took her first futile step. Trembling with fear, she took a scant look over her shoulder and saw only the shadows looming behind her. Her nostrils fancied they could smell the metallic taint of Jessie's blood in the air and the meal she'd eaten earlier rebelled in her stomach, muscles ready to spasm. She swallowed hard and turned her revulsion into momentum, willing her legs into motion and lurching onto the steps. Marla felt numb, catching sight of her faint shadow like that of a puppet in a shadow theater on the wall as she propelled herself up the stairwell.

Each step was an enemy, willing her to fail. Marla pushed on, her breath whistling through clenched teeth. Reaching the first landing felt like a milestone and afforded the opportunity to look behind her once again. Ignoring the voice in her head that pleaded for her *not* to look, Marla glanced over the banister and saw only the stairs winding down into the hallway. Where was her pursuer? Her mind raced, conjuring visions of the monster appearing at the top of the stairs she'd been fighting to climb—cutting her off by way of some secret route. These terrors quickened her panic, but she remained rooted to the spot all the same. Her lungs needed oxygen and her heart needed respite, however brief, and so she stood leaning on the banister daring to catch her breath. The wood was cool and soft beneath her clammy hands. She noticed just how exquisitely carved the banister was for the first time. Devilish details suddenly struck her. Each vertical support was part of the whole, with no discernable join between it and the handrail. Her eye traced the flowing forms carved into the wood, finding suggested physical forms here and there. It was as if the entire banister had been washed up from the beach long ago, swallowing up human swimmers in its wake, then settling here in this big house. More driftwood. Movement between the struts caught her eye and she saw a spider crawling into hiding. Good idea. She pushed on toward the top of the stairs.

The air was colder here at the top of the house and the perspiration from her labors began to cool on Marla's skin. She crept across the landing to the door where she'd left Adam what seemed like an age ago. He'd managed to get the door open and just like he said, there was another door behind it. As she neared the door, Marla whispered Adam's name. No reply came. She whispered it again, repeating it like a mantra. But all was silent, save the muffled banging of Fowler's men from far below outside. She pushed against the inner door now with her trembling hand and it slowly swung open, emitting an agonizing creak as it did so. The air beyond smelled musty, old somehow, and there was something else. A sweet smell, like caramelized onions. *Past its "use by" date whatever it is*, thought Marla as her nose wrinkled. She stepped through the door.

"Adam?"

Her whisper was less a question, more a plea for help. But once more her plea went unanswered as she found herself standing alone in a vast attic. A shaft of silver blue moonlight lit the attic via an open skylight at the far end of the room. Sure enough, a broken shutter rattled in the wind, banging against the skylight's frame—it must have been the source of the banging she and Adam had heard earlier. Where the hell was he? Perhaps he'd wriggled out through the skylight? No. Even if he could fit through such a gap, he wouldn't just up and leave them here. Or maybe he would after seeing them drunk in the kitchen. Whatever, she was alone up here now and she'd have to decide on her next move before that nightmare thing came back.

The open skylight. She had to check it out, see if it was a viable exit. Dirt and debris lined the floor as far as she could see in the scant moonlight. A lump rose in Marla's throat as she noticed that many of the floorboards were missing ahead of her. She would have to tread carefully here for fear of falling through the floor. Looking for signs of rotted wood, she began the long walk, treading as gently as she could and clenching her teeth at every creak and groan of the attic floor beneath her feet. Halfway across and the light dipped as clouds swam across the moon. Marla held her arms out, steadying herself like a tightrope walker as she continued across the rotting beams. She tried to ignore the stench. That sickly-sweet smell had grown more intense the further she'd traveled across the floor. Then, something round squished beneath her foot. Another object brushed the ankle of her other foot and she almost cried out in fear at the sensation. As she took a reflexive step back, the floorboards seemed to moan, mocking her fear of this new unknown. The clouds drifted aside like a curtain, unveiling the moonlight once more, and now Marla could see exactly where she was standing and what she was standing in. Carcasses littered the floor around her feet. Her astonished eyes could make out the rotting forms of birds, rodents, a cat here and a dog there. That sickly sweetness was the stench of their decomposition, a rank herald of the foulness and rot within their bursting little stomachs. Maggots writhed in the skull cavity of what use to be a parakeet, feasting on the pools of jelly in its eye sockets. Marla bit on the knuckles of her right hand to keep from gagging. Focusing on her closest chance of escape from this hideous attic, Marla looked toward the skylight and to her horror and dismay she could see yet more tiny dead forms lining the roof supports and crossbeams. These animals had been nailed to the wall, or lashed to the wooden beams with wire, furry limbs and slick-feathered wings pinned out in cruel mockery of their anatomy. Whoever, whatever, had created this menagerie had torn the other dead animals limb from limb, breaking their little bodies and splitting them open. But those in the roof space seemed special—totems or offerings to something Marla could scant understand, nor have any desire to. Pinpoints of moonlight reflected in the cold, still eyes of the creatures as she moved past through their graveyard. She felt accused here, part of something dreadful just by walking through it to the other side. The skylight was almost within reach now. Just a couple more steps.

Floorboards creaked, split and cracked beneath her. She was falling. Marla grabbed for the roof beam above her, nails digging into rotting wood. Gaining purchase on the beam, she swung her body weight upward and tucked her knees around the beam, which creaked like the hull of an old boat beneath her weight. She looked down at the floorboards where she'd trodden just seconds ago. They'd fallen away, opening up into a void below. She shifted on the roof beam, inching her way to the skylight and welcoming the cool kiss of night air on her cheek. As she moved out of the path of the beam of moonlight for a moment, she saw a reflection through the hole in the attic floor. Black goggle eyes, looking up at her from a room far beneath. Perhaps a dead animal, fallen down there with the rotten floorboards, poor thing. But then the eyes moved, slowly, deliberately, and Marla knew what was looking at her.

She scrambled along the beam in clumsy crawling movements, scuffing the skin of her knees and wrists. The pain didn't even register. That hulking thing had seen her and was charging up the stairs for her right now. She had to get to the skylight. Her fingers brushed the dark, wet wing of a dead crow. She had no desire to join the poor creature, pinned out up here until her own dead organs blossomed with maggots. Marla heaved her upper body off the beam and out through the skylight, legs kicking up dust and animal filth below. Fresh night air choked into her, such a tonic after the corrupt honey of the attic. A moth flitted by, dust from its wings billowing like falling snowflakes in the moonlight. She was frozen in time for a spell, watching it. Then, with an almighty crack, the skylight frame gave way beneath her and she tumbled down the sloping roof, a scream caught in her windpipe as she fell.

CHAPTER TWENTY-NINE

Marla felt her body relax, her heart thudding distantly in her chest as she tumbled down off the lip of the roof. The weight, shape and trajectory of her body caused her to turn slightly in her freefall. She was in a reclining position, hands and feet a little higher than the rest of her. A lock of hair got caught in the spittle at the corner of her mouth and she felt a clear urge to brush it aside. Then she hit something hard. The shock of the impact was enough to delay any feeling of pain. Dazed, Marla tried to sit up and look around. Her body was reluctant to perform such a complicated task, and so she lay there on her back and reached out with her hands to touch the floor instead. The surface that answered her sensory investigations was wooden, not the dirt and foliage of the ground she'd expected. This surprising sensation gave new impetus to her muscles and soon she found herself sitting up and dusting herself off on a second-floor balcony, which had broken her fall. More of the strangely intricate driftwood carvings loomed from the moonlight shadows. Rising to her feet, she peered up at the house looming above her, half-expecting those dreadful eyes to peer back from the spot from which she'd fallen. Marla glanced nervously at the windows to the rear of the balcony. The shutters were still closed behind them, but if they were to open suddenly…. Nothing was certain anymore, save for the urgent need to get off this balcony and go look for help. She turned and looked over the edge of the balcony—elated that she was still alive but dumbfounded as to how the hell she'd be able to get down to ground floor level. She scanned the area, no one around. Fowler's men must have given up; she was all alone here. Then a solution quickly presented itself in a shadow that moved across the balcony's gnarled, knotted handrail. *Tree, big tree.* Her eyes focused on it—her closest chance.

Marla had never been a good judge of distance, and lost count of the number of times she'd nearly been killed by angry London cab drivers in the past as a result. As she teetered on the edge of the balcony, ready to take a leap into the void between it and the thick branches of the great tree, she considered ditching the idea and just waiting it out on the balcony. The concept made her shudder. Every instant she'd delayed on the balcony had put the fear of God into her—a palpable fear of that hulking pursuer crashing through the walls of the house to drag her back in. She licked at her dry lips, balled her hands into fists then released them, bent her legs and flung herself toward the tree. Her fingers were outstretched like a cat's claws and she felt cool air pass through them as she began to plummet, down, down. Branches cracked loudly as she snapped her way through them, her legs flailing in an attempt to break her fall—to hit the ground running. Then she made contact with a larger branch, as thick as a smaller tree's trunk. It struck her in the stomach as she fell hard against it like a clumsy gymnast. Her body folded and wrapped around the branch on impact and she clutched at its rough surface, feeling the welcoming texture of the bark under her fingernails. The branch held, and she onto it. The tree was her savior—a living, breathing thing. She wanted to kiss it just for being there. Catching her breath, she craned her neck to better afford a look at the layout of the tree and the branches below. It would be a precarious climb, but she felt more than up to the task after hurling herself off the side of the Big House.

As she was about to climb down, a light in the distance caught her eye. At first, she thought it was the moon, but no— the moon's silvery light was above and slightly behind her now. She shook her head, concerned her terrorized brain was playing tricks on her. There it was again. The light was *moving.* Curiosity piqued, she now climbed upwards, forgetting for a moment her urgency to feel the ground beneath her feet. She was compelled to discover the source of this new mystery. Reaching up and climbing a couple more branches into the dizzying heights of the tree, she now had a bird's eye view right across the treetops to the coves and the sea beyond. Far from the border of the verdant green canopy in which she stood, Marla saw the source of the light, her eyes following its beam as it swept across the treetops. Her irises shrank as the beam shone directly into them momentarily. It was a welcome light, a beacon, and only Vincent could have lit it—the beam of the lighthouse. Then Marla saw other, fainter, lights that appeared to hover like fireflies above the black of the ocean. She'd have to risk climbing another branch or two higher to get a proper look. She did so and squinted, waiting for the lighthouse beam to turn away once more so she could see these tiny lights more clearly. Almost falling from her crow's nest in shock, it dawned on her that she was looking at the lights of maybe a dozen boats. They were approaching the island.

Adrenaline and elation coursed through Marla's veins in equal measure. She made light work of her descent through the branches and hopped down the last few, lithe as a spider monkey. As soon as her heels hit solid ground, she was off and tearing through the trees in a sprint for the headland. In her mind's eye, those little lights danced their firefly dance and sang to her like sirens, their song one of safe harbor—of a way off the island. She whizzed past a tree and had to duck to avoid a low branch hitting her square in the face. Glancing back at it over her shoulder, she saw a dark shape through the trees. The familiarity of that shape almost made her stop dead in her tracks, for it was not the imposing outline of the Big House she's chanced upon but rather that of its murderous inhabitant—the giant from the basement.

"No..."

The terrified word escaped her lips like a whimper, and Marla began to back away in frightened denial of the shape that was slowly gaining on her. A twig snapped beneath her feet and she replayed the image of Jessie's neck snapping beneath those thick, sinewy fingers.

Run, got to run.

The thought blazed into her skull, like the beam of the lighthouse.

Run, damn you!

Marla pivoted on her heels and ran. The terrain was rough, with unseen ditches and thick roots that conspired to trip her up and deliver her into the blood-slicked hands of her pursuer. She zigzagged through the trees, avoiding yet more low branches and cursing whenever her path was blocked by fallen trees or made impassable by a hidden ditch or steep drop. Glancing over her shoulder in quick terror, Marla could still see the lumbering shape between the dark columns of tree trunks behind her. He had gained on her but she still had the lead. She was faster and more agile than him. This could prove a distinct advantage— her *only* advantage. Determined to widen the distance between them, Marla gritted her teeth and broke into a sprint. She could see the beam of the lighthouse, sweeping through the trees up ahead like a searchlight. Glancing behind her again she could see the killer's obsidian silhouette—further away this time. Elation curled the corners of her mouth into a triumphant smile. Then the wind was knocked out of her sails as she crashed into something.

The something was sticky and stretchy and she fell sideways as she became tangled up in it. On her knees now, Marla struggled to right herself, gasping for breath and clutching at what she mistook for a branch. She quickly let go of the cold wet thing, scrambling backwards to rid herself of its touch. The lighthouse beam swung once again and flooded the area with the revelation of its light. Marla's jaw dropped as she saw what she'd run into. Adam was strung out between two trees, his battered face a dark mockery of the life that had once resided there. What she'd thought was a branch was his arm, dangling useless, out of its socket. The sticky, sinewy fronds that had entrapped her were, horribly, sections of Adam's flesh—flaps of skin and muscle that had been torn open and stretched out between the trees like a fleshy umbrella. Ropes of sinew and the workings of veins lashed the fleshy fronds to wet branches slicked with Adam's blood and juices. A sound like light rain, just as subtle and pervasive, teased at Marla's ears and her horrified eyes searched out its source. It was the sound of blood dripping from within the ruptured cavern of Adam's torso. Her clumsy impact had caused Adam's body to shift and bounce slightly as if on bungee ropes, still held taut in the web of his own flesh. The dripping became more urgent, a constant trickle of blood and steaming bile from his torso cavity. Marla tried not to scream, tried not to yell or cry as the fragile lip of flesh around Adam's stomach gave way and his innards unspooled wetly. Adam's intestines uncoiled and made hideous slapping sounds as they hit the ground at her feet. Blood and stomach juices spattered her face. The lighthouse's beam continued on its journey across the awful scene, catching wisps of warm steam rising from the pile of unfettered organs at her feet and from the yawning hole where Adam's heart used to be. Shock and dismay stilled the very voice of her and Marla struggled finally to her feet. She untangled her arm from a length of Adam's flesh and she saw with raw horror a tattoo on its surface—it was the shape of a creature, perhaps an eagle. Her stricken eyes fancied that the hairs on his skin were standing erect. She felt her own skin freeze, signaling the onset of a deep stomach-churning nausea. A cold tear chilled her cheek as it escaped from the corner of her unblinking eye, and she ran like a madwoman into the woods and away from whatever was capable of doing such a thing to a human being. And that selfsame thing lumbered on after her, his breaths deep and purposeful, his hands ready to fashion more work.

Marla was at the treeline when the light went out. One moment it was there, a rotating beacon in the night sky leading her to the waves and the boats they carried to shore—the next it was simply gone, snuffed out like a birthday candle. *Make a wish*. She wished for this nightmare to be over, for the tumble of images to be gone from her mind forever. Jessie, like a broken doll in that squalid basement. Pietro, shattered and bleeding with his last taste of precious salt water on his lips. Adam, or the abomination that used to be Adam, strung out between the tree trunks. Marla recalled the totem birds in the attic of the charnel house and wondered, feverishly, if the same hands that eviscerated Adam had wrought their intricate work. She remembered her first furtive flirtation with Adam as she'd met him on the path to Jessie's summerhouse and the decomposing cat he'd examined in the leaves there. His body was ruined like that poor wretched animal's. Death was everywhere on this damned island, lapping like blood at its shores, dripping like bile in its most secret of caves. It fell from the very air she breathed in the forms of dead birds. And if she made it through to morning, what then? Would the bright chirps of crickets dispel it? Would death shrink away at the blooming of new tropical flowers, wrinkle its nose at the fresh scent of herb gardens and lie low? No, death would still be there, waiting. Marla could taste it, acrid in her mouth. *Is this what death tastes like,* she thought morbidly, *bitter and chemical and cold?* She shivered and pressed on, glancing up at the scant pinprick illumination of stars. The light in the sky had gone out and all she could do was try to focus on the direction in which it had been shining, until now. Grounding herself in a clarifying thought was the only way she could rise above her myriad fears and keep going. That thought presented itself in the form of Vincent. He was the only one who could have been good to his word and lit the beacon, she was convinced of that. But now that the light had been extinguished, she found herself praying—praying to deities she didn't even believe in—that his life hadn't been extinguished along with it. By powering up the lighthouse, Vincent had proven something to her. He was the only person on this island she could trust. And with a little bit of luck, and boy could she use some of that, she was heading straight for him.

Heart pounding, bladder bursting with the urgent need to pee, Marla pushed on up a steep bank of grass and over the top where she could finally see the lighthouse. No light from its windows, she was prepared for that. But neither could she see the little lights of the boats. Marla began to feel the creeping fear that she had merely conjured them, a mirage of boats to give her hope on this, surely the last night of her life. She felt stricken. The rocks on which the lighthouse made its home were deserted. She could hear the rusty door grating on its hinges in the wind. Her heart descended yet further. She glanced behind her, trying to ascertain the shape of her pursuer in the gloomy landscape. He wasn't anywhere to be seen. The realization did nothing to calm her nerves. If anything, she'd prefer to see him, at least then she'd know where he was. Perhaps he'd taken some secret route around the woodland and was already moving into position to cut her off before she could retreat back under cover. Her clarifying thought returned and galvanized her. Vincent. If Fowler and his goons were responsible for shutting out the lights, then it followed that Vincent would be in the firing line.

Clambering down the rocks and toward the lighthouse she looked up at the tower, monolith-like against the night sky. The rusty door banged shut, then open as she approached it, putting her nerves even more on edge. Up the steps and inside, avoiding the pool of stagnant water. Oh, but it was dark in there, standing trembling at the foot of the stairs too afraid to go up and too afraid to stand still.

A loud bang and a flash burst out from the darkness, causing Marla to shriek in surprise and crouch into a defensive position. Sparks and smoke from the service closet beneath the stairs. She tentatively peered inside, just to make doubly sure. An electrical fault, that was all. A further jolting, loud pop and a shower of sparks made her jump. It provided all the encouragement Marla needed to turn and ascend the stairs, her nerves in tatters.

The control room was eerily quiet and cold to the eye, swathed in a band of cool blue moonlight that reflected, frostlike, off every damp shiny surface in the room. Pietro's body was nowhere to be seen, with only a dirty tangle of bedclothes suggesting he'd been there at all. She crossed the room, eyeing an upturned bucket curiously and following a water stain across the floor to where Vincent's chair lay on its side. She righted the chair, an act of respect for the old man, and walked over to the pile of molding books and periodicals stacked nearest the little coffee stove. Vincent's decaying library had been ransacked, that was for sure. Torn pages were scattered everywhere and broken-backed volumes had been left open where they had fallen, with some lying on their backs looking like fish out of water gasping for air. The mildew that covered the books was like lichen in a graveyard, a headstone for each of Vincent's memories, each tome an epitaph for his stolen years in this island prison. A splash of vivid color caught her eye among the dull fusty books, and Marla peered closer to find a pornographic magazine like the ones she'd seen in the basement of the Big House. She swallowed, her mouth suddenly dry, strangely afraid that these pages might be part of Vincent's collection. And yet, why not? An old man alone for all these years, he would surely miss physicality with a woman. Perhaps his jailers thought it a joke to slip this filth in with his crossword puzzles, eager to get a rise out of a widower whose eyes had seen too much tragedy to care for such lusts. No, something had been here and defiled Vincent's little world, she felt sure of it. Those sickly smells from the basement and the attic of the house were here with her in the room, bringing with them a flavor of decay, of wrongdoing. She suddenly felt more afraid for Vincent than for herself. Had that awful monster of a man been here? Had these high windows played dead witness to the sound of an old man's neck cracking like a twig? She buried the thought, kicking the pages of the vile magazine beneath a pile of sodden encyclopedias. Then, out the window, she caught sight of first one then many of the tiny little lights. They were still adrift on the ocean. She dashed over to the windows, moving along their circle until she had a better view toward the lights. They were heading east, around the headland. If they continued on their course, they would be heading toward the houses, toward the security buildings—and the jetty.

CHAPTER THIRTY

"Get the goddamn floodlights off. How long does it take? Jesus! I told you they like to dock in near-freaking-darkness, the arc lamps play havoc with their skin..."

Fowler's men got to it. All around him a frenzy of black fatigues. Guy ropes were tightened up and tied off, the deck washed down, barrels and other storage containers removed and placed where they should have been days ago. Of all the times for an official visit, they had to pick now. Now, dammit. Fowler stood, his neck muscles tensed so much that they looked about to snap at any given moment, looking out to sea and those little firefly lights. They were a portent, flags heralding a doom about to unfurl in his tight little world. The chief did not like inconveniences of this magnitude. An unannounced visit from these little boats, and the people they carried onboard was the largest inconvenience he could imagine. He barked more orders to his men, *how many times did he have to tell them—all but the emergency lights*, throat sore from all the shouting. A nasty headache was forming from a splinter of pain behind his left ear. He knew it would only grow more painful as the night went on. Good. He needed his pain sometimes to better focus on who, and what, was most deserving of his wrath. The American bitch had started all this and he grimaced at the very thought of her. Without her antics with the laptop and the security network those little lights wouldn't even *be* there—bobbing their way closer to his little empire to peer into the dark corners of his oversights, his ineptitude. Yeah, it was the American girl's fault all right. She'd be put to task for all she'd cost him. If not for her, the old man would still be poring over crossword puzzles and sipping that foul brew he dared call coffee, impotent and insignificant in his rat-infested tower. But no, he'd seen fit to turn on the fucking lights. Christ! Fowler was sure the pilots of those boats had seen them, idling towards the beam for a while like moths to a very big, ugly flame before resuming their collective course to the jetty. The old man would pay for this, but right now he had to focus on the task in hand.

"I want this fucking jetty cleared of non-essential staff now!" he bellowed.

Several black-clad men scurried away into the shadows, quick as roaches under fluorescents, and the boats arrived noiselessly. Their sleek shapes glided into position around the jetty in the movement and formation as effortlessly elegant as dolphins might swim. Fowler could see the silhouettes of deckhands in the scant glow of the emergency lights as they readied their ropes then tossed them to his men, who tied them off efficiently and without greeting. The largest of the boats was directly in front of Fowler, its black hull reflecting the red glow of the emergency lights like angry eyes. He swallowed hard, dry grit in his throat. One by one they disembarked from their vessels and took their places on the jetty. Their knowing eyes commanded respect. Many of Fowler's men had never even seen them before and lowered or otherwise averted their gazes, unable to make eye contact confidently. The eldest, and tallest, of their number disembarked last and made his way gracefully through the columns of his comrades until he was just a foot or two away from Fowler.

"Sir," said Fowler, bowing his head with military stiffness. The address was loaded with reverence and a servility Fowler's men had never until now heard in his voice. There was something else in his diction—guilt, embarrassment, and *inconvenience*.

The graceful man standing in front of him just smiled. White teeth and almost incandescent skin. Hair as lustrous, strong and white as a waterfall. He put a single fingertip to his lips then spoke in a soft, almost musical tone.

"Trouble, Chief?"

Fowler drew breath, ready to answer for all his oversights, all his fuck-ups. *Sentry Maiden* had intercepted an intruder, that was all. Perhaps he would neglect to mention the computer hacker, the Italian boy blown out of the water, Anders gone AWOL. The waves lapped against the jetty's support beams far below his feet. It was a queasy sound and he felt seasick. *Get a hold of yourself, soldier.* Cold sweat began to spread like a sickness across the back of his neck. This was the effect these people had on him, on anyone crossing their path. He fought to gain control of himself, growing aware of a trapped nerve in his thigh as it made a *Saint Vitus's dance* in his leg.

Fowler opened his mouth to speak. The waves lapped sickly on. Then a splash and a black sound from his flank. Everything went red. He clawed uselessly at his crotch. His head exploded.

Vincent stood next to Fowler and pulled the trigger again. Click. Again. Click. Again. Chamber empty, wild eyes staring. No one had even noticed him clamber out of the sea and onto the jetty, distracted by the arrival of these immaculate, shining people. He was sodden from head to toe. Fowler's body fell to the floor, making a dull thud on the jetty as his skull leaked brain matter and blood onto the planks. Seawater dripped off the old man and trickled across the jetty, snaking like cold tongues intent on tasting the blood.

One of Fowler's men took a few unsure steps towards Vincent, his eyes blinking from the aftershock of the murder. The tall man held a hand up, casually, as if placating a child. It was okay, he would handle this.

"Look who's here to see you. Dear Vincent," the musical voice soothed.

No sooner than he'd said it, one of the boarding party moved from the rear of the group. Vincent's eyes filled with tears as he saw her beautiful lithe frame and golden hair. He fell to his knees, dropping the still smoking gun and folded himself into her embrace. She ran her fingers through his wet, thinning hair and kissed his forehead, a lullaby of whispers sighing from her perfect lips. Vincent sobbed, murmuring something over and over again through the pain of his injuries, of his decades here on the island. He was saying he wanted to give The Man his bullet back.

After a few quiet breaths, Vincent stood and started walking away from the group as if in a trance. Nervously, one of the security guards stepped in to block his exit, but the shiny white-toothed man gave the instruction to let the old man pass.

"Let him go. Let him go home. Back to his lighthouse."

He uttered the words like a kindness.

The guard twitched, then pulled his gun and aimed it at Vincent's head, intent on blocking his path.

"I said let him go home." The voice again, like music and starlight.

But the nervous employee stood his twitchy ground. He had seen the old man gun down his boss in cold blood. He was as shocked as the rest of the men. Much as he never liked the chief, the guy had always been on the level with them. He ran a tight ship. These guys had no business letting Vincent go. He explained as much, in exasperated tones. His comrades stood firm with him, an uprising of sorts. They were security; they would handle this. The blonde woman walked towards the nervous guard like a cat. Her gossamer-thin clothing fluttered in the breeze. Sweat licked at his brow as she moved intimately close to him as a lover. She was odorless, smelled of nothing, not like a woman smells. Perfume and product and sweet breath. There was nothing. He sighed involuntarily, a submissive sound, like the breeze at a window about to be shut. She fixed him with her eyes and gently sniffed at the film of perspiration on his neck. One by one, each guard was entwined with such a lover of his own, not all women. Two of the men found themselves in the embraces of men taller and stronger than they, not caring that their secrets were out. Each guard was utterly transfixed. Silence as thick as fog descended over the jetty.

Then their necks snapped and their limp bodies toppled into cold black waters, useless as the weapons that slipped from their fingers and sank beneath the waves.

STRATUM SPINOSUM

He'd had to work the dark boy quickly. Too quickly, for shame. It seemed like an age since he'd performed a field procedure. But then the heat had taken him, reminded as he was of the old days in the forests when his craft was younger and more primitive, rather like those it was visited upon. He'd been a god then and they had names for him that made children cry themselves to sleep and women cradle those children tightly as they writhed perspiring in the humidity of nightmares to come. The dark boy's flesh had reminded him of those villagers and their supple ways. *Too quickly.* Working on the boy should have been a gift. It was a part of the calm after the storm, its opportunity a vital component of ritual. As he'd undressed the carcass, he'd rattled through the root of his base knowledge, tasting the words on his tongue like blood.

The skin is the largest organ in the human body.

Cut.

The skin is formed of three layers—epidermis, dermis, subcutaneous fat.

Slice.

The epidermis is the site of pigment production, melatonin, and keratin (which determines skin rigidity).

Another incision, deeper this time.

Dermis is divided into two areas—papillary dermis and reticular dermis—and contains blood vessels and nerves, gives skin elasticity, and produces collagen.

He carefully stretched out the flaps of skin, peeling back layer upon layer of mystery, pinning them out and making meaning there.

Subcutaneous fat protects the body from physical trauma and is the site of fat metabolism.

Then he'd seen the imperfection embedded into the dark boy's skin. The tattoo was an affront to all his beliefs, a mockery of his labors.

Protects the body from physical trauma.

He lost his patience. He tore the rest of the boy apart.

CHAPTER THIRTY-ONE

Marla cut around the perimeter of the cove, heading for the steep bank of rocks that afforded the quickest route to the jetty, and the boats. The clouds had left the sky, sharp moonlight bringing with it a drop in temperature. Wishing she had more layers to wear, Marla hugged herself and rubbed her arms. Then she saw two figures up ahead on the rocks, walking toward her. She stopped in her tracks, gripped by fear of the murderous giant, but these were no giants. One figure was much shorter than the other and she began to make out its juvenile form more clearly, realizing it must be the little boy who'd run away. Bent over the boy, using his shoulder as support, was a man in his twenties. He looked to be shivering and with good reason—he was dressed only in swimming shorts. His limping gait, and his reliance on the boy for support, told Marla he was injured. He wore a shock of tousled blond hair and an athletic physique. He looked like a surfer. The kid's eyes widened in surprise as she called out to them, her voice echoing off the rocks. For a moment she thought the little one would abandon his burden and make a run for it again, like he did at the house, but he held firm and waited as she ran across the rocks to meet them.

A frenzy of words spilled from her lips, about danger, about the man at the house. The blond man looked delirious and was shivering like he was in a state of shock. He was covered in cuts and bruises, a slick of blood congealing around his ear. Marla could get nothing from the child about where he'd found him. He looked down at the ground, subdued and not speaking. She tried to get through to him, asking how he'd escaped from the house like that—trying to appeal to him with admonishments that he was a clever boy, a brave boy, and everything would be all right. Taking the weight of the delirious swimmer onto her own shoulder, she asked the lad where he was headed. To this he did respond, holding out a lithe little arm and pointing inland where the rocks formed a v-shaped inlet. Marla saw a large circular opening there—what looked like an outlet pipe.

"There? You're taking him in there?"

Now the boy spoke, in that strange little voice of his.

"My daddy can fix him."

"Vincent? Is he your daddy?"

He didn't answer. Marla rounded on the boy, using her free hand to lift his chin a little so she could look him in the eye.

"Are you Vincent's son?" It didn't seem possible, he'd be much older by now, unless the old man was even more confused than she'd credited.

The boy resisted her touch, and her questions, breaking free from both her and the injured swimmer. As she watched him back away, Marla looked again to the black circle leading into the pipe. Perhaps Vincent had managed to get away and hide inside. She pictured him lighting a little stove, making coffee for her, and recalled how tenderly he'd attended to Pietro's injuries. This shocked guy was in bad shape, but not half as bad as Pietro had been. Vincent would know what to do. But what about the boats, they'd be ashore by now? Maybe help was on its way, but then again Marla had no idea who was on those boats. She would follow the boy, find Vincent and they could all leave the island together. It wasn't much, but it was the only plan she had.

"Okay, lead the way."

She helped the swimmer along with her. Together, they climbed into the pipe. The curve of the pipe meant if she walked dead center, they could almost stand fully erect, as if in a tunnel. The floor of the tunnel was treacherously uneven, littered with gritty sediment and moss underfoot. Trickling water that smelled of blocked drains flowed constantly in little rivulets through the pipe and dripped from above. The air was damp, colder and mustier the further inside they traveled. As Marla made her way carefully behind the boy, the moonlight began to fade into the distance.

"Christ, it's pitch-black in here," Marla complained, realizing now just how bright the moon had been outside. She glanced over her shoulder. The opening through which they'd entered now looked a marathon sprint away.

The boy didn't answer. He just made strange little grunts of effort as he walked on into the pipe. The sounds were almost comical to Marla's ears—like the noises of elderly people getting up out of their seats.

"Where...where we going?"

It was the muscular swimmer's voice in her ear. As he spoke, she felt his upper body stiffen in fear. He was having a moment of lucidity and was clearly perturbed to be stumbling into a pitch-black outlet pipe with a complete stranger propping him up.

"It's okay, it's okay. We're going to get help."

"Where the hell am I?"

His speech was slurred like a drunkard's, his accent strongly Australian. Or maybe Kiwi. Marla could never tell, and had often offended Antipodeans back in London by making a wild guess.

"You're...on an island. I'm Marla, I kind of work here. But now I've resigned. And I'm going to... Oh, never mind—we're going to get you some help."

Her voice echoed off the curved walls. The pipe had widened into a tunnel. The young man lapsed into semi-consciousness again, his heels dragging. Marla shouldered his weight as best she could, feeling a sharp twinge in her lower vertebrae. She wondered how long she could keep going like this.

Several minutes of walking and Marla was in near-total darkness, her steps slowing to a crawl. Struggling on, she could vaguely discern a bend in the tunnel and followed the quick shape of the boy around a corner. There was a flicker of sepia light on the wall of the tunnel in the distance and the faint odor of sulfur. The light was immediately comforting to her, now she had something to aim at. The muscles in her lower back screamed in protest as she shifted the weight of the swimmer upwards in an attempt to get a better purchase on him. But as she did so, she lost her footing and they both crashed to the floor. The injured man landed on Marla awkwardly, a dead weight knocking the wind from her stomach. Painfully, she lifted her head and tried to focus on the light up ahead. Still a way to go. She called out after the boy, but he was dozens of feet away now, his little shadow disappearing around a curve in the tunnel.

Then the light was extinguished, plunging the tunnel into total darkness.

"Hey! Hey!" Marla's voice was cracked with fear, and with hurt from her fall. She could feel the clammy skin of the swimmer against her cheek, still pinioned beneath the weight of his slumbering body. Her breaths were quick and shallow, ringing out a heartbeat tattoo in the icy darkness. Another sound joined the frantic rhythm—a dragging, loping sound. Footfalls in the tunnel up ahead, drawing near. Her eyes widened, begging to admit light that simply wasn't there. Then the weight of the swimmer's body was gone from her. It felt as though he had simply levitated into the air like some theatrical illusionist. Blind instinct made her reach out for him, but he was gone. She heard a dull thud and a dragging sound. Marla scrambled backwards in terror, still on the floor, and her hand squished into something moist and spiky. Crying out, she pushed the thing away, smelling rotting fish. The curved wall of the tunnel met her other hand and she struggled upwards into a standing position. Her heart seemed to stop suddenly as she felt something clutching tight around her waist. She shrieked, and pushed at it, feeling the mop of the little boy's hair between her rot-streaked fingers.

"We have to get out of here. Now."

Behind her, heavy hot breaths. She jolted in fear again as a violent spark rang out in the tunnel and her vision was filled with viridian flame. A flare.

"Run!"

The boy was clinging to her too tightly. She looked down at him, intent on quelling his fears even as she felt her own terror falling over her like a tidal wave. But the boy was smiling up at her. His grin made her feel rotten to the core. A rapist's smile painted on the face of a child. Even now she could feel his little hand at her breast, grimy fingers searching out her nipple beneath the fabric of her shirt. She felt the hard throb of his erection against her leg. As the light of the flare danced in his eyes, she realized she was not looking down into the eyes of a child after all. An old man's eyes were looking back at her, through her and into her, perversely knowing and horribly lecherous. How could a look so chilling and evil reside in the innocent features of a young boy? Her heart sank to witness such a perversion of all things holy. Hot tears flooded her eyes and she began to sob in deep despair. She waited to feel the touch of the giant's hands on her neck, for it was surely he who was standing there hot-breathed behind her, just as sure as it was the hideous man-child at her breast that had led her right to him.

Vincent felt like driftwood, bobbing along on the crest of a cold, indifferent wave. His hand still felt the weight of the gun he'd used to shoot Chief of Security Fowler in the face. Even in his catatonic state he knew that he'd feel its weight for the rest of his days. Heavier still was the crushing pressure of seeing her again, his beloved Susanna. There she'd stood, so proud and lovely—majestic—on the jetty, like nothing had happened and not a day had passed since she'd been taken from him. His psyche had flipped cartwheels upon seeing her face. Was he mad? Had he been insane all these years, eking out damp days in the lighthouse? It didn't matter. The events that he'd seen unfold recently, that he'd been a part of, would be enough to imbalance any mind however strong. Cold tears formed as he tried to shun the dread image of his son, crawling like a plaything across the rotting timbers of his home. Fear and anger curled his lip as the image was blotted out by the huge blackness of the giant who accompanied his boy and kept him to heel like a little dog. Vincent allowed the twin images to penetrate his brain in a pincer movement, like vultures pecking at the skull of a dead man. He chuckled through their assault, they couldn't hurt him now; nothing could. He'd remembered everything. When she'd kissed him and held him like that and stroked his hair, *hush little baby don't say a word*, it had all come flooding back to him.

And then they'd let him go, carrying his memories around him heavy as a cursed mariner's albatross, back to his prison of guilt and madness and regret. Shooting Fowler had unlocked something buried deep inside the old man. His lover's kiss had done the rest, drawing his memories out of him like poison from a wound. He knew she'd seen them, too, had sensed that she was feeding on them. How was that possible—how was any of it possible? She'd be as old as he was now, minus a few years of course. But there she'd stood like Aphrodite with her golden hair and gleaming smile and perfect skin. Oh, and the smell of her, like the faintest wisp of cotton candy framed by bee pollen. He'd wanted to dive into her along with his memories, for her to drink every drop of his futile life force until there was nothing left. But even as he'd wished it, Vincent had seen the dark core at the heart of the woman, the taint that exists deep within every treasure. And from that moment he knew that she had not kissed him out of kindness, nor stroked his brow in sympathy. Her motive was to feast on his pain, to gorge herself on the endless loop of suffering that had defined his daily existence all these long years. He was merely a battery to her, a functional thing that existed only to sustain whatever cruel tastes she hungered for. He'd been glad to leave the jetty then, gathering up what he could of his memories, his pain and his old man's pride, reclaiming them as his own.

The sound of the waves crashed into him as he approached the cove nearest the lighthouse, and he began to weave together fragments of past like a spider rebuilding its web after a storm. He saw that night again, when he'd taken to the waves with his boy—intent on escaping the island and all its dreadful secrets. He saw himself as a younger man, saw what he'd done then just as he had tonight. He watched himself murder the security chief from years ago as he fought bitterly to stop them taking his boy away from him, saw the blood on his hands. He hadn't meant to kill him, hadn't meant for a lot of things. All these years he'd carried the guilt of what he'd done and buried parts of it in the dirt of the hole he'd been digging, only to find it uprooted and staring him in the face the very next day each and every time he buried it. History had echoed back on itself, sounding out death like the deep melancholy bass of a foghorn, and here he stood a murderer again. He felt his body folding in on itself, filled to the brim with cold despair and craving the grave. He was a man without hope. Let his mouth be filled with maggots, let his eyes burst like plums, and his belly swell and split with the gas and bloat of his wasted life. He teetered on the rocks and saw a black shape ahead of him. All light had left him, he could not return to his tower nor climb the steep steps there. He gravitated toward the black hole, aching for its darkness.

Brett regained consciousness painfully and in near darkness. The surface he was lying on was hard, wet and covered in silt. He fancied that he could hear waves in the distance, crashing onto far shores. He longed to back in the cool of the ocean. Anywhere but here. Turning his head toward the sound of the waves, he felt a lick of heat warming the sweat on his face. A dry crackle and a sharp spitting sound, like hell's inferno clearing its throat. He was near to a fire. He wanted desperately to get his hands free but they were tied firm behind his back, which arched uncomfortably. Kicking his feet out, he felt only hot air around them. His mouth was salty dry and he remembered the seawater as the boat had been torn apart by the explosion around him. He'd thought himself lucky to bail at the moment he did, just as the explosion had happened, but now he felt only a series of numb discomforts. He wondered how long he'd been lying here, and what had happened to his shipmates. That gorgeous girl. Where had she said she was from? That was it, Ibiza. Was she still alive, washed up on this island like him? Was she sweating hot and cold like him in a dark cave somewhere near? Then the memories came flooding back, a tsunami of eviscerated bodies crashing onto the shoreline of his sanity. He saw the girl's head, *Idoya, that was her name*, bobbing on the surface of crimson waves like a Halloween apple in a bucket of water, her bloodshot eyes fixated on him. Brett wanted to scream, but his mouth felt alien to him somehow. He tried to lick his lips but couldn't. Something was wrong, very wrong. He attempted to cry out and heard his voice, disjointed like someone else's voice, a barely recognizable impotent wet gurgle of a sound. Blood gagged his throat and his fingernails clawed behind him at the silt on the floor. His tongue was gone. Oh, dear God, his tongue was gone. Writhing now, he pulled in shock and fear at his bonds and felt his eyelids blinking wetly. The fire crackled somewhere close by. Perspiration dripped from his matted hair onto his cracked lips. More salt water for the drowning man. He blinked again, and felt the beginnings of a searing pain behind his eyes. If a fire was burning, then why couldn't he see it? Brett cried out, loud as he could. His voice was like out-of-tune music, the desperate discord of a deafened man. Tears fell from his eye sockets. No, not tears. More blood. He shook his head violently from side to side, becoming maddened by the crackling of that damned fire. Even as he asked himself why he couldn't see it he knew his eyes were gone, too. All the breath left his chest in a dreadful rattling sigh and he laid there, a broken thing. His extremities had begun to conspire against him now. Each part of him was awakening and remembering what had been done to it, the nerve endings in his mouth and eye sockets reaching out in a kind of muscle memory for their lost comrades. Nearby, the fire flickered and its amber glow danced on the chrome surface of a surgical steel dish. Inside were his tongue and eyes. Then little hands were on him, attending his most private and tender parts, and Brett screamed a hot gargle of blood and bile until he died.

Marla dreamed of far forests and plains, of bright birds and of a wet humidity that penetrated every pore of her body. These visions were soundless and distant, and she fought to keep them for fear of what she might find when awake. The fight was already lost. She heard the sudden rush of wind through trees and felt herself returning to her body. The sound of the wind diminished, and she opened her eyes to find she was on a cold, hard table in a large, dimly lit room. The walls were rough, hewn from the rock, which told her she was in a cave. But it was unlike any cave she'd ever seen. Spotlights and mirrors illuminated the scene, their sleek modern designs contrasting with partially melted candles that flickered brightly here and there. She was strapped to a large surgical steel table, a spotlight on a snake-like angle poise arm above her. She pulled at the bonds restraining her upper body and ankles. They didn't budge, and caused little spasms of pain to prick at her skin the more she resisted them. So, she stopped resisting and looked around the room as best she could.

Everywhere around her were tables and trays of implements. Knives and saws and clamps, all gleaming. Shiny, shiny things. Jars and bottles stood on every available surface, some perched on nooks and crannies in the cave walls, filled with liquids of a stagnant yellow hue. Floating in the liquid were what looked like organs and tissue samples. Others housed bare bones, swimming above fronds formed of clumps of human hair. Marla could make out a row of teeth in one jar, sharing its glass home with part of a hand. She looked away from these unlikely bedfellows, feeling suddenly and acutely vulnerable lying there on the table. Then, a shadow and a movement from the corner of the room. Her body jolted and she tried to see what was over there, moving in the candlelight. She tasted acid spittle in her mouth, the fear once again holding sway over her body. The roof of the cave seemed to bend and curve as her eyes darted toward the other side of the room in reaction to another movement. She imagined rats scurrying beneath her, seeking out the source of her fear-smell, ready to gnaw at the delicious taste of her dread as she lay there bound and helpless. A chill ran through her hair, each follicle pinpricking icicle cold.

Then the movement was right beside her.

She turned her head and cried out in anguish to see the man-child gazing at her lasciviously not six inches from her face. This close, his breath smelled particularly foul—an undigested mess of seafood and rank rotting sweetness. He appeared to sniff at her, grinning and baring his teeth as he did so, and she saw the rot in his gums for the first time. The look of old man's perverse delight on this child's face was an abomination. His lips were flecked with saliva, which trickled down his chin. He savored the scent of Marla's fear in the same way a normal child would savor the smell of candy. He voiced his enjoyment in little spasms of breathy laughter. Mirthsome little bubbles of snot formed and burst wetly in his nostrils. It was all Marla could do to stop herself from vomiting. He ignored her discomfort, reaching out into her field of vision with pudgy little boy hands then stroking strands of her hair as though she were a stray cat he'd found somewhere along the way. Marla shuddered at his touch, feeling sure it was those hands that had stove that poor pussycat's head in—the one Adam had found by the path that day. The old boy's eyes were filled with dark mischief now, and Marla pictured him at work in the loft of the big house, torturing and maiming his little playthings until they were all dead. The boy sprang up and climbed atop the table, straddling Marla and laughing that peculiar little circus laugh of his as he did so. His voice sounded like it was constantly on the verge of breaking, yet stuck in the shrill tones of a preteen youth. She tried not to look up at him as he knelt above her chest. Then she glimpsed the dirty syringe in his hand, the chamber filled with what looked like chicken fat and blood. He held the needle aloft and Marla winced, waiting for it to pierce her skin.

But then the boy took hold of his twitching member in his free hand and plunged the dirty needle into it, pumping the fatty contents into its head. He moaned in vile pleasure and, discarding the empty syringe, started to rub his newfound erection furiously. He kept rubbing as he rubbed his face in her neck, cold snail trails of snot tracing across her skin. Then, like a rat, he began nibbling at her clothing, tearing it with his teeth and peeling it back to reveal her nakedness beneath. She struggled and kicked, feeling like one of the dead birds in that loft, pinioned and unable to fight back. The boy's rubbing and biting and tearing was becoming frenzied now and Marla felt oily drips of sweat drip from his mop of hair into the valley between her breasts. He began to convulse above her, grunting like a beast, his little legs twitching and knees clenching as though he were riding a rodeo horse. Marla closed her eyes tight and cried out in disgust as the boy lurched into the painful throes of orgasm. His ecstasy at fever pitch, he continued rubbing himself frantically, and Marla felt globs of cold leaden semen spattering her chest and face. His tepid ejaculate tasted of ruin, of heresy, and she spat it from her mouth. Still trembling from his exertions, the boy thing slapped his palms to her chest and began massaging his seed into her flesh. The act was functional and robotic and, daring to look, Marla saw disinterest in her abuser's eyes for the first time. He'd done this before.

The very thought made her gag.

"Have to rub the lotion in. Have to get you ready for Daddy. *All the king's horses. And all the king's men.*"

His casual, sing-song tone was too much for Marla. Her eyes gave way to tears and her breasts rose and fell with great sobs. She felt betrayed by her nipples, which stood erect from the sensation of the semen as it cooled like porridge in the chill air of the cave. She looked straight at him, defiant, as he went on rubbing his filth into her. The boy averted his uncaring eyes, idly distracted by the crackle of a damp candlewick as it sputtered and died in its own puddle of wax. As he turned his head, Marla saw a figure standing over both of them. Heart in her mouth, she recognized the face. Vincent. His arms were stretched out above his head. *What on earth is he holding onto,* thought Marla as if in a dream. She soon realized it was a huge glass jar as it came crashing down on the boy's head, knocking him sideways from the gurney. Vincent released her from her bonds and quickly pulled her tattered clothing over her nakedness as best he could. Only the aftershock of fear and disgust stopped Marla from grabbing the old man and kissing him in gratitude. *Once we're out of here I'll do just that* she promised herself as Vincent helped her to her feet.

They were almost at the opening to the cave when the scurrying boy-thing began to wail. The sound was an affront, only serving to encourage Marla on her unsteady trajectory to the tunnel beyond the cave wall. She turned, sensing Vincent's distance from her and saw that sure enough he'd stopped dead in his tracks. The vile thing's cries were escalating, in that way children cry after a series of sharp intakes of breath when they take a tumble and graze their little knees. *Their little knees.* Marla shuddered, becoming all-too palpably aware of the child's ooze drying and forming a crust on the skin of her chest. She wanted only to be away from here and washing herself in the sea. Even if the waves dashed her onto the rocks bludgeoning the last breath from her body, that was where she wanted to be, not loitering in this cavernous rattrap. But even now Vincent took a faltering step towards the boy-thing, then another, his arms held out in supplication and his unblinking eyes saying *I didn't mean to strike you little man, I'm so sorry, let me hold you, I won't hurt you again!* For Vincent's eyes saw this wretched thing as a child once more, the son that he'd lost so long ago in the stark negative of white foam on black waves. His arms yearned for the embrace of that which he'd lost and he stooped to comfort the boy. *Don't.*

"Don't! Don't go near him! He's a fucking monster!" Marla screamed, giving voice to all that she'd endured at the fat wormlike digits of those little hands.

But it was too late. Vincent looked back at her, his eyes veiled with the membrane of his memories. A single tear trickled from his eye, a pure thing winding its way down the crags of his face.

"But he's my son."

At this, Marla reeled.

"How can that be...your son?"

"He's my son," the old man repeated with sorrow in his voice, "The island took him. The island changed him. But he's still a boy inside."

The notion rang with bitterness in Marla's ears. *A boy?* No. A boy thing that kills, that poisons and maims and despises. An inversion of all that is pure and good about a child. *That's no boy,* she was about to say, when a great jet of blood punched out of Vincent's throat. A huge shard of jagged glass from the jar emerged from his neck. The boy-thing rammed it further through the gruesome hollow where the old man's throat used to be until his little fist began to emerge too. Vincent spluttered and fell to the floor, head swimming in a fountain of his own blood.

"No. No, no, no, no!"

Marla backed away from the murderous thing and bolted for the opening in the cavern wall behind her. She'd been stupid to linger here, but her empathy for the old man had made it impossible to just abandon him. But abandon him she should, even as she heard the sound of sharp glass scraping on old bones as the child began his playtime.

"Pop! Goes the weasel..."

For the love of God, the boy was singing—a vile distorted sound like the nursery tapes she and Jessie had found at the Big

House. A wet popping sound and a guttural giggle followed and Marla turned to see the lad pulling one of Vincent's eyes from the socket, making silly string of the stretchy optic entrails connecting orb to socket.

She ran. Behind her, the shrill laughter and sputum nursery song of the boy as he got to work on his father's tongue.

The tunnel outside stretched out into black in both directions. *Left or right?* It was a tough call, Marla had no idea which direction she'd come from when he, when *it*, had brought her in here. The boy's shrill laughter urged her on and she banked to the right. *Fifty-fifty chance, deeper into this hellhole or out onto the beach.* The tunnel snaked, forming a sly corner and Marla was considering doubling back on herself when she saw a distant light up ahead. That was it, must be, the way out. She ran full pelt, her wet footfalls echoing off the bare rock like mechanical applause. Nearing the light, she saw it was coming from a doorway in the side of the tunnel. Slowing down to a trot, Marla approached the lip of the doorway cautiously and stopped. Back pressed against the wall, she took a deep breath and peered around the doorway. Inside was a large chamber, lit with dim sepia lamps that hung from wires bolted to the walls. The room was lined with rows of shelves that formed an avenue to the other side, and there—another door. Marla looked back the way she came. She could no longer hear the maniac boy-thing and no footsteps were coming from the tunnel behind her. *Into the room then, oh please let that door be an exit.* She stepped inside, struck by the strong smell of mold and dust, and began walking the avenue of shelves to the door. Now she was inside, Marla could see what lined each shelf. The lower ones were stacked to bursting with plain plastic containers, just like the ones filled with cleaning products back at the white stucco house. The containers were neatly grouped according to shape and size and as she walked on, Marla saw further shelves cluttered with the smaller toiletry containers of the type she'd found waiting for her in the summerhouse filled with shampoo, shower gel, toothpaste and the like. Puzzled, Marla paused for a second and took one of the containers from the shelf nearest to her. It was empty. She placed it back on the shelf and saw a stack of screw cap lids waiting next to it—waiting to be twisted on when the container was filled, but with what? Larger shelves up ahead glinted yellow and Marla walked on to better see their wares. These shelves were larger because the vessels that stood upon them were larger and heavier than the plastic containers. Marla was looking at a wall of large glass jars filled with what looked like goose fat. Many of the jars were covered in thick layers of dust, their contents separating like spoiled milk. They must have been here for years, and there were so many of them. Walking further on, Marla was dismayed to see that more of the jars were filled with body parts and tissue specimens, just like the ones she'd seen in the cave before the boy thing had his way with her. She grimaced as her eyes focused on a jar containing the thick tube of a belly button cord, swimming in a dark amber jelly, little flaps of pink flesh surrounding the orifice like a collar. Peering closer, she realized her mistake—this was actually someone's anus, complete with the fleshy rectal opening she'd mistaken for a navel. Dread connections crept into her mind as she equated the contents of these jars with the expectant spaces within the plastic containers. Shampoo, shower gel, toothpaste. *Oh, dear God no.* Marla felt suddenly sick, desperate to wash herself inside and out. Her flesh squirmed sticky cold where the boy had violated her. She backed away from the jars and their disgusting contents and fled for the door, grabbing at the handle with one frantic sweaty palm.

But the door was locked. It was made of old metal, heavy and immovable.

Tears of despair welled up in Marla's eyes. She'd have no choice now but to go back the way she came, and to face whatever lurked in the darkness at the other end of the long tunnel. No, she couldn't do it; she'd be driven mad by fear before a hundred paces, before a dozen even. Nothing else for it, she'd have to break open the door somehow. Studying the door, she saw there was no discernable locking mechanism, just the age and rust that made it looked fused into the rock that surrounded it. Maybe if she could break the door handle with something— that might just do it. She began looking around for an object heavy enough to do the job. The jars had been amassed here over months, years or even decades. They had to be important to someone. Surely they'd keep a fire extinguisher down here, in case of fire? Marla darted to the nearest corner, desperate to see red. But she found only more jars, great stacks of them, each filled with fleshy objects she had no desire to look at any longer. She continued her search, aiming for a gap in the shelves that formed a kind of deep avenue within the tall rows a little way from the door.

She froze. Ahead of her was a dark shape, terrifyingly large and horribly familiar. He'd been here all along, watching her. Marla's head swam, drowning beneath the weight of this new horror. She backed away in slow terror, realizing that she'd run straight into the massive clutches of the giant who'd pursued her through the trees. The candles flickered and she saw him clearly for the first time—a massive Skin Man. His huge physique was clad in black oilskins, but now she saw they were stitched together with a network of leathery off cuts. Horribly, she saw an eyelid forming a buttonhole, the flap of someone's cheek (still with beard hair) grafted onto a pocket at his hip. His greatcoat was literally held together by human skin and sinew. She looked up and her terrified eyes were reflected back at her from his goggle eyes. They were indeed housed in goggles made of bone, eye sockets expertly extricated from a human skull, filled with obsidian glass, then strapped to his head with sickly yellow surgical tubing. The dark lenses bore into every corpuscle of her being, reflecting her horror like hideous inverted scrying mirrors. Marla choked as his great hand clutched at her throat and she felt herself lifted off the ground onto the very tips of her toes. She looked down in terror at the endgame of those black goggle eyes and felt herself falling into their nauseating curves. Like a terrified, naked child Marla slipped beneath the cold black ripples of her fear and gave herself over to oblivion.

CHAPTER THIRTY-TWO

A siren song of waves lulled Marla to and fro like a boat cut adrift from its moorings and set loose upon the ocean. She heard them in the submarine depths of her dreams as she floated above the ground through the trees. The Skin Man was carrying her over his shoulder like a rag doll. Oh, but he was a behemoth, barrel-chested and thick, sturdy as a tree trunk. If you'd seen them crashing through the trees together, you'd be sure to mistake them for something out of a fairytale. *La belle et la bete*. The giant bestial fiend in his greatcoat of skin and the girl fragile and pale in her tatters. But his cold glassy eyes were not party to fairytales, they were filled with the thousand flayed edges of nightmares past and yet to come. On through the woods he trudged—each step a commitment to the darker, higher purpose that drove the engine of his being, each breath a hymn to this eviscerated night. Marla stirred slightly in her fitful sleep, murmuring something of the horrors she'd witnessed under her breath as the Skin Man climbed a steep incline, gravel and dirt fleeing from beneath his feet. He turned onto a path, visible only to his owl-like eyes in the vague moonlight, and cut through a network of tall trees and bushes. Breaking cover, he paused for a moment to draw breath and looked up at the huge white edifice in front of him. It gleamed huge and white as an iceberg—the most beautiful house on the island, unknown to any but him and his brethren. He strode on, his path now lit by an avenue of flaming torches. The torchlight danced across Marla's face, giving her the aspect of a sleeping child curled up in front of a dreamtime fire.

Inside the house, the Homecoming was in full sway. The group from the jetty had made light work of warming up the house and had put on quite a spread. At first glance, the scene looked like any well-to-do gathering of wealthy families. Mothers stood gossiping by the picture window while children ran between their ankles, their play punctuated by joyful exclamations of *"Tag! You're it."* Fathers talked business over the dips, keeping a safe distance from the kitchen door lest they were dragged inside to help with the finger food. Some gathered on the veranda, watching the garden sprinklers, which seemed to be applauding these beautiful rich people with their clockwork display of water jets. Their rhythmic sound was like little chuckles of approval at the urbane normalcy of the proceedings. But the scene was far from normal. Each and every member had shed their clothes—men, women, and children included— revealing bodies of such sheer perfection they'd make even the finest cosmetic surgeon weep tears of blood. They socialized casually, their skin smooth and flawless, not a pair of spectacles or piece of jewelry among them, and not one of them batted an eyelid when the huge, lumbering Skin Mechanic made his way up the garden path carrying a delirious Marla Neuborn over his shoulder. In fact, they let him through as though he were a waiter, here to pass around the *hors d'oeuvres* from a silver tray.

Perhaps he was.

Marla's mind was cloudy. She was still a boat, adrift on the ocean, but something had changed. The sea was becoming unbearably choppy and the clouds were rolling back now. Someone was changing the sky for a new one. Her eyelids fluttered uncontrollably and she began to experience a lunatic flicker book slide show of white walls and white ceilings and luminescent faces peering blithely down at her. Marla wanted to remain as a boat, her back supported by salt water, her face kissed by a fine spray of sea mist. She clenched her eyelids shut tight and fancied she heard joyous laughter from somewhere beyond the field of her consciousness. The dull sensation of heavy hands lifting her crept into her lucid dreaming and she felt her entire body tilt suddenly. The sea was no longer at her back. The waves had solidified into cold steel. Her shoulder blades flinched at the metal chill of her new resting place and somewhere behind her eyes the lights were switched on. Their glare came crashing into her eyes, filling them with the harsh truth of her predicament. She was not adrift, there was no blanket of mist and no sirens sang their lullaby—there was only hard steel and bright artificial light and the sudden, naked horror of being watched by dozens of pairs of eyes.

Marla looked at them. Scores of beautiful translucent faces with big doe eyes and skin so unearthly smooth. Each was stark naked, their bodies hairless and *sexless* somehow, despite bearing the genitalia identifying them as male or female. They eyed her patiently, with soulless tolerance as they might look upon an expensive meal that had taken an age to prepare. She swallowed painfully, her throat craving moisture, but she found only gritty dryness.

Someone moved through the gathering, carrying a gleaming silver tray laden with tall flute glasses. Marla heard the unmistakable fizz of champagne, felt the tempered excitement of the revelers, as the glasses were passed around. Then, a tall man stepped forward and raised his glass. He looked easily as old as a grandfather but had skin as smooth as a newly born grandchild. His evenly tanned features were topped with a well-groomed mane of white hair. He was like a wave, effulgent. His teeth were brilliantly white as he smiled, wide, and then addressed his fellows.

"To this wonderful bounty that nature brings."

Clink.

"To hearth and home."

Clink.

"And to our genius benefactor, our very own Skin Mechanic."

Clink. Applause. Glug, glug, glug.

"Now if you'd all like to freshen up before the ceremony, a warming pool awaits."

Marla listened to the excited chatter as the people filed out of the white room, distant as a dream. She heard a loud metallic clank and felt the trolley to which she was strapped move slightly beneath her. Then a dark form moved over her and she was being wheeled briskly away by the swarthy Skin Man. A mechanic, the glamorous old guy had called him. *A mechanic of what?* Unwanted images of Adam's intestines unpacked themselves in Marla's mind, spooling into memories of the boy-thing's charnel attic littered with dead animals. A breeze passed over Marla as she was wheeled into another, larger space, and she caught the rank intensity of the man's fleshy oilskins for the first time. The smell was one of pickled anchovies and syrup and innards, the most complex and overwhelming scent. Her body wanted to gag, but perversely her nostrils wanted to inhale—provoked by this utterly unique olfactory blend. She heard splashing and laughter a little way off. The ceiling above her had given way to a high glass roof, beyond which twinkled a canopy of tiny stars in a dark purple night sky. The trolley came to a halt and Marla watched as the Skin Mechanic moved silently around her, making adjustments to the metal frame. He pulled a lever and Marla felt the gurney tilt forward, her feet swinging down toward the floor. Held fast by her bonds, the gurney continued to tilt until she was almost in a standing position, then it stopped suddenly with a slight rocking motion and she took in her new surroundings.

She was in a large pool house, constructed almost entirely from glass windows that gave uninhibited views of opulent gardens as far as the eye could see. The floor and columns were made from fine white marble. Flames flickered in stone founts and low-level spotlights illuminated the huge swimming pool that dominated the space. The gossamer-skinned families were at play in and around the pool, some swimming and splashing, others reclining on the pale marble poolside. Marla felt a spasm of revulsion as she saw the dark crimson stains smeared on the white surfaces where the people lay. The pool was a bloodbath—a dark, sticky gumbo of blood and entrails and flesh—and they were all swimming in it, even the children. She looked on in disbelief as she watched two young lovers playfully splashing fluid and guts at each other. The female of the couple pushed herself up in the water before gleefully pushing her beau beneath the surface of butcher's filth. A child swam past them, swimming back crawl, his little legs kicking through what appeared to be yards of tangled intestine. An eyeball whizzed across the vile scene and dozens of tiny hands reached out to catch it, a tiny volleyball. Marla gagged and vomited the last dregs of stomach bile down her front. Her stomach juices bubbled at her breast, mingling with the corruption of the boy-thing.

Then, a hush fell across the room. One by one, the swimmers clambered out of the pool, their games over for the moment. Their eyes and teeth were even more dazzling white now they blazed at her from dark bloody faces. She tried to close her eyes as they approached her quietly, but mortal terror conspired to keep her lids open. First in line was a beautiful woman, her blonde hair streaked with grue, her fingernails dripping livid with the stuff of others. Marla gasped at her sudden touch and looked up, confused, to see the woman was wearing the familiar face of the Australian swimmer. Wearing it indeed, for his face was now just a flap of flesh draped across the woman's features like a mask. The woman tore the mask away, a sick joke. She began to stroke Marla's skin, leaving blood trails on her breasts and belly. Marla looked up at her assailant's eyes, expecting to see wickedness there but found only reverence. One after another they approached her with the same respectful eyes and smeared blood and filth all over her skin as casually as though it were sun block or massage oil. The smallest of the children attended to her legs and feet, the tallest adults to her cranium, face, and shoulders. Marla licked her lips involuntarily and tasted the salt metal of blood there. Her throat raged acid and she tried to find her voice.

"Why...why are you doing this? Plea..."

No more words would come. And why should they? Mere words could make no sense of the *Grand Guignol* playing out before Marla's eyes.

"Hush."

Startled at his voice, Marla then recognized one of the blood-smeared figures standing respectfully in front of her. It was Welland. *Call me Bill.* He looked so at home there in the pool house, naked and covered in blood, just as he had in his office and sharp suit. His shark white teeth glinted from out his mask of congealing plasma. For a moment, Marla thought he might answer her question, answer her prayers, tell her this was all a joke and she could wake up now because the flight was leaving and the gate was closing, so run. But he told her none of those things, just smiled agreeably to his friends and said quietly, "She's ready."

STRATUM BASALE

A needle was all it took to subdue Marla, to keep her very much within sight but out for the count so he could do his work. Her eyes had fluttered slightly when he'd inserted the sharp sting, the only movement in her body and a natural reaction to the invasion being visited upon her. The needle was half in her vein, half out in the sterile air of the chamber where he labored beneath the all-revealing white beam of an overhead lamp. A tube ran from the needle, extending up to a drip feed bag filled with clear liquid. The liquid was formed of a chemical compound developed over ages—an alchemical blend of rare medicinal herbs, worth a fortune on the black market, and everyday pharmaceuticals transformed by the arcane processes he'd subjected them to. This was but a small fragment of his art. He took everyday medicine and augmented it with aeons of forbidden knowledge, turning science into magic and magic into medicine. Adjusting the gurney, the Skin Mechanic gazed at Marla's neckline, her perfection reflected in the domes of his goggles. This really was a fine specimen, perhaps one of the finest he'd ever seen. They were right to send her at this stage of her life, when her derma was just so. And he'd been right to discipline himself, to quell the voices demanding he take her and make good work of her when he'd first laid eyes on her. She'd seen him through the summerhouse window that night; and he'd smelled her blood and panic. He recalled the sanguine odor of the alcohol in her bloodstream, a pollutant his chemicals were even now putting to rights. He'd tolerated the stench—it was, after all, a preservative of sorts for the wondrous specimen of flesh that now lay prone before him. Yes, it had been correct to wait. The others had been fit only for the stock pool, but this girl was worthy of the highest table. He exhaled a slow, long, hot breath and turned to his implements, hoping her innards were as delectable as the skin that sheathed them. The sharp things on the table shimmered beneath the lights. Many of his instruments didn't even have names. Sometimes the sound of an implement was enough to name it and the act of repetition, slicing through flesh or sawing into bone, enough to learn its name forever. He selected a cylindrical, claw-like thing and made the first cut into her mysteries.

CHAPTER THIRTY-THREE

Hiding beneath their lids, Marla's eyes made rapid movements. She was dreaming again, of a hot room that smelled of disinfectant and of huge fingers inside of her most secret self. The fingers were scooping into the matter behind her ribcage like hot spoons into ice cream. In her dream she could open her eyes and breathe steadily, looking up into the face of the man above her. He was a sanguine giant, as big as a wrestler with huge hands as steady as a tiller's working their surgeon's work. She tried to will her dream-state self to rise up off her back so she could get a better look at him. Her body felt distant and she had to scream at every nerve ending just to raise her head closer to his. He stood over her like a waiting storm, those cold, glass goggle eyes regarding her dispassionately.

Then his face was gone, dissipating into cloudburst. The man had evaporated into the ether, and so had the clinical white walls of the room, the conditioned air giving way to the fragrant breeze of a forest. Above her, tropical birds flapped and squawked in the tops of great palm trees, all around her a curtain of verdant green rainforest so huge it faded to black at the extremes of her vision. Hearing a wet flapping sound, she looked down and was embarrassed to see her guts dangling at her toes. She was indifferent to her nakedness but the exposure of her organs, her secret self, made her face blush. Carefully, so as not to have the whole steaming mess topple out of her, Marla reached down and cradled her innards holding them like she might hold an infant. She teased them back into the warm cave of her abdomen, pulling the soft flesh of her belly around them like a sling. Birds sang and distant waterfalls thundered. This place was primal, ancient and alive, far from men and their constructs, their stucco houses of steel and glass. Still holding herself, she began to walk through the massive trees until she came to a ridge overlooking a primitive village in clearing. A single plume of smoke billowed from the center of the village, a fire around which were dotted about a dozen huts, circular in shape with banana leaf roofs. She recalled the decaying grandeur of the Big House and found herself smiling at the simplicity of these huts—yearning, even, for the basic lives that must be unfolding in and around them. Naked children, their lovely skin the color of coconut shells, were playing in the shade of the huts. She longed to join their games and half-ran, half-stumbled down the ridge to the edge of the village. Before she could reach them, to bask in their laughter, the children were gone. Ashes lay where moments ago there had been a fire. The sky darkened with clouds and a great wind howled, threatening rainstorms. A piercing scream rang out from deep within the trees bordering the village, and Marla moved instinctively in the direction the sound was coming from. The scream had been so despairing, so helpless, that she felt all the joy had been screamed out of the world. Rain now lashed at her back, freezing her flesh to the bone, and she plummeted through the trees in search of the helpless screamer who must now surely be dead to have uttered such a sound. The foliage was becoming so dense it was almost impassable, and Marla had to fight her way through leaves as big as doors. She crashed through a great spider's web, disturbing a colony of huge tarantulas, angry black and orange stripes scurrying frighteningly close to her naked body. But Marla was not afraid of them; her only concern was to locate the source of that haunting scream. Then, as she stumbled into another clearing, she found it.

In the trees all around her were natives from the village through which she'd passed. They were strung up like Adam had been, their brown skins stretched out and attached to tree branches like hammocks. Some of them still breathed, driven insane by the physical inversion they were now experiencing as they watched their hearts beat outside of their bodies and saw their colons expel waste onto the leaves and branches above them, defying gravity. Marla looked for the source of all this pain. She found him standing there, dressed in his great fleshcoat, maniac eyes hidden behind those dark goggles. Another of the villagers screamed and died, answered by the terrified pleas and prayers of those others who still lived but who hoped they might expire next. Marla ignored them all, intent now on knowing what was behind those unblinking eyes. She was just inches from him now. She reached out and touched his face, her fingers skittering across the rough surface like a blind woman's. He stood, dispassionate, as she went about her probing and did not even flinch when she slipped her fingers beneath the bone frame of his goggles and into the slick goo of his eyes.

Visions pierced her brain like shrapnel from a roadside bomb. She saw his work, felt his hands as though they were her own. In that moment she knew his life's labors, felt the long dark decades of his alchemical work stretching out in front of her. She heard the terrified voices of the natives as he hunted them down, mercilessly, and understood their tongue. To them he was a demon, come here from the western world to corrupt them and steal their skins. They had a name for this white demon. *Skin Taker*. She tasted salt blood as he drank it from the bowl of a skull, helped him distill spinal fluid into a vial, joined him in his reverie upon discovering an albino child naked and cowering in a mud hut, chanting a spell over and over—a spell that would neither protect it from nor deter the intentions of the Skin Taker looming over it. Marla understood the intricate beauty of the Skin Mechanic's craft, the long dark suffering to which he had willingly subjected himself in return for its secrets. And as night fell in his old Amazonian hunting grounds, she felt the power of the ancient entities to which his workings were offered. Theirs was the lifeblood of youth, every evisceration keeping their dark names alive. Names that whispered through the canopies of this great forest and out across rivers and oceans until they attracted new followers, new disciples of youth and beauty and hot blood. Marla saw them again, pale figures from the West standing naked before the Skin Mechanic. They were begging for his touch. And he blessed them. He was their pastor, their surgeon, and their savior.

CHAPTER THIRTY-FOUR

This island can change you, Marla.

The voice was like warm chocolate, simultaneously stirring Marla from her rainforest dreams and soothing her. Half asleep and numb as a dead thing, she mistook the voice for Jessie's. She opened her eyes without feeling the lids move and looked around without the sensation of having turned her head, expecting to find herself curled up in bed back at the summerhouse after a long dream. But it couldn't be Jessie— she was dead. And the summerhouse was out of reach now, a construct and a dream forbidden. Marla had opened her eyes to a reality as stark and threatening as a scalpel blade.

She was in another white chamber, filled with candles and little halogen lamps suspended like eyeballs from snakelike mounts. Tables filled with reflective dishes and tools could be seen lurking in alcoves, threatening little suits of armor and weaponry. And all around her stood the urbane nudists of Meditrine Island, their passive expressions in a limbo land somewhere between boredom and indifference. She tasted the air and found it powdery and clean, without the sense of having opened her mouth or felt the air leave her nostrils. Marla desperately tried to focus. Something stood between the people and the walls of the chamber, like a vast hospital curtain. She unraveled the structure with her eyes, perceiving it to be a network of wire frames woven all around her. Each frame was lined with pale, tautly stretched fabric and decorated with bright ribbons and bows. The white teeth and bright eyes of her strange, smooth audience glimmered in the lights. Marla felt butterflies in her tummy as they each smiled politely at her and turned away to face the curtains. *They didn't want me to make a speech did they, oh no, please anything but that, I'd not know what to say, I'd be so embarrassed I'd simply die.* But she was safe; she felt no mouth with which to speak even if she had the will. So, her mind raced instead. *Oh my God, my Jesus, what have they done to me?* She saw Welland again, glancing over his shoulder at her and smiling wryly. His voice returned to her, echoing inside her skull. *Comfy? Good. I started out just like you; as a Lamplighter. I loved it so much I joined the Consortium full time. I'm sure once you take the test you'll work out just fine.* Marla could see them all now, in a perfect circle looking in on her like she had dozens of eyes, like a fly. *Oh, what have they done?*

Marla watched them, each and every one, as they stepped forward into the curtain. Her nerve endings screamed, white raw. She *was* the curtain—she knew that now. The taut fabric was that of her own skin, cured and treated and stretched out by way of techniques both ancient and forbidden. The ribbons and bows decorating the intricate frames splaying her unraveled self around the room were her organs and veins. Base tissues and cardiovascular conduits had been reworked into the stuff of miracles, pumping blood and moisture around the living canopy of derma into which the naked beauties had stepped. Marla flinched, *flinched, that's a good one, I don't even have a face anymore,* as each man, woman and child held out their arms and legs in a star formation. Their veins found hers, their hairless bodies fusing with her body until they were one being. The sensation, or rather a million sensations, was mind shattering. Every moment of every life of every person that had joined with her penetrated her consciousness. *My brain? Do I even have a brain now?* And she slipped out of herself.

She was standing inside the bright form of the blonde woman she'd seen wearing the swimmer's stolen face. Still vaguely Marla, she felt herself palpably inside the other woman's body looking out through her eyes. The sensation made her feel slightly nauseated, but it also tickled like feathers and she heard herself laughing. It wasn't her voice that laughed—it was an older voice, distant somehow, perhaps not surprising seeing how it was coming from another's throat, across a stranger's tongue and out through alien lips. Tentatively, she reached up to touch that new mouth with her new fingertips and finding soft moisture there laughed some more via the voice of her host. She closed her host's eyes and began to look inward, into the body and mind she had infiltrated.

Sounds and smells enveloped her like the flesh she was wearing and Marla allowed herself to be carried away by them. She heard the sea and saw lights flashing and opened her eyes to see herself, as this beautiful blonde stranger, on the rocks by the lighthouse. A man was standing outside throwing a ball high into the air and letting it drop, down, down into tiny little hands. Marla fell with it and drew breath sharply, recognizing the little boy instantly. It was Vincent's boy, but as a true child. Every ounce of terrible perversity was gone from his face, and all that remained was wide-eyed innocence. She felt tears trickle warm down her borrowed face as she watched him laugh and shout as he caught the ball and held it triumphant before throwing it back to his father. His father. Yes, Vincent was standing there playing with his son, large as life and several years younger. Her heart ached seeing him this way, so young and in such good health. The clouds in the sky beyond the lighthouse cleared a little and the glow of the sun shone through the glass at the top of the towering lighthouse. A bright beam of sunlight framed Vincent and the boy, drenching them in a glow the color of fresh sunflowers. It seemed as though father and son were surrounded by an aura made of their love for one another. But even as she wept, Marla felt her host's emotions blacken somehow. She was watching Vincent and the boy like a spiteful child might watch a beetle trapped inside a jar. All around her was the bitter feeling of betrayal and the heavy weight of wicked deeds almost dragged her to her knees.

She saw her blonde host, Susanna, worshipping at the feet of the Skin Mechanic and his flock—their naked bodies dazzling her with their impassable youth and impossible beauty. Marla felt herself squirm with despair inside Susanna's body as she felt her give herself over to these new gods of youth and vigor, tried to warn her of the terrible cost she'd pay. But Marla knew she was watching past events unfold and grew still and quiet as they replayed before her eyes. She saw Vincent's beautiful little boy given up as a sacrifice to the huge man of skin and bone science. Hearing the poor little boy's terrible cries as the monster visited unutterable experiments upon his flesh, Marla was desperate to put her hands to her ears and shut them out forever. But they were not her hands, nor her ears, and she had no choice but to endure the howling cries of pain and suffering as the boy was transformed before her into the dreadful, twisted thing she'd encountered in the caves. She saw Vincent, desperate to save him, rescuing the boy and taking to the waves in a little boat. And she watched in mute horror as Vincent was betrayed and dragged back to the island, where he was forced to watch as the Skin Mechanic continued his insane workings on the boy. An experiment, to keep a child young forever. It had succeeded on a physical level only—the body remaining innocent and young, the mind growing old, bitter, and corrupt. Dark decades passed before her eyes and she saw how the boy-thing had become the Skin Man's insane apprentice, copying his master's foul practices on whatever creatures he could find on the island. The birds in the attic of the Big House, his unwitting patients. The Australian boy and Security Operative Anders, his graduation projects. He'd tortured and defiled them just as he had been. It was all he knew, all he'd ever know.

In the midst of all this horror, Marla could almost hear Vincent's mind snap, the frayed edges of his sanity unraveling never to be mended. She looked on helplessly as he climbed the winding stairs of his lighthouse, utterly bereft. The lighthouse was a ruin to Vincent's despair and Marla could feel every brick, every bolt and every sheet of glass sighing. The construct of Susanna's flesh, meanwhile, seemed to be pricking at the memories—infinite arousals playing out across every cell of her skin. The veins that pumped blood all around her were rivers of joy, celebrating the perfect flesh that housed them. Marla saw Susanna remain young and beautiful while Vincent grew old and decrepit. She knew now that through their worship of the Skin Taker and his gods, the Consortium had somehow made Susanna young again, young forever—but her lover and their son had borne the most terrible price for her vanity.

She saw them, the Consortium, for what they really were,

dark demons standing elegant in the proud flesh of bright beings. She saw them at work in their high buildings and at play in their mansions. She could taste their terrible desires, that strong hunger which defined them. They were ravenous for youth, sated only for the briefest of moments before becoming prey to their fear of losing their beauty again. Driven on by this endless cycle, they had enslaved themselves to many lifetimes of death and rebirth, each more painful than the last, each leaving them ever more unsatisfied. Marla watched in shame, for she felt a part of it clothed in Susanna's skin, as countless innocents fed those dreadful desires through the ritual and surgery of the Skin Mechanic. She heard the deep drone of his voice, a litany burning into their brains, promising perfection. They were a cult and their gods were youth and beauty. To them, this island was *Tir na nOg*, the land of eternal youth. To Marla, the island was still a living hell—and one they could no more escape from than poor Vincent ever could. They were addicts, hopeless junkies hooked on the dark promises of their Mechanic's art. And the lengths they'd gone to, just to feel the fleeting benefits of his blade. Their awful history yawned wide before Marla's horrified eyes. She saw them in their places of power, trawling the world for suitable specimens, treating humanity like fish for the net—each writhing innocent destined for their table at a whim. She watched as they collected DNA samples and cataloged tissue profiles, turning their Master's work into a silent crusade. She felt the shellshock of these revelations, as their great conspiracies were unpacked before her mind's eye.

She fell backwards into her drab room in gray London. She watched herself arguing with her landlady, saw her laptop gone from her room, saw her stolen panties laced with her DNA in far dark towers where data was extracted and subtracted and re-tested, leading all the way back to her, Marla Neuborn. She wept hot tears as she felt Welland's hot breath nearby, his strong pulse. He wanted her eyes, all the better to see with. *My eyes, I'll never see that way again.* He was pulling her back, they all were. She jolted back into the bright room.

I'm Marla.

Marla was back inside her body now. But she felt those

other beings pulling at her mind and body. Her nerves seemed to stretch out into infinity. Too many forms, too many hosts wanting her to fill them just as she'd filled Susanna's body moments ago. They not only wanted her flesh, but her identity too—everything that made her who she was. Her desires, her memories, her ambitions were all food to them, accessorized by her fleshy presence on this plane. She steeled herself, trying to hold onto a memory, a sensation, however painful. They couldn't steal her life away from her like this. She had so much potential. She had come to the island to start afresh, it wasn't fair, she had to try to fight it. Marla felt her mind was about to snap any moment, the same way Vincent's had. She visualized the notepads she'd been writing in on the porch of the summerhouse. Each day of her life became a page in the pad and she frantically scribbled each event down, however banal. She was desperate to fill the pages—her lifeblood the ink, her will the pen. But they were closing in, breathing down her neck, clamoring over her shoulder. Each time she filled a page they tore it away along with her memories, forcing her to start over, but she couldn't remember any more. Couldn't even remember who she was…

Marla! I'm Marla…

Even as she thought her own name, it began to dissolve, to diminish like the fading image of someone she used to love. It was as though the letters making up her name had been printed onto photographic paper, which was then bleached out and overexposed before her very eyes. Nothing left but a blank sheaf of paper, nondescript. Her eyes became lost in the white glare. The lights burned so bright, brilliant really, like the perfect teeth and perfect eyes and perfect nails of her beautiful tenants. Marla-as-world shifted. Everything about her unraveled and she felt them, those demons, luxuriating in her flesh and her potential. They basked in her memories and devoured her dreams. Then she felt herself, her sense of self, torn irretrievably apart as the dark star bodies separated, each taking a piece of her with them.

EPILOGUE

It was done. For another season at least, it was done.

Morning broke over the island. Sunlight the color of blood oranges shone on the windows of the great white stucco houses, kissing away the last chill of night. Tropical birds went about their toilet, nuzzling at their feathers to release the natural oils essential to their first flight of the day. Taking to the wing, they glided over the treetops and out over the waves that rolled freshly in from the warming ocean. Crickets began to chirp a gleeful cacophony that would last the whole day through, and butterflies rode the breeze of their music above rich outcrops of wild flowers and grasses.

Atop a ridge, the Consortium stood silently welcoming the dawn, dressed now in understated linens. Some had brought Thermos flasks filled with hot black coffee. Others had dragged picnic baskets all the way up here, eager to breakfast in the first light of a very new day.

Marla Neuborn was among them, too, a part of each and every last one of them, dissolved into their bright bodies and dark hearts. She looked out with new eyes across the ridge and fixed her gaze on the vanishing point where the sky met the sea. Somewhere out there in the world the first pieces of a puzzle were being laid out. A plan was slowly coming to life, like the start-up chime of a computer, the soft glow of a screen. She had already forgotten her name as she stood there, proudly young and virile, with the beautiful people. Marla Neuborn had ceased to exist, even as her youth and beauty lived on. The dying whisper of her name had joined a new call.

A call to new flesh.

A call to The Lamplighters.

ABOUT THE AUTHOR

The Lamplighters was a Bram Stoker Award® fnalist for "superior achievement in a first novel".

One of Frazer's early short stories received a Geoffrey Ashe Prize from the Library of Avalon, Glastonbury. His short fiction has since appeared in numerous anthologies including the acclaimed Read By Dawn series.

Also a screenwriter and filmmaker, Frazer's movie credits include the award-winning short horror films *On Edge, Red Lines, Simone, The Stay,* and the critically acclaimed horror/thriller feature (and movie novelization) *Panic Button.*

Frazer is Head of Creative Writing at Brunel University London and resides with his family in leafy Buckinghamshire, England, just across the cemetery from the real-life *Hammer House of Horror.*

Official website: www.frazerlee.com
Facebook: www.facebook.com/AuthorFrazerLee
Twitter: www.twitter.com/frazer_lee
Instagram: www.instagram.com/mr_frazer_lee

Curious about other Crossroad Press books?
Stop by our site:
http://store.crossroadpress.com
We offer quality writing
in digital, audio, and print formats.

Printed in Great Britain
by Amazon